CLUBBED

A Story of Gay Love:
Trials, Tribulations and Triumphs

Robert A. Karl

Self-published by the Author

CLUBBED is a work of fiction. Names, characters, businesses, events, locales and incidents are either the products of the author's imagination or used in a fictitious manner. Where real-life locations, businesses and/or products are named, the situations, incidents and dialogues which take place are entirely fictional and are not intended to depict actual events. The mention of a product is not intended and should not be taken as an endorsement of that product. With the exception of public figures, any resemblance to actual persons, living or dead, or actual events is purely coincidental.

Cover Design: Hussnain Designz

Dedicated to all the Beautiful Souls who were lost
to the AIDS pandemic
and to all those who still remember and mourn them.

ONE

Now that I think about it, the idea was genius for its time. The bar was divided into two parts. If you entered from the back alley, you were in a straight bar, complete with female strippers in their skimpy thongs and glitter pasties. That scene was a sure draw for the frat boys in this small college town in rural Pennsylvania.

But if you entered by way of the bright red door on the main street, you entered a forbidden world, a gathering place for the people the locals called "faggots" and "queers."

I was drawn to that red door. I walked by it hundreds of times, usually on the other side of the street. My imagination ran wild with what might go on behind that door. I wasn't sure that I would ever find out. The peer pressure to be straight, to act straight and to hate "the fags" was intense.

I felt the pressure from friends, family and all of straight society. For example, if I was in the car with my father and he saw anyone who looked out of the ordinary, he would let loose with a string of profanities, talking about the homos and the queers.

"Look at that, can you believe it?" he'd shout at me. "That guy looks as queer as a three-dollar bill!"

I hated when he talked like that. It made me uncomfortable, and I felt a little guilty. I wasn't sure what I was, but there was no one I could talk to. No one at school. None of my friends. Certainly not my dad.

When I first started feeling different than other people, I didn't even have the words to describe how I was feeling. In my imagination, I was the only person in the world who felt like this. I was sure that something was very wrong with me. The best word to describe my feelings at the time was that I felt completely alone.

As I got older, and started to hear words like queer, homo and faggot, it was so clear to me that anyone who fit that description was someone I was expected to hate, to despise, since they were somehow inferior beings. I didn't know why I was supposed to feel that way, but I tried my best to act in the way I was being taught to act.

I had no idea what these fags and homos did to make everybody hate them. But that hate came through loud and clear.

The other guys at school were no different than my father. As we reached that age where guys start getting interested in the opposite sex, I acted like I was interested in them too. For a while, I even managed to convince myself that I liked a couple of girls.

All through high school, I was popular. But even as it seemed that half the girls in my class were getting pregnant by senior year, I couldn't bring myself to do anything more than make out with a girl. Clearly, my male classmates were far beyond my level of experience, since I was still a virgin on graduation day.

A virgin, but not totally inexperienced.

I was on the swim team in high school, and one day, another guy and I had to do extra laps after practice because we had been late arriving. All the other guys on the team had already showered and left the gym by the time the two of us hit the showers. Even the coach was gone.

Two of us, naked and alone together in the shower room. I couldn't help myself; I just had to watch as he washed himself. Incredibly, he got himself excited as he washed his private parts. He looked in my direction, but avoided looking me directly in the eye. Then he turned to face away from me, as I watched him work on himself, till he brought himself to climax. At that point, he finished showering, wrapped a towel around his waist, and went out to the locker area where he quickly got dressed and left.

I couldn't stop thinking about him. I wondered what he was thinking. Why did he do that in front of me? Was he a queer? Was I? I mean, I watched the whole thing. I couldn't stop watching and honestly, I wanted to see more and know more.

That wasn't the last time I saw him. We had one class together, Chemistry. I hated that class. I didn't really understand the concepts and I had no interest in trying to understand. But after that scene in the shower, I had a sudden interest in attending Chemistry. Funny, right?

One Friday afternoon, right after lunch, I was looking forward to the opportunity to stare at his back during class, when I saw him waiting outside the classroom.

"Hey, man," he greeted me at the door.

Without realizing it, I looked him up and down, my eyes pausing at his crotch, before I realized what I was doing and quickly met his eyes. I saw his smile as he realized I was checking him out.

"Hey, Brainiac," I returned the greeting, using the nickname that everyone used, acknowledging his status as the smartest kid in the class.

"Joey, I'm sick of school today. I'm thinking about cutting and heading out for a little fun this afternoon. You up for it?"

He didn't have to ask me twice. I only went to Chemistry because of him. If he was cutting, there was no reason at all for me to go.

We tried to sneak out of the building without being seen. Since it was Friday, there was no need to stop for any books or backpacks. The weekend meant no homework.

"Can I trust you?" he asked me as we reached the street.

"Of course," I answered, not sure what he was thinking.

I was surprised when he reached into his pocket, pulled out a pack of cigarettes and offered me one. Although a swimmer, I was already a heavy smoker, easily ignoring the warnings about the dangers of smoking. No one cared about what might happen in 40 or 50 years. At least, I didn't.

"I have a secret spot," he said, almost in a whisper, though there was no one anywhere near us. "Can I show you?"

"Cool," I said.

Being out of school early, missing Chemistry class, and in the company of a boy I had watched in the gym shower, that sounded like a perfect Friday afternoon to me. I would have followed him practically anywhere.

Walking briskly, we headed towards a house that had been empty for a few years. The lot was overgrown with weeds and the fence surrounding the property was broken in a few spots. Not bothering to look for an opening, Brainiac, whose real name was Nelson, just hopped the fence. I followed him with ease, since we both had strong lower bodies from hours and hours of swim practice.

I had never gone into this yard before, but Brainiac knew his way around the property. He headed straight for the cellar door, loosening the latch and opening the creaky door. It was dark down there and the pungent air made me briefly consider whether this was safe. But Brainiac scooted down the stairs without hesitation, so I wasn't about to question his judgment.

"Welcome to my hideout," he said, heading towards a pile of blankets. He threw himself on top of the heap and reached for a radio, playing the music softly enough so there was no chance that anyone passing by would hear.

4

An old coffee can half-filled with water was nearby, with about a dozen cigarette butts floating lazily at the top.

"Damn," I said. "All the comforts of home."

"It gets even better," he confided to me, pulling a towel off of a cooler. "Sorry, it's empty right now. I gotta make a beer run soon."

We were quiet for a few minutes, listening to the radio and smoking. I showed off by exhaling a few smoke rings, hoping to impress my new friend.

"What did you think?" he asked me.

"About what?"

"In the shower the other day. What I did. You saw it."

I took a minute to think, not sure what I should say or what he wanted me to say. So, I decided to be honest.

"That was cool. I liked it. I liked it a lot."

"Really?"

"Yeah, really," I answered.

"I wanna do it with another guy. I wanna do it with you, but I've been too afraid to tell anybody. I was too afraid to tell you."

The next Monday morning, Brainiac and I were both called into the principal's office and given a week's detention for cutting class. Personally, I was happy to spend a week after school in the same room with Nelson. Though we both knew that we couldn't risk cutting class again, because the principal warned us that another infraction would get both of us kicked off the swim team. And neither one of us wanted that to happen.

But of course, we were free to meet at Brainiac's secret spot after school, and he invited me to join him as long as I followed his rules. No kissing. No touching each other. Only stroking ourselves. As many times as we wanted to. No limits there. But Nelson wasn't ready to do anything more with another guy. I wasn't so sure about myself; maybe I wanted more, but I agreed to his terms.

5

I lost count of the number of times I met Brainiac at his secret hideout. We drank, we smoked, and we...well, you already know what we did. But always following those rules. So, as much as I enjoyed our times together, I always felt that something was missing. Still, it was fun, and I never turned down an invitation to spend time with him.

A week after we graduated from high school, Brainiac was leaving for a summer program at one of those Ivy League schools in Boston. I was staying right here, right in my hometown.

He didn't even say goodbye. One day, he was just no longer there. That's when I realized, I was stuck.

Not only stuck, but utterly confused. During the times we spent together at the hideout, we didn't talk much. Especially not when we were doing our thing.

He was always completely silent from the moment he first opened his pants. Never a word. I wondered what he was thinking. About girls? About boys? Maybe about me? I never knew. I never asked. He never shared that information.

After he left for school, I started to wonder even more. Was that what gay people did? Meet in some secret spot, never touching, never kissing, and just basically stroke themselves? I wondered if somehow Brainiac knew the rules for gay people, and I hadn't gotten the message. Or was he giving me the secret message about how to act by showing me?

I didn't even know for sure if Brainiac was gay. The same for me. Did those actions mean that I was gay? Or was it more my thoughts that defined me?

In the 1970s, there was no place I knew of to find out such things. My one possibly gay contact was now gone, and I didn't know what to do next.

I did know what straight people did for sex. At his 16th birthday party, Clark, another boy at my school, had a secret room where he was showing a videotape of a straight porno. All the guys at the party were allowed to watch for a short time, but not too long so his parents wouldn't get suspicious about what was going on. The man and the woman in that movie did a lot more than Brainiac and I did. They actually touched each other. There was penetration. Were there different sex rules for straights and gays? How was I going to find out?

These were the thoughts that led to my fascination with that bright red door. It led to a place that I could only imagine, where the secrets of the gay world might be exposed. At the very least, once I became aware that a gay bar existed, I was comforted in knowing that I wasn't all alone in the world. But I was too nervous and scared to explore that world, at least for now. I would have to approach this one step at a time, somewhat delicately, at least until I felt more secure with myself.

My plan was to get into the building, but to do it discreetly. I decided to go with my straight friends, to the stripper bar, figuring I could just casually watch what was happening over on the other side of the place, the queer side.

So not long after we had all turned 18, newly graduated from high school, my friends and I, armed with our fake IDs, successfully got past the bouncers at the back entrance. My buddies were there to ogle the strippers and drink as much as possible, typical behavior for teenage hormonal dudes. I was more than happy to get drunk with them, but I was unable to see my real goal, the gay side of the bar. My friends had no idea that I was on a secret mission. But unfortunately, I found that a wall separated the two sides, and you had to go through a door to enter the forbidden zone. It was impossible to accomplish this without being noticed.

At closing time, we sprinted through the pouring rain to my friend's car. During the ride home, they talked excitedly about the strippers. Which ones they liked, what they wanted to do to them, the size of their breasts, etc. I was really too drunk to talk, but the topics held no interest for me, anyway. I vaguely heard my friends talking about the strippers' titties, jugs, bazongas, boobies, etc. They seemed to have a million names for them. But the funniest was when my buddy Josh would try to pronounce the word "breasts." He couldn't quite say that word properly, instead calling them *breastesses*. I quietly laughed every time I heard him say that.

I was sitting in the middle of the back seat during the drive back home, squeezed tightly between Josh and Chase. Josh had taken off his wet shirt and while he continued to jabber on about those big *breastesses*, I was trying not to be noticed as I stared longingly at his left nipple. To my eyes, it was beautiful. It was hard...it was taut...it was...erect! I watched in fascination as a small drop of water from the rain ran down his smooth chest, and paused as it hung precariously on that hard brown little hill on the left side of his chest. Oh, how I wanted to lick it off! But of course, I could do no such thing. So instead, I continued to watch in absolute fascination as that small drop of moisture formed perfectly at the very edge of his masculine, yet erect nipple, wondering if it would ever fall and continue its journey. Amazingly, just as Josh pronounced the word *breastesses* for what seemed like the millionth time, I gasped as I saw that small drop of moisture fall from his nipple, onto his chest and travel the length of his torso until it was swallowed by his little belly button. I was drunk, but I felt like I was in love with Josh at that very moment.

I could feel a tightness in my private area as I watched that show, feeling the pouch of my briefs being filled and then stretched, pushing against the tightness of my jeans, close to exposing my desires at what I was witnessing. Just as I was about to reach between my legs to adjust myself, hopefully inconspicuously, Josh jabbed my chest with his elbow.

"It's your stop, Joey! Don't let your dad catch you coming home drunk again!"

Josh wouldn't move out of the car, so I had to climb over him to exit the vehicle. I reached for the car seat for support, but instead found my hand right between Josh's legs, and I felt...yes, I felt his hard dick inside his pants. No doubt that was caused by him thinking about those gigantic *breastesses*, but the cause of the reaction meant nothing to me. I knew I shouldn't do it, but I just couldn't help myself. As I leaned heavily against his manhood, I gave that mound a little extra squeeze. If he minded, or was even aware of my transgression, he never said a word about it.

Finally out of the car, I vomited in the street before staggering into the house. I could hear my friends laughing drunkenly as they drove away.

The next day, I saw that the rain had washed away all signs of my drunkenness, so I was spared having to explain anything to my stern, old-fashioned father.

As the summer of 1975 drew to a close, I found myself increasingly in the area of that red door. Walking by, hesitating, thinking, considering what if, but not taking the big step of opening the door. The feelings of frustration were growing to a breaking point. I was missing those regular sexual encounters with Brainy, and I had no other connections for any releases for my urges.

I had always felt safe experimenting with Brainiac, but what I was considering was different. It was dangerous.

After all, the Stonewall Riots had only occurred a few years before, in 1969, so being openly gay was not looked on as favorably as many in today's society view it. Not only was anti-gay discrimination legal, but it was openly practiced throughout most of society, especially in an area like where I lived.

Just as the college football season was starting, I saw a guy I had never seen before, hanging out in the same area where the gay bar, Uncle Teddy's Tavern, was located. Probably one of the new freshmen, I thought. He was cute, with a nice but average body, and long hair framing his face like a young rock god.

"You really need it, don't you?" he said as I walked past the park bench on which he was perched.

"What?"

Was I really being that obvious?

"I see you out here all the time. You really need it, don't you?" he repeated.

My first instinct was to deny knowing anything he was talking about, maybe even to run away. But I was intrigued. His hazel eyes were irresistible, and those lips, with a cigarette dangling between them, looked absolutely delicious.

He pulled a joint out of his shirt pocket. "Wanna smoke?" he asked.

"Sure, man," I replied, as I sat next to him on the bench. "I'm Joey."

"I'm Tommy," he replied, tossing aside his cigarette and lighting up the joint. He took a deep drag before offering the joint to me, which I eagerly accepted. As I took the joint, our fingers brushed lightly together, and I felt a surge of electricity pass through my body, just to be so close to him.

The next few minutes were spent silently smoking, allowing our highs to relax our bodies and our minds. But even in a relaxed state of mind, my brain was racing with the possibilities that this encounter might bring.

After finishing off the joint, we started that typical undergraduate chitchat..."What's your major?" Blah, blah, blah. Honestly, I don't remember the rest of the conversation until I suddenly blurted out, "Whaddya mean, I really need it?"

"You know what I mean, man. Dick. You're lookin' for some dick tonight."

I didn't know what to say, and I felt my face turning hot and red. Tommy leaned further back against the back of the bench and spread his legs even farther apart.

"Whaddya say, dude, you wanna come back to my place or you just wanna hang out here by yourself lookin' at guys?"

I nodded my agreement, and he stood up to lead the way to his apartment, located 5 blocks away. I immediately started following him, basically at his side, but letting him lead by being just slightly ahead of me.

It's funny what people think sometimes. During the slow walk to his place, I remember thinking that I was glad that I had already jerked off earlier that day. At such a young age, and thinking about sex all day and all night, I knew it wouldn't take much to bring me to my climax, so having already jacked once might let me last a little longer tonight. I was also glad that I was wearing my tight blue bikini briefs, instead of my usual tighty whities. I had been stupidly nervous when I bought the bikinis, and I even hid them from my father, hand washing them in the bathroom sink and letting them air dry in my bedroom. How do you explain to your dad that you want to wear little bikinis?

Tommy's apartment was on the third floor, but neither of us could wait that long. As soon as we entered the building, we were on each other. Laughing, giggling and panting, we explored each other as we made our way up the stairs. By the time we reached the third-floor landing, we were both excited almost to the point of no return.

I didn't see any of the details as we entered the apartment. All I could see...and hear, taste and smell...was him. He was strong, and he wasn't afraid to use his strength on me. But I was equally strong and showed him that I was his equal as we tore at each other's clothes.

Grabbing, licking, panting, grunting. Whispering words of desire as our bodies slid against each other, until we came to a position where his hardness was in my mouth, and mine in his, a classic 69. His salty taste was all I could think of as my body shuddered, releasing a flood into his mouth that was met a minute later with his creamy essence filling mine.

As expected, the actual sex didn't take very long. But for me, the best was still to come, as I lay in his strong arms and felt his warmth against me. He rubbed his hand on top of my head, playing with my short cropped blonde hair.

He reached across me, grabbing a pack of cigs from the nightstand. We sat in the bed, still naked, both smoking, with his arm around my shoulders, softly playing with my left nipple. It felt so warm, so comforting, so safe to be held by him. I hoped the moment would never end, but moments like that just don't last long enough.

Crushing out his cigarette, he then lit up another joint, handing it to me as he headed to the fridge for a couple of beers. Holding the beers in one hand, he came back to the bed, as the smoke from the joint filled the room with its sweet perfume.

The combination of weed and alcohol went to my head, as I felt the room spinning around me. But that feeling quickly passed as I fell back into Tommy's arms, back into my comfort zone.

During our ensuing conversation, I learned that my first impression that Tommy was an incoming freshman was incorrect. He was actually a junior, majoring in engineering. Clearly, he was a guy with a plan for the future. But more importantly, at least to me, I found out that he was a musician, playing bass in a local rock band that frequented some of the straight bars in town.

I thought about my situation, comparing myself to him. I had just graduated from high school a few months ago, not even applying to college. My part-time job at the sandwich shop was highlighted by making submarine sandwiches with super-hot peppers to satisfy the cravings of the college kids when they had the munchies.

Having no real direction in life, and no role models I wanted to emulate, I was fine with just drifting along for now. After all, through all of high school, I was well-liked and had plenty of friends. I had the nice, smooth, athletic body of a natural swimmer, with strong legs and an awesome ass, round, smooth and muscular. My face is best described as cute, with a winning smile and bright blue eyes. No one would call me a 10, but I graded myself as at least an 8, possibly 9, when compared to some of the less attractive guys.

But school didn't really interest me, and I was mostly a C student. Not stupid, but really just not that interested in academic pursuits. I loved swimming and spent hours upon hours practicing. I also liked the results from my physical exertions, and I knew that guys admired my physique. Strong shoulders, arms, legs, and of course, my best asset, so to speak, was my fat ass, accentuated by my small waist.

"You know, I've seen you around Teddy's a few times," he was saying, as we continued to talk while lightly touching each other playfully. "I like the way you walk.

Something about the way you move your ass," he said, laughing lightly.

His tone changed suddenly. Rather than being playful, he was serious. Maybe a little too serious for my comfort.

"Get on all fours," he commanded.

"What?"

"Don't act like you didn't hear me. Get on all fours."

I hesitated, not for long, but long enough to bother him. He got up on his knees and literally picked me up from the bed, placing me into the position he wanted.

I wasn't ready for this. My previous sexual experiences had been totally hands-off and I had just now given and gotten my first blow job. I had almost choked having him inside my mouth. Burying my face in the pillow, I was prepared to scream if he tried to enter me from the back.

My body tensed.

"Are you a virgin?" he asked me.

"Of course not," I lied.

"Yeah, you are. I can tell. That's nothing to be ashamed of."

I felt him rubbing up against me. But there was no penetration. No fucking. Just rubbing against me, harder and harder, faster and faster. More grunting and groaning. More sweat.

His second orgasm came almost as quickly as his first, leaving a trail of wetness extending from my lower back all the way to my shoulders. Without cleaning me up, he rolled me onto my back and looked directly at me, smiling again, back to being playful.

"To be honest, I'm not really into fucking, but I did want to see what your reaction would be if I tried it. And I wouldn't put it in you unless you really wanted it," he continued.

He was being honest with me, but I stupidly continued to lie, claiming that I was not a virgin. At 18, I felt like I

14

was off to a late start, and I really didn't want anyone to think I didn't have experience.

"Okay, okay!" He was laughing now. "I'll tell my friends that you're a good fuck and you can tell your friends that I'm a great fucker that gave it to you three times in one night. Then we'll both be happy."

That made me laugh, too, but I never told him my secret. That I was still a virgin. And besides that, I didn't have any friends that I could talk to about what had just happened. I wondered if he was lying about having gay friends and telling them about what happened tonight. Or at least, some version of what had happened.

We spent the next half hour or so just relaxing. Then I stood up and told him I had to go. "No problem," was his curt reply, as I walked naked into the bathroom.

I came back out to the combined living/dining/bedroom to get dressed. Tommy was standing in front of the bed, still naked, but holding my blue bikini briefs in one hand, and his red bikini briefs in the other. "Wanna trade?" he asked, with a mischievous grin on his face that could have come from the devil himself. "We wear the same size."

"Sure, honey," I replied, reaching for his bikinis.

"Not so fast," he said, taking both pairs of briefs and rubbing them in my face, forcing me to inhale the musty, exhilarating odors. "Let's get something clear right now. I'm not your honey, I don't wanna be your honey, and I don't want you to ever call me 'honey' again."

"Ok, I got it," I replied, trying to hide my disappointment, but at the same time surprised that I had even called him "honey". I had never called another guy "honey" before, and I didn't even know where that came from. "But you still wanna trade, right?" I asked hopefully.

15

"Sure, bitch," he replied, tossing his briefs into my hand. We both noticed that I had no objection to being called a bitch. That made him smile, as I pulled on his bright red underwear, then getting fully dressed.

Still clutching my briefs, still totally naked, he walked me to the door of his apartment, which was just a few steps away from the bed. Before he opened the door for me, he wrapped his arms around me and gave me a tight squeeze that lasted for more than a few seconds. Then, taking my face in his hands, he gently pushed me down so he could kiss me lightly on the top of my head.

"Oh, hon..." I started, but then quickly corrected myself.

"Thanks, Tommy. I had a great time."

With that, he slapped my ass playfully one more time and opened the door. I had a lot to think about on my way home.

I started to compare what I did with Brainy with what happened with Tommy. The Brainiac had never touched me during our silent sessions. Tommy had been all over me, talking to me, both before, during and after the sex. And of course, Tommy let me suck him, and he returned the favor. I remember thinking how much better it was when the two people touched, communicated, had a connection, then thinking that it was foolish to even compare the two situations. What Brainiac and I had done was really for beginners, for amateurs.

But there was one striking similarity. Neither one of them had ever kissed me. I felt my previous doubts about sex between two guys creeping back into my mind. Was there some unwritten rule that a guy couldn't kiss another guy? Was that something I was doomed to be denied?

A few nights later, I found myself sitting on the park bench across the street from Teddy's, the same bench where I had met Tommy. And yes, I was wearing his red bikinis under my tight jeans, hoping to run into him and recreate the fun we had that night. As I sat there, casually smoking, I watched the red door to Teddy's Tavern. It was early evening, around 9:30 PM, when I saw a young guy walk right into Teddy's. A few minutes later, another one. And after another few minutes, one more guy.

There was no hesitation on their parts. They confidently entered the gay side of the bar, seemingly without a second thought. They didn't look strange or weird. Just regular looking young guys. I wondered for the millionth time what went on inside that place.

My heart started pounding as I thought about actually doing it, actually going into a gay bar. Then my hands started to sweat in the cool autumn air, as I started to seriously consider it. What was I afraid of?

I tried not to think about all the things that might happen. Someone I know could see me going into the bar. Or someone I know might already be in there. I could get branded forever as a faggot. Shunned. Beat up. Robbed. Killed.

I put all that out of my mind as I walked towards the red door. By the time I reached it, I could feel my heart pounding in my ears. I reached for the door, opened it, and after taking a quick look back, I stepped inside. There was no bouncer, no one to check ID, which meant I didn't have to try to pass for 21 with my fake ID.

It was dark inside, and I needed a few minutes for my eyes to adjust. I could see that the room seemed to be a little smaller than the stripper bar on the other side of the building. The air was filled with a smoky haze, making it hard to see the bar on the far side of the room. I noticed that a few tables and chairs were scattered along the other walls. Soul music was blaring from the jukebox, and two couples were slow dancing in the center of the room. One couple consisted of an older looking guy, maybe 35 or so, dancing with a drag queen, resplendent in her sequined

17

gown, high heels and feather boa. I heard her high-pitched giggle as her dance partner squeezed her ample ass while they swayed to the music. The other couple consisted of two younger men, more my age, who were barely moving. Their dance was more of a combination makeout/hip grinding session, with no regard for the beat of the song. Oh, and there was one other guy on the dance floor, performing a rather flamboyant erotic dance all by himself. I remember thinking I wanted some of whatever drug he was on.

There were only two other people in the bar - me and the bartender. I was disappointed, having expected something different, though I wasn't quite sure what I had expected. I headed for the bar, wondering if the bartender would ask for ID, but he placed my beer in front of me with nothing more than a nod and a smile. Getting comfortable sitting at the bar, I turned to watch the dance floor. It wasn't long before the place started to fill up with guys. Some came in through the front door, while others, usually looking a little more nervous, entered from the stripper bar side.

One of the men who came in from the stripper side was short, a little older, with hair that was just beginning to turn slightly grey. He sat down on the stool next to me, patted me on the knee and said to the bartender, "Hey Sal, it looks like we got ourselves a newbie here. Make sure he has a fresh drink all night. On the house."

I took a second look at this guy. He was dressed more formally than the other people in the bar, including me. I was in tight jeans, an even tighter tee shirt that had been cut off at the bottom to show off my abs when I stretched, and sneakers. On the other hand, he wore dress pants, dress shirt and shoes, with a tie loosened at the neck. He may have been wearing a designer label, but at that point in my life, I lacked the sophistication to be able to tell the difference. "Thanks for the drinks, but how? Why?" I stammered.

"Relax, hon. I'm Teddy. I own this place."

"You're Uncle Teddy? I didn't even know that was a real person."

He gave a slight laugh, trying to act like he hadn't heard that same thing at least a thousand times before. I didn't want to come across like an idiot, so I tried to extend the conversation by asking why the bar was divided into two sections.

"You ever hear of gay liberation?" Teddy asked me. To be honest, I had never heard of that exact term, but I was smart enough to know the meaning of the words, so I replied, "Of course."

Teddy explained to me that he was interested in equal rights for gay people, so he wanted to provide a place where they could safely gather and meet other gay people. But he also understood that not everyone would feel comfortable walking into a gay bar, so he decided to make half of the bar into a straight stripper bar. That way, anyone trying to hide their identity could come and go through the straight side, and pass through to the gay side when they felt comfortable. But he felt it was important to also have a direct entrance to the gay side, to encourage people to come out and let their identities be known. And besides, in a college town, a straight stripper bar was a sure money-maker, so he made enough profit to cover the costs of the gay side if it got off to a slow start.

While I was listening to Teddy, I was paying attention, and what he was saying made a lot of sense. But at the same time, I was a horny 18-year-old guy in a gay bar for the first time, so I wasn't exactly looking for a long, serious conversation.

I could hear Teddy talking, but my mind began to wander. I was watching the two guys who had been

19

dancing together, kissing deeply while grinding their bodies against one another. I noticed that, while they weren't dressed alike, their clothes were complementary, as though they had planned a way to look similar, yet different.

While I never really got to know them well, I did learn more about them from other guys who sometimes hung out with them. David and Chris had grown up on the same block, meeting in kindergarten, and becoming best friends at that time. From the age of 5, they were basically inseparable, doing everything together. Clearly, they enjoyed each other's company, enjoyed the same activities and bonded closely. As they reached sexual maturity, they found they had even more in common, as they felt a mutual attraction.

During the time I was watching them perform their slow sensual dance, they were both enrolled at the local college. David was studying journalism, while Chris was in the pre-law program. Both would go on to have successful careers in their chosen fields, and against all odds, they would stay together for many years into the future. Some people, especially in the gay world, spend years searching for their true love. These two had found each other at such a tender age, and they nurtured their love into a life-long relationship. There was a hint of that future success that night in Teddy's Tavern, as they gazed longingly at each other, clearly madly deeply in love.

"So, whaddya think?" Teddy asked, as I realized that I wasn't paying attention to the conversation.

"Well, uhhhh..." I stammered.

"No worries, my dear boy. We can talk about it some other time," he said, with a smile. "Hey Sal, remember to keep the drinks comin' for our new friend here," he said, as he started to get up from the bar stool. "That's my song, I gotta dance," he continued, as a Barry White tune started playing.

Teddy walked over to where the glittering drag queen was standing and started dancing with her. The queen, whom I later got to know as Gracie, wrapped her boa around Teddy's neck, pulling him closer to her, as she shook her supple breasts and moved her ample hips. Her name was Gracie, "In honor of Her Royal Majesty, Princess Grace of Monaco," as she explained to everyone she met. Actually, she told me that every time I ever ran into her. I wondered if she did that with everybody.

I turned to order another, more expensive drink, from Sal. "Why not, since they're on the house," I thought.

A minute later, I felt an arm on my back. For a moment, I thought that Tommy had come in while I wasn't looking, and I turned, expecting to see him. But no, it wasn't Tommy. A guy I had never seen before was inches from my face, leaning into me, trying to get his balance as he had tripped while walking by me.

"I'm so fuckin' sorry," he slurred. as he steadied himself halfway on me and halfway on the empty stool where Teddy had just been sitting. "Hey man, can I bum a smoke?" I handed him one and gave him a light.

I checked him out as he took a deep drag on the cig. Tall and skinny, shaggy brown hair, a hint of a moustache, and a hoop in his left ear. Wearing hip hugger jeans, sneakers and a flannel shirt with the sleeves rolled up to the elbows. Looking very much like the typical college kid at that time.

"Hey man, I'm gonna hit the head. You wanna come?"

"Nah, I'm good," I replied.

"No, c'mon with me. I got something to show you. I promise you're gonna like it," he said, pulling my hand. I let him pull me up from my chair, and he led me towards the men's room. Still holding my hand, he led me straight into a stall. If I had been thinking clearly, I might have resisted, but after a few drinks and with a cute boy, I was willing to go along.

The stall door slammed behind us, and I was wondering what was coming next. I had heard of guys having sex in bathrooms, but I wasn't really ready to try it. Even before I had completed that thought, he reached deep into his pocket and pulled out a plastic baggie. "You like reds or yellows?" he asked. "Only three bucks."

Now I was a teenage boy in the mid 1970s, who had been smoking pot since the age of 13. And of course, I knew guys who took drugs, and I had been offered different drugs on more than one occasion. But I had always declined, happy to enjoy the pleasant high that smoking a joint or two or three provided, with no real desire for anything stronger.

But this time, it just felt different. So I asked him which one he liked. He shrugged and told me that both were equally good, but the reds got him off quicker. So I said, "Sure, I'll take a red," and handed over the three bucks. Unfortunately, I had left my drink sitting on the bar, so he offered me his beer to wash it down.

He stuffed the baggie back into his pocket, took my hand again, and led me to the dance floor. I wasn't much of a dancer, so I clumsily tried to follow his lead, eventually pulling away to free style without touching him. It wasn't long before I felt a tingle in my fingers, leading to feeling somewhat numb. Same for my feet. I felt like I was dancing on air, found the beat, and moved more smoothly than I had ever danced before. At least, that's what it felt like. By the end of the song, I was higher than I had ever experienced before, and it was a feeling that I would try to relive many more times in the future. But there's nothing quite like that first time, right?

I felt warm and giddy and horny and silly. We went into a dark corner and started feeling each other with the abandon of mindless teenage boys. I felt my hand reaching between his legs, rubbing against the hardness in his jeans. Unexpectedly, he went stumbling away towards the bar, wanting another drink. I tried to keep my eye on him, but the bar had gotten quite crowded, and I lost sight of him for a minute. I was having a little trouble focusing my eyes, but I thought I saw him leading another guy into the bathroom, just as he had led me a few minutes before. I didn't realize it at the time, but I later came to understand that to him, I was just another customer.

While he was conducting his business transactions in the men's room, I scanned the dancing crowd. For just a brief moment, it struck me what a cool scene this was. Guys...gay guys...openly dancing with each other, talking, laughing, having fun.

But in my current state, it was hard to keep a coherent thought for more than a few seconds. My body was becoming even more numb, and I truly couldn't think straight. I started to walk around the perimeter of the bar, only able to focus on whomever or whatever was right in front of me, unable to see the big picture. That's when Troy came into my view. If I could've opened my eyes wide, I would have, but they were not cooperating at that particular moment. But I was quite sure that was Troy, a guy I knew from high school. Not only did I know him, but he was one of my secret crushes for the last four years. And there he was, leaning against the wall at Uncle Teddy's. I wasn't sure if I should turn around and hide or what.

"Joey, what the fuck're you doin' here!?"

I have to admit, I had spent more than a few nights thinking about Troy when I was lying awake in my bed, stroking myself. He was one of the finest boys in my class, very handsome with a bright smile and the body of a star athlete. So it would be stupid to turn and run now.

"Hey, Troy." It seemed to me that I was speaking more slowly than usual, and I wondered if he would notice. But almost immediately, a couple of guys came off the dance floor and joined Troy, making it clear that he was there with a group of friends. One of them grabbed me by my waist and twirled me around before letting go.

"How long have you been out?" Troy asked. "I've been out for a couple months now," he continued.

I knew what he meant by the question, but since this was my first night at Teddy's Tavern, on the gay side, I didn't even have time to process whether that meant I was "out" or not. So I just avoided the question.

"What's up, man?" I asked. "It's great to see you!"

He introduced me to his friends, and we engaged in the typical "Nice to meet you" chatter. Of course, I was having trouble concentrating and couldn't even remember one name after the introductions were completed. Besides, my eyes were glued on Troy. Oh my God, here was Troy, an object of my desire, standing right in front of me, in a gay bar, no less!

I was feeling almost unbearably horny. I wanted to feel Troy in my arms, under my thrusting body, my hands running through his beautiful, thick black hair, licking and kissing all those special areas of the male anatomy.

Troy suggested that we go outside for a minute, to smoke a joint. Although I didn't want or need to get any higher, I jumped at the opportunity for a little alone time with him. The night had gotten a little cooler since I had gone into Teddy's, although I was too numb to notice. But Troy put his arm around my shoulders and suggested we go sit in his car to have a little talk.

"Yeah, right, a little talk," I thought.

We got into the back seat of his car, and his hands were instantly all over me. Before I knew it, he had opened my pants and was furiously pumping me. Although both my body and my mind were numb, I still felt the sexual pleasure washing over me. I watched as he opened his jeans and stroked himself with one hand while he continued to work on my erection.

At that point in my life, I was certainly no expert on dicks. But it isn't like I hadn't already seen plenty of naked boys - in the locker rooms, in the showers, and up close and personal while sexually exploring. I had spent four years fantasizing about being with Troy, but my fantasy never included the reality that I encountered, that Troy had the tiniest dick I had ever seen.

It didn't take long for both of us to reach our climaxes. Surprisingly, after we both finished, Troy pulled a couple of cocktail napkins from the bar out of his pocket, cleaned us up, and threw the napkins out the car window. I wondered if giving hand jobs in his car was part of his regular sexual routine, and I was later told that was indeed the case.

After I fumbled my way out of Troy's car, I went home, a little disappointed in how my first night in a gay bar had ended.

It seemed like my ventures into the gay world were actually sliding backwards, going from masturbating myself with Brainiac, then moving on to oral sex with Tommy, only to slide back to mutual masturbation with Troy. Even the location didn't seem right. First, a secret hideout, then a guy's apartment, and now sneaking in the back seat of a car in a parking lot. The more I thought about it, I was actually more depressed than disappointed. I had always been attracted to guys, but this wasn't how I had expected things to be.

A few days later, I was busy working at the sandwich shop, when my friend Josh came in. It was Friday, and every Friday night since we had gotten our fake IDs, a small group of us always went to Teddy's, on the straight side of course, to party.

"Hey Joey, we're still goin' to Titty's tonight, right?" Josh asked, with a huge grin on his face. We had started calling Teddy's "Titty's," a clear reference to the strippers who provided the entertainment on the straight side of the place. "You bet," I replied, wrapping a sandwich for a customer. "Can't wait."

All the members of our group were still living at home with their parents, so Josh drove around the neighborhood, picking us all up, before we headed over to the bar. During the entire trip, Josh talked incessantly about titties. He had a true fetish for female breasts, or as he continued to call them, breastesses. Every other word out of his mouth seemed to be titty, or some other term that men use for breasts. He was clearly excited to be on our way to the bar, the same as he was every Friday night. Among all of us, he always had the best time, tipping the strippers and enjoying the attention he got from them.

This particular night, it was clearly different for me. I had been to the other side. I had not only been there, but I loved it over there. Seeing gay guys acting naturally and without shame was very appealing to me.

But I went into the straight side with my buddies, sitting at a table and taking turns paying for the pitchers of beer. The main conversation was comparing the sizes of the various girls' breasts, followed by macho talk about what we would do with the girls if we ever had a chance with one of them. My friends had no idea that I had absolutely zero interest in girls. I knew how to play the game. But the question for me was, did I want to play that game?

Did I want to blend in and pretend to be something different than my true self?

I made a decision, right there, right then. I stood up and told the guys, "Hey. I'm gonna go check out the other side." Although the bar was loud with music and the chatter of the customers, a stunned silence came over our table. Everybody knew what the other side was. "Ok, faggot," Josh said, thinking that I had to be joking.

"No, man. I really mean it. I don't belong over here," I said, and I abruptly left my friends and walked through the door to the gay side. Things were never the same between me and that group of guys, but that was my decision and I was okay with that.

The gay side was fairly crowded, but I didn't stay long. I didn't really want one of my buddies to get curious and leave the straight side to check up on me. And I definitely didn't want to run into any of them at closing time. So I found myself walking in the direction towards Tommy's apartment.

I hadn't seen him since the night we met outside of Teddy's. His exact words to me that night were, "You really need it, don't you?" That's exactly how I felt, as I strolled more quickly with each passing block on the way to his building. I felt like I needed it, needed it badly. When I reached his building, I didn't even hesitate, ringing the bell to his apartment.

"Who's there?" His voice sounded gruff over the intercom.

"It's me, Joey. Remember me?" I asked.

There was no answer, but the door buzzed and I pushed it open. I bounded up the steps, two at a time, up to the third floor. I knocked and the door opened wide.

I was surprised that Tommy was already naked and even more surprised that he was already hard, his erection pointing straight up, extending an inch or two beyond his hairless belly button.

"You wanna come in?' he asked, stepping aside so I could see into the room. There on the bed was another guy. A sexy, good-looking guy.

"Yeah," I said. I walked into Tommy's apartment, about to experience my first gay threesome. But you can be sure, it wouldn't be my last.

TWO

During the next few months, there were some dramatic changes to my life, as I adjusted to my new reality of being an out gay teenager. I didn't tell everyone, but when you live in a small town like I did, word does get around. No one told my father, so I didn't have to deal with his bullshit. But I was hanging out with a new group of friends, spending less and less time at home, and by the time I turned 19, I was seriously thinking about moving out. I figured I could get started by having a roommate and then eventually get my own place.

Sitting on the swing on our front porch, thumbing through a magazine, I barely saw the pages in front of me. I was thinking about guys. Not unusual. I was obsessed with them. More specifically, I was obsessed with kissing a guy.

By this time, I had a few sexual experiences, but they were always quick, secretive oral sessions. There seemed to be plenty of guys who were quite happy with sucking and getting sucked. Jacking and getting jacked.

I replayed those scenes in my head, over and over and over. Now, don't get me wrong; I was having fun. I was discovering that I could feel comfortable with these other guys, and it was a major relief that I wasn't all alone in the world.

My fantasies included being topped by a strong guy, but I had another, stronger fantasy. I wanted to kiss. Not a peck on the cheek. Not on my forehead. I wanted a boy to kiss me hard, wet, on the lips, feeling his tongue in my mouth. But anytime I tried to kiss a sex partner, they shied away from that contact. Some of them specifically told me, "No kissing. Ever." I had to wonder why.

Was it a fear of intimacy? Was it normal? Again, I asked myself, is it a rule? An unwritten rule that somehow everyone knew about except me?

My thoughts were interrupted by the sound of my father's voice, calling me from inside the house. "Phone!" he hollered.

I was surprised to hear Troy's voice at the other end of the line, asking me if I wanted to go to the movies with him that night. Having no plans, I agreed to go.

Even on a Thursday night, there was a line to get into the theater. Troy wanted to see *The Omen*. I imagined Troy holding me in the darkness as we huddled in terror, watching the devil try to take over the world, but of course, that didn't really happen.

We sat in the back row, and surprisingly, Troy left an empty seat between the two of us. I thought that was odd. Did he really think it would be suspicious if the two of us actually sat next to each other?

I forgot about my annoyance as I was swept up into the drama of the story. "I'm going for another popcorn. You want anything?" Troy whispered.

When he returned, he handed me a box of candy and slid into the seat right next to me. Moments later, I felt his hand on my bare knee, rubbing me suggestively.

"Oh hell, is he really thinking about stroking me right here in the theater?" I thought, feeling his hand creeping upward.

But his hand never went past my inner thigh, though he rubbed my leg throughout the rest of the movie. Squeezing my knee, gently tickling my upper leg, almost reaching the place where I was feeling the tension build, but then moving back down to my knee. It was exciting and frustrating at the same time.

Before I knew it, the closing credits were on the screen, and I realized I had missed the entire second half of the movie. "Did the devil win?" I wondered.

Troy got up to go, but I had to whisper, "Wait. I can't stand up right now."

He sat back down, giggling uncontrollably, but trying to keep it quiet. We were still sitting there as the theater emptied and the lights went up.

"You ready yet?" He was still laughing, though more calmly.

"Almost!" By that time, I was laughing too.

"What now?" I asked as we left the theater. I was expecting some sort of sexual encounter, as it struck me that I had just gone on my first date with a boy. And don't boys always try to get it in with their dates, even if that date is with another guy?

As we walked towards his car, I wondered if he wanted to play the same way we did in the parking lot at Teddy's. But no, he just started driving me home. After the short drive, we pulled into my driveway and he just sat there. I didn't know what he wanted.

But I did know what I wanted. I leaned towards him, reaching for his chin, pulling his face towards mine. I wanted his lips. Those beautiful, luscious full lips.

"No," he said firmly. "I don't kiss guys."

And that was it. I was deflated, rejected. I figured that there had to be something wrong with me, to want so badly to feel a guy's soft lips against mine. My desire turned to anger.

"Okay," I shouted. "Thanks for the movie," I said, with as much sarcasm as I could muster. I can only imagine what Troy was thinking as he watched me stomp my feet on my way back into the house, frustrated at my inability to understand what guys wanted, and wondering why they didn't want what I wanted.

31

And if anyone had asked me, I would have had to admit that I really didn't know what I wanted except to feel that kiss. Maybe that would make me feel that sex with guys was somehow more valid, more acceptable, more "normal," if we acted more like straight people did. But later I would realize that gays didn't have to act like straights. We could have our own style. Our own culture. Our own ways. But dammit, I still wanted someone to kiss me.

July 2, 1976, was a Friday. In two days, the United States would be celebrating the Bicentennial, two hundred years of American history. The city of Philadelphia was planning a huge celebration, since the country was basically born there. I was thinking about driving down there to spend a long weekend celebrating America, and maybe check out the gay scene there at the same time.

My father and I lived in a single-story home in a small town, a 75-mile drive from Philly. I rarely went into the city, but my father worked there. He drove 75 miles, back and forth every day, to get to work and back home. In his opinion, Philly was a good place to work, but he always said that he would never live there.

In 1976, the country was just coming out of a recession, so the economy was improving for some people, but my father's business was suffering. He owned a factory, running a company that produced parts used in automobile manufacturing. A series of bad business decisions and the lingering effects of the economy were driving him out of business. Maybe one of his bad decisions was to pay off the mortgage on the factory as early as possible, but he thought that owning the building outright would provide economic security. Instead, it actually threatened his business, since all his profits were going to pay off the mortgage.

So on that day, July 2, my father drove into Philly to inform his employees that he was forced to lay all of them off. Not the news anyone wants to hear at the start of a holiday weekend. But he did what he had to do, telling the employees how to apply for unemployment compensation. The looks on their faces wore heavily on my dad, and he was feeling a lot of stress as he got on the highway and had to fight holiday weekend traffic on the way home.

About a mile from the exit to our town, my father suffered a massive heart attack, as he was on what would be his final trip home. He lost control of the car, and crashed into an overpass. I was informed not long after, when the local police showed up at the house to escort me to the hospital.

Although we weren't particularly close, it wasn't like I hated him or wished him any harm. But the fact is, I didn't think I would really miss him, either. So not having the opportunity to talk to him before he died wasn't the tragedy for me that it would be for some people.

Of course, I couldn't go to Philly for the Bicentennial celebrations. I spent the weekend making arrangements for his funeral. My aunt, who lived nearby, helped a lot. She even offered to let me move in with her. "Hell, no!" I thought, but I was actually much more polite when I declined the offer. I had recently been making plans to move out of my dad's house, so there was no way I would even consider living with my aunt.

Because of the circumstances of his death, an autopsy was required. It was determined then that he had a heart attack, but the actual cause of death was the car accident. For me, that seemed like a detail with no significance, until I was told that his life insurance policy would pay double in case of accidental death. And I was his sole beneficiary.

After the funeral, I had a lot to think about. I was living alone, on my own for the first time in my life, with responsibilities that I had never even considered before. Once the check from the insurance company was delivered, I really felt like I had enough money to live on for a very long time, maybe even a lifetime. One choice would have been to just stay in the same house, in the same town, and live out my life there.

I also had to make a decision about the old factory, which I now owned. It had been a few years since I had been there, so I decided it was time to check out the place.

The night before I was planning to drive down to the city, I found myself once more relaxing, swinging on the front porch. Troy drove up and stopped on the street right in front of my house. I was always surprised to see him. But he wasn't alone, making me wonder what he was thinking. Rather than parking and coming up to the house, Troy let out his passenger, then drove off.

I recognized him instantly. He had been with Troy the night I first saw him at Teddy's, and I also knew him because I had bought weed from him a few times back when we were both in high school.

"Joey!" he shouted as he ran towards me. I wondered why he seemed so excited to see me, but in reality, I had been feeling a bit lonely, so I was glad to see him.

"Drizz! It's fuckin' good to see you!"

Everybody called him Drizz because his last name was Driscoll. And he hated his first name, Abner, bristling whenever a teacher insisted on calling him by that name.

Before I could get up, Drizz was already seated next to me on the swing. "Damn, dude, I like your new look."

Though he was just a small-time dealer, Drizz always had plenty of extra money, spending more than most guys on fashions and accessories. Clogs, bell-bottom jeans, tight tee shirt with wide red, black and white vertical stripes, a string of puka shells around his neck, his normally brown hair now dyed a shocking shade of platinum blonde.

"You like these?" he asked, pulling his ears forward to show that he had just gotten both ears pierced, sporting one small gold stud in each lobe.

"Awesome!" I said, gently touching each one. "Did it hurt?"

"Just a little, but definitely worth it. Me and Troy both got them done. They got a stand down at the carnival."

"I knew you were at the carnival! I can smell the cotton candy," I said, laughing.

"I got something for you, too," he told me, reaching into the bag he had brought with him from the car. "Close your eyes."

Feeling just a bit silly, I did as he asked. "Open!" he commanded.

I laughed when I saw what he handed me. A small pink stuffed toy kangaroo.

"I won it tossing rings onto Coke bottles," he explained. "When I saw it, I thought about you. 'Cause it's a joey!"

We both started laughing. "You're a sweetheart," I said, looking at Drizz but giving the little toy joey a hug and a kiss on its head. Grinning, I thought that was just about the cutest thing a guy had ever done for me.

"I got something else for ya, a couple of joints, but we should really go inside first, right?"

I almost never turned down an offer to smoke, so we both headed into the house, where we could smoke without the neighbors getting suspicious. Drizz lit up while I turned on the TV and joined him on the couch.

It wasn't long before I was flying high, totally relaxed, feeling myself sinking deeper and deeper into the cushions of the couch.

Eyes closed, listening to the drone of the TV, but not hearing anything that was being said. Feeling his knee pushing against mine. His foot against my foot. My eyes still closed, I felt the soft touch of his hand against my cheek. Smiling, laughing just a little, as I could once again smell the sweetness of the cotton candy on his breath. I started to speak.

"Don't," he whispered, placing one finger against my lips. "Just enjoy the feeling."

I lay back on the sofa, feeling his body pushing mine down onto my back, his weight leaning into me. I let out a sigh when I felt his soft lips kissing my eyes, and he once more brushed his fingers softly against my lips.

I opened my mouth slightly, just enough to extend an invitation.

He accepted that invitation and pressed his lips against mine. That was the single most intense feeling of pleasure that I had ever experienced. He pulled back, his lips just millimeters from mine and then he kissed me again. My response was to moan softly, losing myself in the sensation. Reaching back and running his fingers through my hair, he kissed me again, this time using his tongue to open my lips just a bit more, sliding into my mouth in an act of sheer intimacy.

We did more that night, as our passions took over and we enjoyed the satisfaction of sex between two young guys, but I'll never forget, not for as long as I live, the sheer beauty of that first kiss with a boy.

The next day, I was ready for my trip to Philly, placing the toy joey on the dash of the car, reminding me of the pleasures of the previous night during the long drive. Once I arrived and found the old factory, it didn't take long for me to figure out that it was located just a few blocks north of the area known as the "Gayborhood" in Center City Philadelphia. The area was mostly industrial,

36

with factories and warehouses, that years later would be converted into expensive condominiums. But this was 1976, and the area could best be described as run-down and maybe even a little dangerous. No one really lived in the area, but plenty of people worked there. After leaving work, they traveled to other parts of the city or to the suburbs to go home. Besides the factories, there were a few restaurants in the area where people went for breakfast and lunch, basically diners and pizza/sandwich shops, nothing at all fancy or sophisticated.

I contacted the former manager of the place and asked him to give me a tour. The factory was located on a corner, taking up an entire small block running from north to south, and about half the block running east and west. It was a larger building than I had remembered, five stories tall. It was filled with machinery, but what struck me were the wide-open spaces inside. I was starting to get an idea for how to use the space, but I wasn't sure I could pull it off.

The disco era was in full swing, quickly gaining in popularity with young people who flocked to the dance halls, partying till dawn. I pictured this old factory being converted into a disco, but a gay disco, hopefully drawing the residents of the Gayborhood a few blocks north for a night of fun.

I decided to spend a week or two in Philly, to get acquainted with the area and the people there. Finding a cheap hotel room was easy. Although I had money, I wasn't about to start spending like crazy. I had a feeling I would need a lot of money to put my plans into place.

My exploration began just by walking around Center City. In those days, Center City was defined as the area between Spring Garden Street on the north to the southern boundary at South Street, and between the two rivers, the Delaware and the Schuylkill, from east to west.

There was a lot to see in that area, but I tried to concentrate on the Gayborhood.

I also needed advice and guidance from other people, and an important resource for me was found in a new publication at the time, the Philadelphia Gay News (aka PGN). That paper not only had stories about what was happening in gay life, but there were lots of ads for gay establishments in the area. That helped me to easily find the bars, clubs, bathhouses, coffeehouses and other shops and places that were gay-friendly. I first saw the paper stacked in piles at the doors of various gay establishments, but I later came to rely on getting my weekly copy from one of their iconic plum-colored vending boxes.

The back section of PGN was packed with classified ads from gays seeking other gays. For example:
"GWM Gr/pas Fr/act w/7.5 cut sks dom GBM for close encounters. Can't host. Reply to Box xxxx."

In other words, a White male bottom (Greek passive, French active referred to anal and oral sex, respectively) with a 7.5 inch circumcised dick was looking for a dominant Black top. Stating that he couldn't host usually, but not always, meant that the guy placing the ad was married, but in any case, needed to be discreet. Having our own language like that used in the ads was one of the many parts of gay culture that I found appealing.

Something that surprised me as I went to see the locations of the gay bars in Center City was that they were almost always located on small side streets or in alleys. My best guess was that, even in an area informally called the Gayborhood, gay people still felt the need to be somewhat discreet. One reason, of course, was that the gay lifestyle was just starting to come into the mainstream of American life, so it was still somewhat of an underground community. In addition, there were still laws against homosexuality, and Philly cops were sometimes overly enthusiastic in their attempts to keep gay people "in their place."

Besides their somewhat hidden locations, most of the bars catering to the gay crowd were in bad shape, sometimes to the point of actually being dilapidated. One time, I was in a crowded bar located on the second floor of a building, where I could feel the dance floor bouncing from the weight of the dancers. One reason for the unsafe conditions at some of these places might be due to owner neglect or lack of money, but looking back, I also think there was a deliberate attempt to make gay people feel that they didn't deserve a nice, safe place to congregate. Today this might be described as institutionalized homophobia, but at the time, people seemed to just accept those conditions without really questioning how or why they occurred.

Another observation I made was that the gay places were clearly racially segregated. In my hometown, I had never even noticed that Teddy's Tavern was filled completely with whites. I also never paid any attention to the fact that the schools I attended were 100% white, simply accepting that as a fact of my surroundings. But now that I was in Philly, I was suddenly aware that other races actually existed in real life, beyond the occasional sighting of a Black person on a TV show.

I needed some time to think about this. Back home, the only people we considered "different" were the kids who went to Catholic school. Sometimes we laughed at them, as they wore their school uniforms that set them apart from the rest of us. But I never felt any real hostility towards them. I just perceived them as different, though if you had asked me what set us apart, I wouldn't have been able to tell you any real facts.

I didn't feel like I harbored any prejudices against people of other races. The fact is, I didn't really know anyone who was a different race. Of course, I had heard the ugly names that some whites called other people, and I knew that plenty of people, even those I knew, wanted to keep society segregated. Back in my hometown, I didn't consider it an issue that was important to me, and I just accepted it as natural that my surroundings were totally populated with white people. I never questioned why it was that way.

As time went on, my views on race changed dramatically. Some people later described me as being "color-blind," but I rejected that description. To me, being color-blind was to refuse to acknowledge an important part of any person. Instead, I strived to be accepting and appreciative of the diversity of the human race, including diversity of gender, race, sexual orientation, age, or any of the many factors that make all of us unique individuals. Did I always succeed? No, but at least I started to acknowledge the issues and to take a stand on the side of inclusion.

My plan was to spend two weeks in Philly. During that time, I went out to as many places as I could, concentrating on places popular with gays. I not only wanted to have fun, but I also wanted to see how these businesses were conducted. How did they attract gay people there? How did they treat their customers? What made people return or what made them decide not to go back to a particular place?

Remember that during this visit, I was a 19-year-old cute guy with a winning smile and a very cute butt. When I went to a bar, I was never carded, not once. But it didn't escape my notice that some people were always carded at certain establishments, specifically anyone who wasn't white. Sometimes, Black or Brown people would be turned away, even if they had valid ID and really were old enough to drink legally. I would hear the bouncers accuse some guys of not looking like the photo on the ID, or of having altered something. The bouncer always got the last word; there was no avenue for appeal.

The truth is, some of the customers inside those white clubs actually wanted it that way. They wanted to be with "their own kind." Others never even thought about it; it wasn't their problem.

For me, being with my own kind meant being with other gay people, in all their different colors and flavors.

During those two weeks I spent exploring the gay side of Philly, I found that there were plenty of places outside of bars to meet guys. The Museum of Art, the Free Library, and various parks were known areas for guys cruising to meet other men for sex. I even heard about the Merry-Go-Round, a one block stretch along Spruce and Pine Streets, where men in cars would circle the block, looking for sexual encounters. I was open to all these possibilities. I didn't see any reason to restrict my cruising for men to bars and clubs.

One evening, while hanging out on a park bench in Rittenhouse Square, I met Henry, a young Black guy who had the most intensely beautiful eyes that I had ever seen. He was of average height and on the skinny side, wearing a crop top that showed his tight abs. But it was hard to look at anything besides those gorgeous brown eyes.

Henry sat down on the bench beside me and immediately started talking to me as if we had been best friends forever. I would later find out that he was that friendly and engaging with almost everybody, a truly friendly and likeable individual. He asked me if I wanted to go out for a drink with him, mentioning the name of a club that I hadn't yet heard about. This was a club that wouldn't be advertising in PGN or any other publication.

It was more of an underground place, only advertised by word-of-mouth, keeping the secret only among those who would be interested in a place like this. Feeling adventurous, and always wanting to know more about the gay life here, I readily agreed.

We took the subway to a station in North Philadelphia and then walked a few blocks west of Broad Street. The club was located in a basement, under a corner store. A hand-written chalkboard sign identified the club as Sharkey's. Inside, it was packed with men, almost all of them Black men. There were two bars along the walls, a dance floor in the middle, sort of a typical layout. Although the air conditioners were set to full blast, the heat inside was almost unbearable. That heat, combined with the odor of strong perfumes and colognes, cigarette and marijuana smoke, almost took my breath away. But there was no denying, from the moment we entered, that the atmosphere here was electric.

Without this crowd, the bar would just be a typical place for hanging out and grabbing a drink. It was the clientele that made this place so very special. After all, these were gay men, in a relatively safe space for them, so they felt free to express their true selves. Many of them did so in their manner of dress. To me, it resembled a fashion show, with guys dressed in the latest fashionable attire, with plenty of flamboyance meant to catch the eye of an attractive male.

There were also a couple of men in drag, with make-up done immaculately, sporting large wigs, gowns and high heels. Later that night, they would be putting on a show, lip syncing to the songs of the divas they adored.

The music was so loud I could barely hear Henry as he introduced me to some of his friends. Most were friendly, but a few acted like I was an unwanted outsider. That surprised me a little. I had been noticing how the white clubs in Center City were less than welcoming to minorities, but it never occurred to me that some people in a Black club would prefer to see only Black men there.

As Henry continued to chat with his friends, I took a step back to take a really good look at him. His skin was dark brown, glowingly beautiful. He had those very high cheekbones that you might see on a supermodel and eyebrows that were somewhat more arched than those of most men. His mannerisms were not at all effeminate, though he was beautiful in a way that was more feminine than masculine. He was clean-shaven, with no hint of a beard or moustache. I wondered if he had to shave at all.

We all have our types of guys that we like, and not everyone would find Henry attractive, but to my eyes, he was handsome, sexy and desirable. Another point in his favor - I had already discovered that Henry enjoyed kissing me as much as I enjoyed the feeling of his lips against mine.

His eyes were as hypnotically beautiful as they had been when I first met him. I watched as one of his friends, who was several inches taller than Henry, patted him on his head, slightly rubbing his short curls, making me wonder if they had a history between them. Henry arched his back just a bit at the man's touch, stretching his broad shoulders upward. His body was so sleek, so smooth, and I saw how his slightly muscular arms were starting to glisten in the heat of the room. The more I gazed at him, the more I felt a very strong sexual attraction to him. He pulled me forward to engage me in the conversation and I let him hold me as the group talked, feeling his strong legs leaning tightly against mine.

We stayed to watch the drag show. Tricksie was the first to perform. Unfortunately, she tried to incorporate high kicks into her routine, but she just wasn't limber enough to be successful. Although her choreography needed a

43

little work, her lip syncing was flawless and her enthusiastic delivery won over the audience. I was a little distracted by seeing that her stockings were somewhat worn, with a few runs and even a small tear here and there. And her shoes looked for sure as if they came from a second-hand store. Despite these observations, I admired the fact that she had the courage to get up in front of a crowd, dressed in drag, and put on a show. It isn't easy to do that, to open yourself to criticism, in order to express yourself the way you choose to do so.

I didn't tip Tricksie that night, but plenty of other guys did, including the three guys in jheri curls, who all worked as hairdressers at a shop called Black Beauty. They encouraged her, and to me, that was cool. I hoped the tips and the encouragement would be enough for her to feel empowered to come back and perform again, maybe the next night, maybe the next week. Maybe she could at least use her tips to invest in a new pair of stockings. I mean, come on girl, let's be real. You gotta look good, right?

When I told Henry what I was thinking, he gave me a look. "Joey, you really gotta learn that not everybody has things as easy as you. Tricksie is unemployed and was just kicked out of her place. She's putting on a show tonight to make some money to eat. And you're gonna stand there and criticize her for her stockings?"

I admit it. I felt guilty. Of course, I knew that some people struggled to survive, but I didn't really know anyone in that type of situation. I told Henry how stupid I felt, but he assured me that everything was okay. However, it was clear that he expected me to have more empathy for what other people were going through in their lives. Like I said before, Henry had already thought about things and had formed opinions on subjects that I had never even considered.

The clear favorite of the crowd was BaeBae, dressed all in red and moving with the grace of an Olympic athlete. Midway through her set, she ripped off her gown, working her way around the dance floor wearing panties and bra, garter belt, stockings and heels. When she passed by me, I slipped a few bucks into her garter belt, and she gave me a kiss on the cheek. At the time, I didn't know anything about tucking ("Why would anyone ever want to do that?" I would have asked), but I did notice that she seemed to have nothing between her legs.

Henry knew the stories of more than a few people in the bar, including BaeBae. In her life outside of the club, out of drag, she went by her given name, Ernest, working as a makeup artist. She made a good living, with a huge following, mostly ladies who would patiently wait for her services at the department store counter. A few gay guys could also be counted among her clientele. And every theater company in Philadelphia always utilized her skills whenever they were having a show.

Whether as Ernest or BaeBae, she was always meticulously and flamboyantly dressed. For example, Ernest might strut around Center City in a lavender suit, a large, floppy hat, dark sunglasses with huge frames and the highest platform shoes he could find. Being effeminate was part of Ernest's nature, and he embraced it fully.

If asked, Ernest would describe that side of himself out of drag as his "church-going" side. He didn't mean that literally; Ernest never went to church. Instead, he used that term as a way to describe wearing men's clothing as a costume, a sham, putting on a show for the world. Ernest's view of the world included the opinion that people who went to church did so for show only, not because of any true belief.

He would also describe his life as BaeBae as the only time he was really being true to himself, or to describe it more accurately, that was the only time she was being true to herself. BaeBae insisted that she truly was a female, but born into a body with male physical characteristics. In those times, this idea seemed novel at best, and downright unbelievable to many people.

BaeBae was not at the club headlining the drag show because she needed money. This was when she felt like she was truly alive. The night we saw her, she had not quite reached the point of living her life full-time as a female. But that was her ultimate goal, and she even sometimes talked about having full reconstructive surgery to make the transition complete.

BaeBae thought of herself as a sweetheart, but the truth is that she had developed a tough exterior shell around her vulnerable spirit. Not surprising, considering how society viewed and treated feminine boys. Rejected by her family at an early age, treated with contempt by the other kids at school and in her neighborhood, of course she developed a number of defense mechanisms. She often used her sarcastic wit and bitter tongue to lash out at others, in anticipation that they would eventually reject and/or abuse her anyway. She didn't let her guard down often, but when she did, those who got to really know her knew that she could be kind, loyal and lovable, all the while maintaining a fiercely independent streak.

A little later, Henry and I left the club, arm in arm, laughing and enjoying ourselves. I was feeling a little buzzed and uninhibited. Somehow the conversation turned back to Tricksie, and I told Henry again how badly I felt for judging her so harshly.

"You salty!" Henry said, laughing almost uncontrollably as he brushed a few imaginary grains from my shoulder. "I told you that story about Tricksie because it does bother me when people jump to conclusions. But the truth is, I don't really know anything about that queen. Maybe she's unemployed, maybe not. The hell if I know."

My first reaction was to be mad at being fooled like that. But I quickly realized, even in my buzzed state of mind, that Henry had used an effective technique to teach me something.

"Ok, one point for you," I said, making a motion with my index finger to draw an imaginary "1" in the air. "But watch out; the next point's gonna be mine."

The next morning, I woke up on the mattress of a sofabed in the living room of Henry's apartment. I was naked and alone, but then I saw that Henry was in the kitchen area, making coffee. He was naked too, and I admired his sleek, sexy body. Before I could say anything, another guy, his roommate, a slightly older white guy, came out of the bedroom, apparently in a hurry.

"I'm gonna be late for work," he said, reaching for the door to the apartment. "Oh, hey," he said to me, then turning his attention to Henry, he continued, "Be back later. See ya, sweetie!"

Henry explained to me that he had recently moved in with John, and although they were roommates, they didn't sleep together. John had the bedroom, since the apartment was originally his, and Henry slept on the sofabed. The arrangement was strictly for economic reasons, with Henry needing a cheap place to live and John wanting someone to help pay the rent.

I always woke up with an erection, and today was no exception. The sight of Henry, standing stark naked in front of me, casually drinking his coffee, struck me as so incredibly sexy. I started to think about the sex we had the night before, remembering it as passionate, hard, and over much too quickly. I threw off the sheets that were covering my passion as Henry put down his coffee and joined me on the bed for a second round.

From a very early age, I knew I was attracted to other males. My fantasies were often sexual in nature, but honestly, I always thought about being with other males in all aspects of my life, whether it was playing sports, going to the movies, or just hanging out. I was never interested in girls, not even socially. Later on in life, I learned to appreciate women, but at this time, I was really focused on being with other males.

At that young age of 19, I didn't really consider all the implications of my feelings. Was it possible for another man to fulfill more than my sexual needs and desires? Could a man satisfy all of my social, emotional, even spiritual needs as well? There were no role models for me to consider at the time. I never heard of two men building a life together. Could it happen? I admit that those thoughts were going through my head after meeting Henry.

"I'm off till 4 o'clock this afternoon," he said, getting out of the bed. "You got any plans?"

After showering together, we walked over to my hotel so I could change my clothes. Then I took him over to my father's factory, well actually, it was now my factory. I took him inside, gave him a tour, and told him that I was thinking about converting the place into a gay nightclub.

Henry was immediately on board with the idea. "This place could be awesome!" His enthusiasm was contagious as we walked around, imagining how the place could be designed and decorated.

"I already know that I want the front door to be red," I told him, describing my attraction to the red door at Teddy's back home. "And I like the idea of decorating with neon sculptures...you know, maybe something sexual, definitely gay," I continued. Other than that, I was open to ideas, and Henry shared what he thought could add to the overall design of the place.

By the time we left, we had a pretty good idea of how that first floor could be converted into a very cool place to attract the gay crowd.

Henry had another idea. He suggested that I consider trying to get a license to run a private club. The closing time of a regular bar in Philly was at 2 AM. With a private club, my place could serve alcohol until 3:30 AM, with the last customers needing to be out the door by 4 AM. That was a new concept to me, but it sounded like a good option to explore.

The day flew by very quickly, as we went to a deli for lunch and continued to talk excitedly about our plans. Conversations with Henry were so easy, never feeling forced just to fill the dead air. He had an opinion about everything and he encouraged me to discuss all kinds of topics, whether we agreed or disagreed.

He was also persuasive, highly intelligent and more mature than I was. He was a few years older than me; already in his senior year at Temple University, soon to earn his Bachelor's in Business Administration. Or, as he liked to joke, he would have his B.A. in B.A. He would always finish the joke by declaring that it was better than a B.S. in B.S.

Technically, he was working towards his Bachelor of Science degree, a B.S., but the difference between that and a B.A. was lost on me.

"You're so corny," I told him, laughing at his lame joke.

"Yeah, corny and horny, all the time. That's me!" he agreed, with his dazzling smile and infectious laugh making it impossible for me to do anything but agree with him. I could feel his knee rubbing against mine under the table at the deli, and I felt a rush of excitement when he said he was horny.

49

While in school, he was also working part-time behind the counter at Paulie's, a pizza parlor not far from his apartment. I was impressed with him. He really seemed to know where he was heading and was making all the right moves to succeed at reaching his goals.

After we finished eating lunch, he said he was going home to study for a while. I asked him if he wanted to meet up later and go to TRAX, one of the gay dance clubs in the Gayborhood.

"Well..." he said, his voice trailing off. That was the first time all day when he seemed to be at a loss for words.

"Well what?" I asked.

"Well, first of all, I don't get out of work till midnight, so you know I might be too tired to go out tonight."

"Henry, c'mon man, I think I know you better than that already. What's up for real?"

"Okay, Joey, the truth is, I always get carded at TRAX, and even with my ID, they don't always let me in there."

I took a minute to process that information. I guess if a club turned me away, I wouldn't be in a hurry to admit it, either.

"Let's try it anyway," I said. "If we can't get in, then we can always find some other spot, right?"

I didn't tell Henry, but I had a plan. In those days, no one used the term "white privilege," but that didn't mean that we were unaware of the concept or that we didn't know how to use it. And I had more than white privilege in my favor. I was young and cute, and I already knew that those traits were getting me into the clubs, never even having to show my fake ID.

When we got to TRAX later that night, it was a little after midnight and there was a small line of people waiting to get in. As usual, the bouncer was checking IDs of any Black or Brown guys who were trying to get in, as well as any females. I ignored the line, grabbed Henry's hand, walked right up to the bouncer and said, "He's with me." The bouncer already recognized me from previous visits, and he casually waved both of us in.

The club was starting to get crowded, so we made our way to the bar for drinks. Henry had a pocket filled with cash, his tips from working at Paulie's that night.

With our drinks in hand, Henry kept his arm around my waist. I liked that feeling, and I was thinking that we made a really cute couple.

"Joey, see that guy over there? Do you know him?"

Henry gestured unobtrusively towards a dark-haired guy who was deep in conversation with a small group of guys. I didn't know him, but I watched as the entire group headed to the men's room. A minute later, the entire group, except for the one that Henry had indicated, walked out of the bathroom.

"C'mon, let's go!" Henry said, pulling me towards the bathroom.

"Hey, Arthur! This is my friend Joey." I shook Arthur's strong hand and smiled.

"How many?" Arthur asked. "It's really busy tonight and they're going fast."

"We'll take 4," Henry said, handing over a twenty-dollar bill. Four white pills were now in Henry's hand, and we headed back to the main bar.

Henry popped one as soon as we hit the bar and offered one to me. I took it without even asking what it was. I felt safe with Henry, but after swallowing, I did ask him.

"Dude, you never tried a Quaalude?" He seemed incredulous, as they were quickly becoming THE party drug of the disco crowd. "You're gonna love it," he continued, pulling the other two pills out of his pocket. "But always look for the number 714 on the pill, so you know it's legit. There's a lotta guys tryin' to pass fakes out there." He showed me the 714 imprint before stuffing them back into his pocket for later use.

"Yeah, back home we called them Sopers, but I never tried one yet," I explained.

"You're gonna love it, babe."

"Babe." That's the word he used. That word excited me, intoxicated me. Maybe I was already feeling the effects of the lude, but at that very moment, that described exactly who and what I wanted to be. His babe. Maybe just for that moment. Maybe for that night. But maybe for more than that. Maybe I could be his babe for days, weeks, months, years.

Henry was right; I did love the high from the lude. It was a smooth high, not as harsh as the reds and yellows I had taken before. I felt like I was almost floating, my mind and body both relaxed and feeling nothing but pleasure. And I would find out later, when I woke up the next day, that there was no hangover, no after effects. From that night, I was a fan of taking ludes at the clubs, until they were eventually banned from being manufactured in the US in 1982.

Most of that night is a blur, the kind of fuzziness where you know you had a great time, but you can't quite recall all the details. I know that Henry and I spent a lot of time together. At some point, Henry challenged me to see which one of us could pick up a cuter guy. So, the hunt was on!

Not long after the challenge began, we got together to show off and compare our "catches." The guys we had met separately were eventually let in on the joke, and the four of us ended up having fun dancing, joking and drinking, with a few make out sessions thrown in for good measure.

The combination of the ludes and the alcohol were making all four of us horny as hell, so as a group, we headed back to my hotel. The ludes definitely contributed to the lack of inhibitions, as we engaged with one another in our little orgy.

When I woke up, I was being held in Henry's arms. The other guys were nowhere to be found, having left at some point during the night. I felt a sense of comfort and contentment in his arms, and I wished that feeling could last forever.

I had no way of knowing what the future would bring, but I liked Henry enough to want to include him in my plans, at least for the immediate future. So I told him that I had definitely decided to leave my small hometown and move to Philly. That meant I had to drive back, collect a few things from my father's house, and put that place up for sale.

I asked Henry if he'd be interested in helping me put that plan into action. The next day, Henry was sitting in the passenger seat of my car as I headed back home.

Music was playing on the AM radio as we sped along the highway, casually tossing our cigarette butts out the windows as we talked about plans for the club. Henry was actually making some sketches of possible layouts for the main bar on the ground floor, though his drawings were simple, almost child-like. But they didn't have to be artistic, as long as we could show our vision to the actual designers and construction workers.

"Why do you want the door to be red?" he asked. "The only red doors I ever saw were on churches."

I told him again about the red door at Teddy's, which had been my introduction to the gay bar scene. But he wasn't really listening, as he continued to talk about the doors on churches being red.

"So maybe the red door is a sign...like a sign of salvation for gay people," he said. "No, it isn't salvation, really." He was thinking out loud, as he considered various possibilities.

"No, it isn't salvation," he repeated. "It's more like a sanctuary. A sanctuary for gay people to get away from our everyday lives."

"Hey, how's that for the name of the club?" he asked. Up to that point, we had discussed possible names, but no definite decision had been made. "You could call it Club Sanctuary."

That was the perfect name for the place.

Sanctuary.

THREE

The next few months were a whirlwind of activity. The design and construction of the club were one area of focus, but we also had to work on networking within the gay community, to inform them about this new club and to garner their support. While we would be competing for business with other clubs in the area, we really weren't trying to form adversarial relationships.

One advantage we had in that regard was that Henry, who was basically acting in the role of a general manager, had managed to pull a few strings, getting us that coveted social club liquor license. Since we would be able to stay open after the regular bars closed, we were not in direct competition with them, so those establishments were more open to the idea of cooperating with us.

Our official name was The Sanctuary Society of South Philadelphia, but the club would simply be known as Sanctuary. The club wasn't in South Philly; it was located in Center City. But in order to get the social club license, Henry had reached out to a City Council member who represented a section of South Philly. That member of City Council was instrumental in getting our license approved, so we agreed to rent an office in a South Philly building owned by that City Councilman, as a gesture of thanks for his help. That office would be the club's official headquarters. This move would not only help us in case of problems with zoning, but it would later be invaluable in providing assistance and protection for the club from harassment by the police and other governmental authorities.

Our outreach efforts were wildly successful, with 5000 annual memberships sold in advance of the club's opening, at $20.00 per membership. That provided us with $100,000 in working capital, on top of the money I was investing in the operation, to set everything up exactly how we wanted it.

Henry pointed out to me that there were many people in the community who would not or could not pay the membership fee. I tried to find a solution, by providing the ability for members to sponsor guests to get into the club for one night, paying only the small cover charge, and for others to purchase an extended guest membership for a week or weekend.

Those 5000 annual memberships didn't come easily. We had an extensive advertising campaign, focusing on the gay and alternative newspapers and posting fliers on just about every telephone pole in the Gayborhood. We also spread the word just by talking to people, informing anyone we came into contact with, and making an effort to reach individuals who already had a voice in the community.

My goal was for the club to be inclusive, but I also wanted to maintain an air of exclusivity, because I was determined to keep my club as a safe area, a sanctuary, for gays, lesbians, and those who were friendly with us. It was inevitable that there would be conflicts along the way, if only due to the diversity of our intended audience, and I hoped we would be prepared to meet any and all challenges.

I knew one thing for sure. The best way to make a diverse group of people feel welcome at the club was to be sure our staff reflected the diversity in the community.

Now of course, when we talk about diversity, that word can mean different things to different people. It would be impossible to try to address every possible difference. So we made a conscious decision to focus our diversity on race, but with a policy to have an open mind about any other types of diversity.

I wish I could say that the gay community, recognizing their persecution by most of the straight world, would band together in peace and harmony, with all gay people accepting and loving all other gay people. However, that would be denying the way it is in the real world. Gay people almost always had their own preferences, prejudices and judgmental attitudes about other individuals and/or groups within their own community.

The people most admired and desired in the gay community were the young and the beautiful, preferably those blessed with both of those traits. Wealth was probably the third most desired trait. Those lucky enough to possess all three liked to assume that they automatically belonged at the top of the pyramid and some of them would only socialize with others they considered their equals. Of course, not everyone had those narrow attitudes, but many did. And of course, they also had to deal with the envy of those who didn't fit into their cliques. These issues were the source of much drama, including those in attendance at Sanctuary.

Our goal was to open on Friday, May 27, 1977, the Friday at the start of the long Memorial Day holiday weekend. We realized that lots of Philly gays went out of town for summer weekends, or even for the entire summer. However, even with that, there were plenty of gay people who would still be in town, and opening at the start of the summer season would actually be an opportunity for our staff to develop their skills before what would surely be a huge weekend when everyone would be back in town after Labor Day.

But there was another reason why we selected that date for our grand opening. It just so happened that Henry and I shared the same birthday, May 27, though he was three years older than me. That means that we were both born under the sign of Gemini. One day, we actually went for a consultation with a tarot card reader, who also specialized in the study of astrology. She told us that two men born under Gemini would most likely have an extremely strong connection, with laughter being one of the bases drawing them together. Two Geminis would bond together in a way to form a strong pair, often with identical outlooks and goals. She assured us that we could have a relationship built on an unending desire for each of us to constantly entertain the other one, while also doing, seeing and learning new things together as well.

Dress rehearsal for our Grand Opening was held on Thursday, May 26. The designers had done an impressive job, transforming the first floor of the old factory into a gay showplace. Quality materials had been used in the construction and the furnishings, hopefully giving them a long life. Images of gay erotica were dispersed throughout the main floor, highlighted by a red neon sculpture of a male couple in the midst of a sexual embrace, with erections prominently displayed. This sculpture was suspended from the ceiling, at the main entrance, the first thing you would see after passing through the lobby/coatroom area. All of the art had been purchased from members of the Philadelphia art community, with a specific focus on supporting local gay artists.

Huge speakers were placed on stands surrounding the dance floor, with the sound system controlled from the DJ booth located 18 feet above the ground, providing those in the station with a clear view of what was happening below. Laser and strobe lights were scattered throughout the area, controlled by the lighting technician, who shared the DJ station. As the owner, I would spend many nights up there with the DJs, watching the interactions of the club members with great interest. It wouldn't take long for me to develop a few favorites that I enjoyed watching, while also identifying a few people that I didn't care for at all. As the years would go by, the individuals would change, but I always had my favorites and not-so-favorites under my watchful eyes.

We tested all the systems, double-checked to be sure we had adequate supplies of everything, and discussed our goals with all the team members. We didn't anticipate having many problems, since most of the staff had been hired from other clubs in the area. We expected them to know what to do and how to handle most circumstances.

Once the team meeting was over, everyone left except for me and Henry. I poured us a couple drinks while he climbed up the steps to the DJ booth, turning the music up to a blast and starting the light show. He came down with a backpack, carrying it to the middle of the dance floor, where he started unpacking, spreading a blanket and a couple of pillows on the floor.

"We gonna sleep here?" I asked innocently, knowing what his intentions were.

"Maybe," Henry answered, with a wink. We sat cross-legged on the blanket, surrounded by music and lights, as I raised my drink and offered a toast. "To us and our gay sanctuary!" I said, clinking our glasses and drinking up. In the next instant, Henry was on top of me, tearing at my clothes and grinding into me, kissing me with the hot passion of youth.

A minute later, I was totally naked, on my stomach, with Henry on top of me, penetrating me as he sucked on my neck so hard I knew that I'd have a hot hickey the next day. He started slowly, rhythmically moving his hips as he dug his way deeper and deeper inside me.

He knew what I liked and how I liked to be treated. He whispered hoarsely in my ear, grunting earnestly, as he called me his little bitch, his ho, his pussyboy, telling me that he owned my ass and more.

As he was forcing me to answer "Yes, Sir!" to his questions, demanding I answer louder and louder each time, we suddenly heard the door to the men's room in the back open. Apparently, two of the new bartenders had decided to spend a little quality time in there, enjoying a quick encounter after everyone else had left. When they saw what was going on, with Henry dominating me thoroughly, they hurried towards the exit, giggling the entire way.

"Good night, Boss!" they called out in unison.

"Good night, boys, see you tomorrow," Henry answered, as he kept his strong hand tight against my mouth so I could only remain silent.

"You know I'm the real boss, right?"

"Yes, Sir" was my immediate answer, as he shook in spasms, coming to his climax, seeding me right there on the dance floor.

The grand opening finally arrived at 10 PM the next night. I made sure that all the team members were in their proper positions, and I made a grand gesture as I flung open the door - that big beautiful red door - to NOTHING. No one was there to hit the new club at the very first minute.

"Calm down," I thought to myself. I had to remind myself that this is an after-hours club, and who really would go to a place like this at 10 PM? The real action at the regular bars wouldn't even really get started for another hour at least.

So the DJ kept spinning up in his booth, along with the lighting tech controlling the lasers. The bartenders tried to keep themselves busy, wiping down the bars and rinsing glasses that were already clean.

11 PM, still nothing. I was starting to get a little nervous. Did we do all this for nothing? I was a small-town guy in the big city. Maybe this was a dumb idea.

Henry came over to talk and he was his usual self, full of positivity. He told me that he personally knew over 100 guys who had promised to show up for the first night. At about 12:15 AM, a group of four guys finally came in through the door. A feeling of sweet relief came over me that at least we had a few customers, though I could see the disappointed look on their faces as they realized they were the only people there. But that quickly changed as guys started to trickle in, slowly at first, then turning to a steady stream.

By 1:30 AM, the club was more than half full, with the line of customers waiting to get in getting longer with each passing minute. By the time the bars in the Gayborhood closed at 2 AM, groups of rowdy, drunken gay men were making their way a few blocks north, turning our grand opening into a truly grand night for Sanctuary.

As the night progressed, I was drinking a little too heavily, getting excited as I watched the crowd from the DJ booth. While it was a mostly white crowd, I was happy that it wasn't exclusively white, signaling that an integrated club just might be acceptable in this town. Despite my drunkenness, I noticed a few details that surprised me.

First, a group of 10 to 12 guys, mixed black and white, congregated in one area of the club. They were all members of the gay deaf community, which was something new for me. I had no real knowledge or experience with deaf culture, and I watched them using ASL for communication, while other people were trying to shout over the music, which was blasting. I admit I was surprised when I saw them dancing, though I should have known better. Everyone could feel the vibration of the music, so no surprise that deaf people could follow the beat. I made a mental note to myself to learn more about this group and their culture, which I found intriguing.

Although the majority of people in the club that first night were in their 20s, we had also attracted a sizeable number of older gays, mostly in their 30s. I noticed that they seemed to be attracted to one particular area of the club, at the bar all the way in the back of the club. Two bartenders were assigned to work back there, the same two who had been in the men's room while Henry had been fucking me on the dance floor the night before. Both of them had previously worked at TRAX, but sensing a better opportunity, they had both accepted positions working at Sanctuary.

It looked to me that they had both made the right decision to come work at my club. Not only did they bring their fans from TRAX to the club, but they were also gaining new fans now that they were working at Sanctuary. Those fans were loyally buying their drinks from them, always returning to the same bartenders when they were ready for a refill. And they showed their appreciation for being served by these two hotties by throwing tips their way, very generous tips.

The two guys behind the bar worked well as a team, keeping the drinks flowing quickly and smoothly at their bar. However, they were really a study in contrasts. London, known to all as Lonnie, was a tall lanky Asian, born in Hong Kong but raised in the Chinatown section of Philly. London was his Americanized name. When he decided to change his name, he chose London because at the time, Hong Kong was a colony of the British Empire and Lonnie was a fan of the British monarchy.

Sometimes, he found himself fantasizing that he was a royal prince. At other times, he thought about being the royal princess. He was actually comfortable with both roles.

During the Bicentennial celebration, while I was attending my father's funeral, Lonnie was at the Independence Hall Visitor's Center, where Queen Elizabeth II was presenting a gift to the United States, called the Bicentennial Bell. In a crowd of mostly white tourists, Lonnie stood out just by nature of being Asian. However, in the spirit of celebrating British royalty, Lonnie had decided to attend the event while wearing a rhinestone studded tiara, feeling today just a bit like a princess.

This was an historical event, so there were plenty of reporters and photographers covering the festivities. One photographer took a picture of Lonnie, who was sitting on top of a wall, legs crossed in a manner that some would call effeminate, clad in very short shorts, a tank top, sandals, and his precious tiara.

The next day, one of the daily tabloid-style papers in Philly featured a photo of Lonnie on the front page, with a photo of Queen Elizabeth taking up the second half of the page. The caption read:

"Battle of the Queens, Philly vs. Britain"

Lonnie had no knowledge that this was going to happen. He was never interviewed by the paper, and had never given permission for his photo to be used. The paper had an anti-gay agenda, and Lonnie was now their latest victim. One of Lonnie's neighbors made sure to show the paper to his mother, who broke into his bedroom screaming in Chinese, accusing Lonnie of bringing shame to the family.

Lonnie's mother was a small woman, but her rage filled the room, as she was beating on her son's chest, screaming into his face, telling him he had to leave immediately. Lonnie grabbed a few of his belongings, stuffed them into a bag and fled the house, tears streaming down his face.

Lonnie was never permitted back into his family's home, and his mother forbade anyone in the family from ever mentioning his name again. She simply couldn't bear the humiliation and shame of having a son who was now publicly identified as being gay.

Angry, confused, dejected and rejected, Lonnie felt like he had hit rock bottom when he was forced to go to a homeless shelter, located on Vine Street, near his family's home. He felt humiliated, not at being outed as gay, but by suddenly being part of the homeless population in the city. He didn't want to ask for help, but after a few nights sleeping on a cot in a large room filled with other homeless men, he finally reached out to some friends for help. It felt as though a huge weight had been lifted from his shoulders when a friend offered him a temporary place to stay. Shortly after that, he landed the bartender job at TRAX, enabling him to support himself and find a room, soon to move into his own apartment. Not long after that, he started working at Sanctuary, where he was sure to be one of the most popular bartenders there.

His work partner, Antonio, was a short, muscular Italian guy, born and raised in South Philly. I was one of the few people who knew his name was Antonio, since I had to use his real name on his paychecks. To everyone else, he was BJ. And yes, for the obvious reason. He loved to give blowjobs to anyone and everyone, and he was famous for his technique that made his mouth and deep throat feel like heaven for all those who entered. There was a rumor that even his mother called him BJ, though I was never able to confirm whether that was actually true.

Lonnie wasn't in a relationship, but he was extremely selective and picky when it came to sexual partners. He would tease all of his fans with the possibility that they might eventually get him into bed, but in reality, Lonnie was only interested in effeminate twinks. The more delicate a guy's features, the more Lonnie was interested. He also liked when one of those twinks wore feminine clothing. He wasn't usually interested in guys who wore full drag; he was more attracted to a guy who hinted at his effeminate side rather than shouting it out. For example, some lipstick and eye shadow were sure to catch his eye. If you carried a purse, you might be Lonnie's choice for the night. If you bent over the bar to grab your drink, and Lonnie would spy a glimpse of women's panties under your clothes, he would be in hot pursuit.

On the other hand, BJ was much more interested in quantity over quality. If you had a dick, he would suck it, never turning down an offer and always looking for fresh meat. Hell, the meat didn't have to be fresh. He just wanted it. All the time. From anyone. From everyone.

On the night of our grand opening, BJ found the time to give blowjobs to five different guys in the bathroom that was located just a few feet from his station. As soon as the requests for drinks slowed even a little, BJ would indicate to one of his customers to meet him in a stall for a quick blow and go. By the end of the night, BJ's tip jar was jammed full, but to be honest, the same was true for Lonnie, so BJ wasn't really blowing guys for tips. Something inside him just made him addicted to getting as much dick in his mouth as he possibly could.

There was so much going on at the club that first night, I really couldn't take it all in. Over a thousand gay guys crowded into Sanctuary, drinking, taking drugs, dancing, making out, passing out, making connections, gossiping, arguing, and more. At one point, I decided to have the DJ stop spinning, so I could make a speech to the crowd gathered below. Luckily, Henry talked me out of that idea, since I was flying high on a mixture of ludes and

65

vodka tonics. No need to intrude on everyone's good time with a speech from me, when I could barely hold on to a coherent thought at the time anyway.

Being the owner of the club, I sort of expected that I'd be the star of the night, adored by my fans who would somehow be aware of my every move throughout the evening. Of course, that didn't happen, not even close. The crowds of people were all engaged in their own thoughts, urges, desires. But there were people who stood out, gaining the attention of many, if not everybody in the club.

A group of four guys from South Philly had all come to the club together, with a plan to put on a show. They were all friends with BJ, and after the club started to get crowded, they signaled to BJ that they were ready to put their plan into action. BJ had stored their bags under his bar and he handed them over as the guys headed to the men's room.

When they emerged, they were dressed in jockstraps and Timbs. Their jocks were color coordinated to match the sashes they wore over their chests, like the type worn in the Miss America pageant. Written in glitter on their sashes were the names of the streets they were representing. For example, Giuseppe lived on Snyder Avenue, so his purple sash proclaimed him as Mr. Snyder Ave., matching his jock that had been dyed a deep shade of purple. Matteo was Mr. Packer Ave., sporting his pink sash to match his pink jockstrap. Tito, in red, was Mr. Washington Ave., and Rocco, in blue, was Mr. Two Street.

They positioned themselves in strategic areas around the club, jumping up on various tables and stands, and started their gogo boy routines. A cheer went up from the crowd as the boys gyrated to the pulsing music. We hadn't planned on having gogo boys in the club, but their presence added to the air of decadence we were looking to achieve. I climbed down from my perch and stuffed a few bills into the pouches of their jocks, enjoying the intimacy of the moment. It wasn't long before all four of the boys had dollar bills lining the waistbands and leg straps of their jocks, the pouches bulging with bills.

Perhaps the biggest star of the night was DJ Thunder. He had earned that nickname because everything about him was loud; I mean LOUD. His voice, his personality, his demeanor. All loud. His current hairstyle was a Mohawk, worn sky-high, dyed a deep blue. He was often clad in leather, and tonight was no exception. A studded leather dog collar was tight around his neck, with matching studded cock rings worn as bracelets on both wrists. His black tee shirt clung tightly to his muscular chest, with taut nipples jutting against the fabric. Tribal tattoos adorned both biceps, bulging from many hours spent at the gym. Leather pants and black boots completed the look. This was the look of a man who would clearly be in charge in any situation, and he took control of the crowd on the dance floor the same way he would control any of his submissive bottom boys.

Instinctively, he knew when to keep the beats super heavy and when to slow things down just a little to provide some time for the dancing crowd to breathe, as well as to refresh their drinks. Spontaneous applause erupted several times throughout the night as the partiers showed their appreciation for the mix of his tracks. At 3:45 AM, Thunder closed the dance floor with the last songs of the night, "I Feel Love," by the number one diva of the disco era, Donna Summer, followed immediately and finally by Thelma Houston's megahit "Don't Leave Me This Way." Thunder took a bow from his DJ booth, acknowledging the love from his adoring fans.

Since the bartenders had to stop serving at 3:30 AM, and they had to move from their stations, Lonnie was out on the dance floor. One of his fans from TRAX had been hanging out near him all night. He used the name Chanel, after the designer, and he was drenched in Chanel perfume that night. Although his face had masculine features, with a square jaw and prominent nose, his body was petite, just the way Lonnie liked them. And best of all, to Lonnie's mind, was the fact that Chanel enjoyed dressing in feminine clothing. Tonight, he wore women's high heels, with black bell bottom pants, a white sheer blouse and a black bra that was clearly visible. As they danced, Lonnie was thinking that he really hoped to find a pair of lacy black panties under his clothes. Later that night, he was not disappointed. And although Chanel wouldn't be the love of his life, he was at least good enough for that one night.

Depending on what you were looking for, the night of the grand opening was more successful for some than for others. Some were there just to dance, drink, socialize, have fun. Others wanted more, maybe drugs, maybe a hookup, maybe searching for love.

For me, the night was wildly successful, as the club had been packed, and we were sure to make a huge profit that first night. Besides the financial success, I wanted to establish a place in the community, and I thought we were off to a good start in that regard. And even though my thought processes were blurry from my usual combination of drugs and alcohol, I was in a great mood as Henry and I grabbed one of the many taxis waiting outside at closing time and headed back to my place.

Later that night, after giving him my ass as one of his birthday presents, I had another surprise in store for him. That night, I asked Henry if he wanted to move in with me.

The night wasn't successful for everyone. When the club closed, some of the guys were hanging out around the front door. A few were making last minute drug deals. Others were exchanging phone numbers with potential lovers for some other time. And a few others were just waiting, hoping they might make a last-minute connection with someone, anyone.

Charlie was one of those waiting. He felt like he was always waiting. Thirty-five years old, already balding, with a saggy body and a sad sack face, he had been trying for years to make some impact at the clubs in town. He had been excited for weeks about going to the new club, thinking this might be a new beginning for him. The reality, however, was that it was just more of the same. Moving with the beat of the music, he hovered near the dance floor, hoping someone would ask him to dance. No one did. No one ever did.

Every time he went out to a club, he drank too much. All the bartenders knew him, because he left very good tips. But he was always there by himself, seemingly having no friends to go out with for a good time.

As he stood outside the club, waiting, Charlie watched as a group of five close friends stumbled out the door, shrieking with laughter. He noticed, just for a moment, that not all of them were young pretty boys, though two of them would certainly fit that description. The other three were just average guys as far as their facial appearances, and one of them could only be described as fat. Yet they enjoyed one another's company, and Charlie wondered what they had in common, what made them friends.

But he didn't dwell on that thought for very long because just then, the object of his desire appeared. It was Thunder, in all his glory, walking between two guys who appeared to be twins. All three of them were dressed in their leather gear, and Thunder had his arms wrapped tightly around both of their waists. Charlie was close enough to overhear Thunder say, "You're both gonna be my fuckboy slaves tonight, you understand me?"

Charlie was almost insane with jealousy. He wanted to be Thunder's fuckboy slave. He would give almost anything for the opportunity to serve as Thunder's fuckboy slave. He pictured himself being kept captive in Thunder's basement for the rest of his life, and that thought excited him to the point that he was walking while sporting a major erection.

He followed the trio at what he considered to be a safe distance. He wanted to be noticed, to be invited to join them, but he also feared rejection. He never ever ever made the first move. Being turned down for him was an awful experience, and he was not able to handle that. So he continued to follow them all the way to Thunder's apartment on Spruce Street, like a puppy following his master.

Thunder and his boys disappeared into his apartment. Charlie was left outside, a little lost about what to do next. So he sat on a stoop across the street, just watching and waiting.

When he woke up, still on the stoop, the sun was already shining brightly on what would be a hot summer-like day. There was no sign of Thunder or the twins. Dejectedly, Charlie slowly walked the few blocks to his own basement apartment, where he masturbated furiously, thinking about those three guys and how he wanted to be used by all of them, most especially Thunder.

And as for me, I felt a rush of excitement when Henry said "Yes," he would move in with me.

FOUR

Every society has a structure, including gay society. And like all societies, a person's place within the structure might depend on many different factors. For example, you would expect that those people who chose to be out and active in the gay community would probably have a greater influence within that society.

Other factors played a part as well. Many gays placed a very high value on outward physical characteristics, such as youth, beauty, and even race. Factors such as these could go a long way in determining what your social life was like.

Social and peer pressures often guided our expectations for ourselves and others. Certain people would somehow manage to exceed the expectations of others, while other individuals would fail miserably, falling below the expectations set by themselves as well as society at large.

Sometimes, the reason for someone's relative success or failure is fairly easily determined. Other times, it remains a complete mystery.

For example, looking at Richard, most people, especially gay people, wouldn't think of him as a star. In a club, there was nothing about Richard that made him stand out in the crowd. If you even bothered to cast a glance in his direction, the overwhelming impression would be that Richard seemed average to below average in every respect. His clothes were boring, his glasses were boring, his haircut was boring. You get the idea.

But in reality, to see Richard in a club, or anywhere for that matter, he was constantly surrounded by guys who literally adored him. How did Richard manage to exceed the expectations you would have of him if you didn't know him?

Richard was one that was fairly easy to figure out. He was smart, successful, funny, kind and generous, just to name a few of his positive traits. He took a genuine interest in everyone he met. He wasn't trying to use anyone for anything. He really cared about everyone he met, and he wasn't afraid to let people know he cared. People responded to his positivity because it was infectious. He brought out the best in people.

From the moment he came out as gay, Richard was also committed to bettering the lives of gay people. During this time, gays were subjected to ridicule, discrimination in all areas, including housing, employment, educational opportunities, and even faced imprisonment. Straight society was adamant in their efforts to suppress and repress people who identified as gay and lesbian. And trans people bore the brunt of society's wrath. Richard was committed to changing all of that.

He also knew how to have a good time, becoming a fixture at the Philly clubs, including Sanctuary. You might think that I would have met Richard at my club, but that isn't how it happened. One afternoon, on my way to the club to help set up for that evening's opening, I happened to walk by a new bookstore, a gay bookstore. A small group of people had gathered outside the store, demonstrating against it. A woman was screaming that the books in the store would be used to turn young straight people into gays.

I was getting quite close to the area of the confrontation when I heard Richard say, "Honey, what makes you think a book can turn someone gay? I've been subjected to images of straights my entire life, and all that never did anything to change me!"

I literally bent over with laughter as the woman sputtered, "But...but...but," before Richard dismissed her with a wave of his hand.

"Get the fuck outta my neighborhood," were his final words before he disappeared into the store. I followed him inside and immediately introduced myself to him. Richard was the kind of person I wanted to know. Unapologetically, proudly and loudly gay.

For every Richard, who exceeded people's expectations, there were ten, twenty, maybe even more who failed to live up to expectations. There are many reasons why this is so. Among the gay community, internalized homophobia is a major contributor to feelings of low self-esteem and self-worth.

Richard explained to the lady outside the bookstore how images of straight sexuality did nothing to change his feelings of attraction to other men. However, that constant onslaught of images portraying straight sexuality as normal and desirable, with no images portraying gayness as normal, took an enormous toll on so many people. Lots of guys with gay feelings would go to great lengths to deny, suppress and reject what they knew they truly felt. The pressures came from everywhere. Some religions would damn gay people to hell, just for being who they are. Businesses could and would fire people just for being perceived as gay. Laws were enacted and enforced to try to stamp out gay behaviors. The medical community identified being gay as a sickness, a disease, something to be cured.

It took enormous courage to stand against those pressures.

Some people couldn't or wouldn't put up much of a fight.

To look at Lucas, you would have the opposite reaction than you would have looking at Richard. Lucas looked like a winner. Young, sexy, handsome, athletic, these were the words people associated with Lucas. But of course, the straight world assumes that everybody is straight. No one looked at Lucas and thought he might be gay. Yet that was his deep, dark secret. At least, that's how he thought of it.

He tried to hide it. Desperately. He did not want to be gay. Society told him that gay people were dirty. They were perverts. They were sinners. Lucas thought of himself as a good person. How could he possibly be gay?

It used to be easy to hide how he felt. He had girlfriends and he would take them out on dates and make out with them. He never felt really excited by them, but he figured that was okay. The important thing was to make the girl think he was interested, and then she would tell her friends, and no one would ever know. At least, that was the plan.

As he moved into young adulthood, it became more of a chore to act straight. Young women expected more than his tongue in their mouths. They wanted sex, real sex. They expected it; some of them demanded it. His excuses for being unable to perform satisfactorily with them became more ridiculous and convoluted.

He tried praying. He tried alcohol. He tried drugs. He tried abstaining for weeks, in the hope that his sex drive would become so intense that anyone, even a female, would become the object of his lust.

Sometimes, his plans worked. Other times, they fell far short of the desired effect, and he failed to show any signs at all of arousal. Those were the times he would become most despondent, desperate for an answer to his dilemma.

Every day, he hated himself more. He would catch himself looking longingly at some young man, feeling that familiar stirring of desire in his pants and then despising himself even more.

Lucas knew about the clubs. But he absolutely refused to go, worried that he might actually become the thing he hated the most - a faggot. He had no real plan for getting through life. When every day is torture, it's hard to see a way out.

He was dating a young woman named Anna Marie. She was fun, always ready to go somewhere for an adventure. She had made arrangements for her and Lucas to travel to Atlantic City for the weekend with another couple. Lucas had no problem with the plans. Maybe it'd be good to get out of the city; maybe a change of scenery would help alleviate his depression and anxiety.

Anna Marie made reservations at a small motel at Pacific Avenue and St. James Place, just one block from the beach and the famous boardwalk. The four of them would share one bedroom, with two double beds, so each couple would have their own space. Lucas wasn't sure if that meant he would have to have sex with Anna Marie while another couple were in the room, or if it meant he would be free from performing sexually that weekend.

They arrived on Friday night, leaving Philly right after all of them got off work. After they checked in, they headed out for a night of drinking, with plenty of clubs in the area from which to choose.

First, they decided to spend some time on the boardwalk, so they walked one block to New York Avenue, which provided direct access to the boards. None of them knew that New York Avenue was the center of gay nightlife in Atlantic City at the time, with the entire street lined with gay rooming houses, bars and nightclubs for several blocks, all the way to the beach.

Considered a safe area for gay people, gays cavorted freely, with many letting loose with behaviors that would not be tolerated in straight areas, where they lived most of the time. The street was loud, with the sound of music blasting from the clubs as kings and queens went from one bar to the next, freely expressing their gay selves.

Lucas, Anna Marie and their two friends were confronted with this scene as they walked along New York Ave. "Oh my God, look at all these fuckin' queers!" was the reaction of Cal, who was holding the hand of his girlfriend, Molly.

"I hate all these fuckin' faggots," Lucas agreed, grabbing hold of Anna Marie's hand.

Three guys in hot pants and midriff tops were walking hand-in-hand, swaying their hips, showing their effeminate sides, as they walked towards the two couples.

"Who wants to suck my cock?" Cal asked as the two groups neared each other. "I got a big one for ya."

"Oh honey, sorry, you ain't really my type," said one of the gay guys, as he turned and started making out with his friend.

Cal spat in their direction, as Lucas threatened them, saying, "I'll knock your faggot teeth down your throat, you queer homo pussy."

Anna Marie and Molly grabbed their guys and started dragging them faster down the street, to get away from the situation. By the time the four of them had walked a half block along the boardwalk, three of them had already forgotten about the incident. But Lucas was in a rage as he thought about the nerve of the fags acting like that. He was going deeper and deeper into denial about his true feelings as he thought about violence against any gay he might see. In his mind, he was dehumanizing them, not recognizing them as real people, with their own very real lives and loves.

By the time they were ready to go back to their motel, all four had gotten drunk, as they had hit a number of bars and clubs, the last of which was on the other end of town. They took a taxi back to their room, so they missed out on seeing all the gay action still happening all along New York Avenue.

76

The next day was gloriously warm, with cloudless skies, perfect for spending the day at the beach. They decided to walk, avoiding New York Ave., hoping to just enjoy themselves without being distracted by the presence of the queers. They had no idea that the gay beach was located a few blocks from New York Avenue, at Park Place, but luckily for them, they actually headed in the opposite direction to find their place in the sand.

While Lucas was still seething inside, he didn't let on to his friends, so it just seemed like a normal, straight outing to the other three. They spent their time at the beach alternating between body surfing in the waves and relaxing on the beach in the blazing sun.

The four of them shared a gigantic beach blanket, talking about mostly nothing. At one point, Cal pointed out a pier to Molly and said, "I can never remember. Is that the Atlantic side or the Pacific side?

"What?" Molly replied, having no idea what Cal was talking about.

"Well," Cal continued. "I know that on one side of that pier, it's the Atlantic Ocean, and on the other side, it's the Pacific Ocean. But I just can't remember which ocean is on which side."

"Dude, all of that is the Atlantic Ocean. Who told you that you can see the Pacific from here?" Lucas asked.

"I know I heard people talkin' about the Atlantic side and the Pacific side," Cal countered.

"Maybe you heard them talking about Atlantic Avenue and Pacific Avenue?" offered Molly. Anna Marie just rolled her eyes at the entire ridiculous turn of the conversation.

"No," Cal insisted. "I know there are two sides here. The Atlantic and the Pacific. You mean you don't know that?"

"Man, I think you must've failed Geography in school," Lucas said, trying to think of a way to change the topic.

At that point, Lucas volunteered to walk up to the boardwalk to get some drinks and snacks. On the way, he made a mental note that he didn't want to go on any more trips with Cal and Molly, especially not with Cal. He didn't think he could be friends with a guy who was that stupid. Before buying the snacks, he stopped into one of the restrooms, which were located all along the boards, often used as changing rooms by the visiting sunbathers. But he wasn't there to change, just to take a quick leak.

He stepped up to the urinal and started peeing. As he did so, a young man stepped up to the urinal right next to him, with no divider separating the two. Out of the corner of his eye, Lucas saw that the guy next to him wasn't peeing; he was stroking himself to a full erection. Lucas felt himself beginning to panic. "Why are these queers always around me?" he wondered.

While he always told himself that he hated gays, he was conflicted because he secretly desired them as well.

Lucas's mind was racing. He felt that he had three possible ways to act and he had to decide immediately, without time to consider the possible consequences. First, he could finish peeing, zip up and leave, totally ignoring the hard dick next to him. Second, he could punch the guy in the gut, unleashing his fury by attacking this guy, and then make a run for it. Or...

In an instant, Lucas chose the "or" option. That option was to give in to his hidden desires, just this one time, and take the offer the guy was obviously providing. So, very quickly, Lucas reached out and took hold of the guy's rigid cock.

"You're under arrest, you fuckin' queer!"

He felt his heart drop into the pit of his stomach as two guys grabbed his arms from behind, with a third flashing

78

his Atlantic City police badge. The guy next to him quickly fixed his clothing and disappeared out the door. Lucas was ordered to fix his own clothing before he was shoved against the wall and cuffs were placed on his wrists.

"These sick fuckin' fags are always looking for sex, even in public," one of the cops said, with obvious disgust.

This was clearly a case of entrapment, an attempt to literally place temptation right in front of a gay man, but Lucas couldn't think that far ahead to even consider hiring a lawyer. He felt intense shame and anger, with that anger mostly directed at himself. Why did he make that decision to reach for that man's dick? He had spent years denying those desires and just when he finally gave in, the worst possible thing had happened.

Since it was Saturday, Lucas was taken to the local jail, where he would be forced to wait until the following week for his preliminary hearing.

Anna Marie, Cal and Molly couldn't imagine what had happened when Lucas didn't return from his trip up to the boardwalk for snacks. They waited for a while on the beach, then went back to the motel, hoping Lucas had gone back there for some reason. It wasn't until Sunday when they called the police station that they learned he was there, charged with indecent assault.

When they got to the station, the officer at the desk told them what happened, explaining in detail how Lucas had attempted to sexually assault another man in a public restroom. Anna Marie went into the area where the holding cells were located.

"Is it true? You're a queer?" she demanded to know.

"Get out! Get the fuck outta here!" Lucas screamed, turning away from her to face the wall, so she wouldn't see the hot tears streaming down his face. Anna Marie didn't have to be told twice. She stormed out, ready to go back to Philly and forget about this disastrous weekend with a guy she thought might be a potential husband.

It wasn't until Tuesday when Lucas was released, after a date was set for a few months later for him to return to face the charges. He went back to the motel, wearing his swimsuit, tank top and sandals, since that was what he was wearing when he got arrested. Of course, his friends were long gone, and they had packed everything when they left the room, including Lucas's clothes.

Lucas couldn't have possibly felt any worse. He walked dejectedly to the train station, trying to think what he should do next. He already knew that he could never accept the fact that he was gay. If his first attempt at making a gay connection ended this badly, he could only imagine what the future might hold for him. He didn't want to face his friends and family, knowing what they would be thinking about him.

It was already dark as the train approached the station in Philly. During the ride, Lucas had a long time to think. He had finally calmed down, so he could think more clearly at this point. He couldn't think of any positive way to handle his situation. All he could imagine was a future where he was branded as a sex pervert, a queer, a homo. He could not envision himself joining the queers on New York Avenue or anywhere else, acting all girly and queeny, all the things that made him sick about the fags.

Maybe Lucas could have found peace in the gay world, maybe even love. But he accepted what straight society told him about gay people. That they were worthless, perverted, sickening.

He had no friends to confide in, no one who would provide support or guidance or help him find a way to deal with what he considered to be an unsolvable problem. He knew what he had to do, so he headed towards his destination.

Twenty minutes later, he found himself walking along the pedestrian walkway of the Ben Franklin Bridge, 135 feet above the Delaware River. As he climbed over the ledge, he took one last look at the city that he loved, and wondered how his life had ever gotten to this point. But he knew he had to act without hesitation, fearing he might lose his nerve. He took a deep breath and pushed himself off the ledge.

No one heard his screams as Lucas plunged those 135 feet. Screams of terror. Screams of hatred. Screaming at the unfairness of everything that had happened to him. The screams only stopped when his body was crushed as he hit the water.

If anyone saw him jump, no one reported it. There was no desperate search or attempt to rescue him. And no one would ever know the full truth about what happened. Two days later, his body was found, washed up on the riverbank, a few miles from where he spent his last minutes alive.

Lucas had wanted nothing to do with gay life. But there were others, such as Charlie, who wanted nothing more than to be accepted into that life. After Charlie had followed DJ Thunder home that night after Sanctuary opened, his obsession with Thunder only grew stronger

He started stalking the DJ, following him whenever possible, without making it obvious that he was following him. But he didn't want to be totally invisible. After all, his plan was to meet Thunder, seduce him, and he was sure that Thunder would fall deeply, madly in love with him.

Lucas and Charlie. Polar opposites. Taking different paths. Different outlooks, different desires, different fates.

FIVE

As Sanctuary continued to grow in popularity, my relationship with Henry was growing in intensity. We were living together, working together, and yet I never tired of his company. Our sex life was great, and although neither of us felt that we needed to include others to spice things up, we did it anyway. In the 70s, this was a fairly common setup. We just accepted it as part of the fun of being free and gay. And Sanctuary provided plenty of opportunities for us to share our bed with just about anyone we wanted.

At this point in the late 1970s, plenty of gays acted like we did. We felt no need to be monogamous. There was a debate in the community about sexual freedoms, with some advocating for having multiple sex partners as a way to rebel against the moral confinements of straight society. Others disagreed, arguing that being promiscuous only validated the view of most straight people that gays were degenerates who were incapable of having meaningful, lasting relationships, doomed to a life of one-night stands, with loneliness and despair in their future as they would lose their ability to attract anyone as they got older.

From my observations of the people who frequented the club, most were constantly on the hunt for new partners. Of course, that was one of the main purposes of going to a club. To hook up. So that particular group of people who went to Sanctuary wasn't necessarily reflective of gay culture in its entirety.

Like I said, Henry and I were in a relationship, but we also enjoyed inviting other guys to join us for sex. One reason is that it was fun, simple as that. We didn't really consider that we might be using guys who might want to develop an emotional attachment with one or both of us. We only occasionally invited anyone back for a second time.

If either or both of us caught an STI, that was taken care of with a quick trip to the clinic for some antibiotics. And we damn well knew that no one was going to get pregnant. So, we engaged in lots of casual sex. Lots of it.

Between the two of us, Henry was more sophisticated in the ways of the city, and he easily blended into what could be called the A-List community. He enjoyed musical theater, taking me to see a few shows in Philly, usually at the Forrest or the Walnut Street Theater. We even made the trip to New York a few times to see shows on Broadway.

He was also more accomplished academically, now enrolled in the MBA program at the Wharton School, part of the University of Pennsylvania. I was also taking a few classes, studying ASL at community college. I wanted to learn more about the gay deaf community and learning how to communicate with them was important to me.

I was more of a small-town guy, and I enjoyed the outdoors. I talked Henry into getting a bike. We enjoyed biking along the Schuylkill River paths, even stopping sometimes to go into the Art Museum. To see the art, of course. We weren't there to cruise the bathrooms, no.

It was summer, 1978. Sanctuary had already been open for a year, and I was amazed at the level of success we were enjoying. Not that it was easy; a lot of hard work was involved. But the financial rewards were substantial, and Henry and I were enjoying the life we were building.

One hot weekday afternoon, we took a day trip to Bucks County, just outside of Philly, for a day of tubing down the Delaware River. Henry was so involved in city life that he would never have even considered spending a lazy afternoon floating on an inner tube, enjoying the fresh country air. But he enjoyed it, and he said he hoped that we'd do it again sometime.

The rest of the week went by as usual with days spent sleeping and nights at the club. By the weekend, Henry mentioned feeling tired, but we didn't think much of it.

Henry was especially busy, because we were using the profits from the club to expand. The main floor would always be the heart of the club, catering to a diverse crowd of gay people looking to enjoy the club scene. But we also wanted to provide spaces for other groups, a little outside of the mainstream gay club-goers.

The old factory where Sanctuary was located had a basement, and months had been spent converting part of that area into a club for men who were into the leather scene. We called it The Hole. Any member of Sanctuary could enter, but they would have to use a separate entrance and pay a separate cover charge. It was decorated in such a way that no one could be mistaken about the intended clientele.

Of course, there were several bars and a DJ booth. The walls were painted black and ultraviolet lights were used to enhance the menacing atmosphere. Whips, chains, paddles and other sadistic devices hung on the walls and from the ceiling, making the place resemble a dungeon. We even set up a few private areas by adding cages that looked like prison cells, for the enjoyment of those who liked to go to extremes.

An area on the second floor was also being converted, but that one was designed to attract lesbians and their friends. There was a separate entrance, but it could also be accessed through the main club, with no separate cover charge. We called the club Aphrodite's, for the Greek goddess of beauty. The decor consisted of various symbols associated with Aphrodite, including swans, roses, doves, sparrows and dolphins. A mural of a scallop shell with doves soaring around it dominated the room. There were some small private rooms here too, but they were designed more for comfort and relaxation, rather than the prison cells in the basement bar.

Henry had appointments scheduled all week to interview applicants for staff positions in the new bars, which would be opening soon. As he met with some of the candidates for work at Aphrodite's, he began to feel weak, with a dull ache throughout his body which was starting to sweat, though he felt chilly. In the middle of his interview with Chrissie, a lipstick lesbian, Henry passed out, falling to the floor, shivering, having difficulty breathing.

An ambulance was called, and Henry was rushed to the hospital.

When I got the word, I was in a panic. I had no experience dealing with serious illnesses, and no one could even tell me what was wrong with Henry. He had a high fever, nausea, couldn't keep any food down and complained of feeling sore all over. But the most serious problem was the respiratory distress, which continued to grow worse until he was eventually transferred to the ICU.

I went to the hospital every day, but I also had to go to the club every night. Without Henry, there was no one to manage the place, and I was hardly equipped to handle the job. I postponed the opening of Aphrodite's and The Hole, hoping to muddle through with the main business until Henry recovered.

In less than a week, it was clear that I was losing control of the club. I had no management skills whatsoever. I actually thought about closing down temporarily, but I never took that step. I held onto the hope that things might just run themselves until Henry could get back and restore order.

Henry always managed to control the flow of the crowd and kept some degree of order in what could only be described as a chaotic scene. A gay disco by definition has some chaos built into the atmosphere. People were there to let go, have fun, express themselves. Some people took things to extremes, but Henry kept a close eye on every situation and intervened when necessary. I had no idea how to decide when to take any action to control the activities of the crowd.

There's no question that drug use was rampant in the club, with MDMA, aka Ecstasy or Molly being one of the most commonly used drugs at the time. Club goers on E would sometimes dance for hours on end, their energy fueled by the drug.

Miles and Beatrice were regulars at Sanctuary. They weren't there for hooking up with others, but they did like to party with a group of friends. They used Ecstasy every time they went to the club, enjoying the feeling, the music, the endless dancing. They actually made a beautiful couple, wearing the latest fashions, moving together on the dance floor effortlessly, setting a high bar for people who wanted to be just like them.

They trusted their dealer, always buying their supply from the same source at Sanctuary. Sometimes they took a little too much, not wanting to allow the effects to wear off, and the day after could be brutal as the hangover effects were sometimes severe.

But the first Saturday night while Henry was in the hospital, the dealer who was trusted by Miles and Beatrice had made a mistake. He made his own drug concoction to sell at various clubs. This time, he was distracted during the process and somehow mixed the various ingredients to create a potentially lethal combination. He had 200 capsules from this batch, all ready to go.

Lots of customers felt the difference in the caps that night. People were getting sick in the restrooms, vomiting violently, while others literally felt numb from head to toe, losing control of their bodily movements to the point of falling down, but laughing the entire time. One young lady got scared, as she was half carried out of the club by her friends, crying hysterically, unable to control her emotions.

Miles felt his heart beating rapidly as he danced as usual with Beatrice. He began to sweat profusely, which was unusual for him. He developed a pounding headache that he tried to ignore as the music engulfed his senses. Beatrice took his hand and led him off the dance floor, telling Miles she needed a break, out of breath, with legs that felt rubbery, thinking she might fall at any moment.

They left an hour before closing time, which never happened before, and they skipped their usual visit to the pizza shop for a couple of late-night slices. Their usual routine also included taking a taxi to their Society Hill neighborhood, but that night, they started to walk home. Their judgment was clouded, because they both felt like they had a lot of pent-up energy, though they were barely able to walk a straight line.

Halfway home, they stopped to rest on a park bench in Washington Square. And although they still felt that strange rush of energy and lethargy, due to the combination of chemicals reacting in their bodies, they both fell asleep right there on the bench. A park ranger found them there the next morning. Beatrice was in a coma. She had been found lying on the ground in front of the bench, covered in her own vomit. Miles had died during the night, his blood pressure spiking so high that he ended up suffering a stroke. Blood had poured out of his nose and his shirt was stained with a mixture of blood and mucus. It was a gruesome sight to see a young beautiful couple end up like that.

It took a few days for the police to solve the puzzle of exactly what had happened. Witnesses described the problems with the drugs being used at Sanctuary that night. The local papers reported on the story, concentrating on the fact that the couple had been partying at a gay nightclub, as they sought to cast blame for what happened.

The headline on the front page of one of the papers described the situation simply:

"CLUBBED TO DEATH"

The article below that headline described the gay club scene in Philly in the most negative terms possible. The reporter portrayed the death of Miles and Beatrice's coma as somehow being caused by gays, specifically by being involved in the gay club scene.

Of course, Black, Brown and poor white people died from drugs every day of the week, and their deaths never caused any concern. They were never mentioned in the papers. But when a young, affluent straight white couple from a so-called "decent" neighborhood were the victims, the alarm was sounded by the press. Add in the fact that the last place they visited had been a gay club and the press was calling for blood, expecting the citizens to rise up and storm the place like the villagers attacking the monster's lair in some old horror movie.

The press wrote what they wanted, but they hardly knew the real story. Miles would never have chosen Sanctuary as his preferred club for dancing. He wasn't gay, had no real interest in gay culture, but he was deeply in love with Beatrice, more than she would ever know. Miles would have gone anywhere to spend time with Beatrice and in the haze of their drug intoxication, it mattered little to Miles that they were dancing in a gay club. His entire focus was on his love.

Beatrice was tall, slender, elegant, with a love for fashion. Her thick blonde hair was worn at a medium length, with beautiful highlights done impeccably by her stylist. She loved to wear long dangling earrings, along with intricate necklaces and gorgeous bracelets. She spent a lot of money on fashion, although she sometimes visited the consignment shops to get deals. Her love of fashion and designers gave her something in common with a lot of the gays who went to Sanctuary.

But that wasn't her real reason for taking Miles to a gay club. As a teenager, Beatrice had been sexually abused by both her much-older brother and her uncle. Those incidents had made her fear straight men. She felt safe when surrounded by gay men, thinking that none of them would ever exploit her or attack her. The only straight male she trusted was Miles, and she was just beginning to trust him, due to his gentle and kind nature and the way he treated her with respect.

Although both Beatrice and Miles would be described by friends and family as respectable, responsible young adults, the truth is that they truly enjoyed getting high on Ecstasy. They started using it occasionally, but that quickly changed to using two or three times a week, as many nights as they went out, mostly on the weekends. Since they trusted their dealer, they weren't worried about any problems. For Miles, the mistake was fatal.

Beatrice eventually came out of the coma, but she was never really the same after that night. She lost the one man she was learning to trust, and she wasn't sure if she would ever find another. She was also left with some neurological issues and walked with a slight limp for the rest of her life. She also had to deal with the feelings of

89

guilt, an issue faced by many survivors. We never saw her at Sanctuary again.

The attempts by the press to demonize our club ended up being a minor nuisance. The club was raided by the Philly cops the first two nights after the story broke in the press. The raids were meant to harass the employees and the customers, with cops barging into the club, walking around looking for violations, but finding nothing. A couple of police cars were parked on the street, right in front of the club, trying to scare customers away.

To end the harassment, I had to contact the City Council member who had helped us obtain our club license. He used his influence to bring the harassment to a quick end. But of course, there's always a price to pay, and our monthly rental for the office in South Philly was doubled.

Some reporters actually expected people to boycott Sanctuary because of the incident involving Miles and Beatrice. But that never happened. In the late 1970s, nothing would stop the club-goers from seeking their thrills. Our customers were no different. If anything, the publicity made more people aware of our existence, and the crowds just kept coming.

In the meantime, I was still trying to deal with Henry being sick and unable to help me. It took two weeks for the doctors to finally diagnose the problem. Henry was suffering from a severe case of anaplasmosis, which is caused by a tick bite.

"Oh, hell," I thought when I heard the diagnosis. The only reason Henry was sick in the hospital was because I had talked him into that trip to go tubing on the Delaware. That's the only time it would have been possible for him to get bitten by a tick.

The feeling of guilt only added to my problems. Luckily, once the diagnosis was made, the doctors knew that an aggressive treatment with antibiotics should result in a complete recovery. It took two days before he was able to leave the ICU, but he had to remain hospitalized for another 10 days for treatment, rehab and recovery.

While the doctors certainly played an important part in Henry's recovery, the nurses at the hospital took care of him on a day-by-day basis. I visited every day and it didn't escape my notice that Javier, a young, dark-haired and handsome Latino, paid a lot of attention to Henry's care. It seemed that Javier made an appearance in Henry's room every time I was there, and he always made a fuss about how Henry was such an excellent, cooperative patient.

The first time we met, Henry was still too groggy from his meds to participate in the conversation. "Hey, I'm Javi," he said, taking my hand and shaking it firmly, but at the end of the handshake, he let his wrist go just a little bit limp, just enough to send me a silent signal. I learned that he had moved to Philly from Puerto Rico with his family ten years earlier, and had been working at this hospital for the last 3 years, starting right after graduating from nursing school.

I had nothing to hide, so I introduced myself as the owner of Sanctuary. "Maybe you've heard of it," I said, hoping for a positive reaction.

"Hell yeah!" he laughed. "That's my hangout! I thought you guys looked familiar."

As the day for Henry to be discharged drew near, I spent as much time as I could visiting him at the hospital. The day before he was set to leave, I felt a panic attack coming on when I entered his room and found it empty. I quickly reminded myself that this didn't necessarily mean an emergency, as I went looking for a nurse. Before I got to the nurse's station, I saw Henry out of the corner of my eye, sitting at a table in the solarium, having an intense conversation with Javi.

"Hope I'm not interrupting anything," I said as I approached them.

The smile on Henry's face gave me all the assurance I needed that everything was okay.

"Actually, we were just talking about you," Henry told me. "But first, tell me how things are goin' with the club."

I filled them in with the latest details about my struggles managing everything. "It's turning into a bigger operation than I expected," I confessed.

"I've been thinking about that a lot," Henry told me. "I have a suggestion."

Henry had an analytical mind, and he approached problems systematically. Unlike me, who sort of did my best just to muddle through and hope that things might work out on their own.

So Henry began by describing his responsibilities at the club and how his absence impacted many areas of the operation. He wasn't trying to make himself sound important. He was really just stating facts. Then he told me how placing too much responsibility in the hands of one person was a mistake that could prove to be costly. And of course, since Henry was thorough, he not only described the problem, but he was also ready to propose a solution.

"You need an organization, a structure, like a Board of Directors."

"Exactly!" I said. "Uhm, what's a Board of Directors?"

Henry smiled at my innocence and naiveté. He explained to me how a Board could be used to divide responsibilities among a greater number of people, and if the right people were chosen, how they could help by using their expertise to not only solve problems, but also avoid problems before they occurred.

At this point, Javi jumped into the discussion. He described the way the Board of Directors ran the hospital and how each director used his or her expertise to provide advice concerning the hospital's operations.

"Chairman of the Board, President, Vice-President, Secretary, Treasurer, sounds kinda boring to me," I said.

"I think you're right that we need a way to spread out some of the jobs at the club, but can't we be a little more creative...a little more gay?" I asked.

Javier got what I meant right away and he started joking about possible positions on the Board of Directors for Sanctuary.

"The guy in charge of security would be the Cockmander in Chief! Or, or, the Cum, that's C U M... Cumander in Chief!"

"We don't need no Treasurer...but we gotta get us a Pleasurer!"

Henry and I were giggling at Javi's antics. But he wasn't finished.

"The head of the training department is The Dicktator."

"The Secretary is the SuckYoutary!"

"We need a Director of Dance too, that's gonna be the Primo Baller-eeeeeno! And part of his duties gotta be to ball those fat queens who can't dance for shit!" Javier exclaimed as he stood up and completed a glamorous twirl right there in the solarium, raising both arms and snapping his fingers with a flick of both wrists and moving his hips, mimicking a flamenco dancer's moves. All three of us ignored the looks from the other patients in the room.

"And of course, the Leader of the Pack, that's Queen Josephina herself!" Henry added with a sly smile.

"You better bow down to the Queen, honey!" I said in the campiest voice I could manage, as the three of us continued to giggle like schoolgirls at the table. For a minute, we could forget that we were still in the hospital,

93

still waiting for Henry to be well enough to go back home.

Once Henry was back home, safe and sound, we did form a Board of Directors. Of course, we took it a little more seriously than we had during our fun conversation with Javier. We recognized that it was important to have a support network, not only in case of emergencies, but also to build the business.

We offered a spot on the Board to Javier, but he declined, explaining that he was focused on his nursing career. His goal was to eventually move into healthcare management or education. I chuckled at the thought of him teaching nursing students, knowing that his enthusiasm for the work would surely be a positive influence on his students. And though he chose not to be on the Board, he was a regular at the club, and became a trusted friend.

Javier did have a suggestion for someone else to participate on the Board. His friend Alejandro, a young blonde Puerto Rican, worked as an entertainment planner at one of the largest hotels in Philly. He knew how to plan large events, how to get a good mix of diverse groups together, and he was expert at planning down to the smallest detail. Javi recommended him as someone who could help us plan special events at the club, as well as someone who would be successful at community outreach efforts.

Jando, as he liked to be called, proved to be a valuable Board member. He was the one who came up with the idea for Latino Nights, held every Wednesday at the club, featuring the latest in Latin music and expanding our base clientele. That idea led him to pitch Black Fridays, where every Friday night from 10 PM to 1 AM, the music would feature the latest in hip hop, drawing in members of the African American gay community.

I thought the three of us, Henry, Alejandro and I, were enough members to fill the Board. Other positions could easily be filled by hiring employees. I told Henry that since the club was really just a small business, there was no need to overdo it with a large Board of Directors.

Henry agreed that a small Board would be sufficient, but he also wanted the Board to reflect our community to the greatest extent possible.

"It does reflect the community," I said. "We got one white guy, one Black guy, one Latino guy. If that isn't our community, what is?"

"Listen to yourself, Joey. Guy, guy, guy. You're leaving out a big part of the community. And with Aphrodite's opening soon, how can you so easily forget about the lesbians?"

I had to admit, my focus was on men...gay men. That was always my focus. Even though I had a steady partner in Henry, I was always looking at guys, thinking about guys, lusting after guys.

"You got a good point," I told him. "We could probably use some advice about what the ladies might want. To be honest, I don't even know what lesbians do with each other!" I said, laughing.

So we agreed that we could use some input from a lesbian, but I had to point out the obvious. "Ok, Henry, I don't know any dykes. Do you?"

Henry, Jando and I were on our third interview to find the lesbian member of our Board. We were conducting the interviews at a small coffee shop on 13th Street that was known to be gay and lesbian friendly. Today's lunch crowd was almost entirely female, except for our table.

I had just informed our prospective board member that we wanted to add a dyke to our board, when she asked quite loudly:

"You want WHAT?"

The look on her face showed her exasperation with me, but I had no idea what I had done wrong.

"Honey," she said, looking directly at me. "Do you have any idea how many times I've been called a dyke? What makes you think you have the right to use language like that around me?"

"How would you feel if the positions were reversed and I told you I wanted to hire a faggot?" she continued.

"Oh, I didn't think..." I stammered.

"You're right about that. You didn't think. Now I do understand that I'm here to interview for a job with you, but that doesn't mean I'm gonna sit here and not say what I think. And I already know that you guys probably call each other bitches and faggots. Am I right?"

I nodded in agreement while Henry just stared at her and Jando seemed to be very busy watching the clouds of smoke he was exhaling into the air.

"I get that," she continued. "But when you talk like that, you're doing it as friends. It's even affectionate. But you know it's different if some guy passes you on the street and calls you a fag. He isn't saying it with affection. If anything, he's probably saying it with nothing but pure hatred in his heart."

"Do you even know why they call you a faggot?" she continued, making me feel a little like I was the one being interviewed.

"No, I don't really know," I replied. "When I was a kid, I looked in the dictionary, and all it said was that a faggot was a bundle of sticks."

"Exactly!" she said. "Not that long ago, if someone was accused of being gay, people would gather a bunch of sticks, tie that gay person to a stake in the middle of that pile of sticks, and set the whole fuckin' thing on fire. So when a straight guy calls you a faggot, he's really saying he wants to burn you alive."

"Wow! I never fuckin' knew that," I confessed.

"So maybe you understand why I'm sensitive about being called a name that straight people use to put us down. Words like dyke, bulldyke, bulldagger. The only exception is if another lesbian uses them, like that new motorcycle club called Dykes on Bikes. When we call ourselves dykes, it's like we take the power of the word away from the straights. But I don't want to hear anyone else using those words in a way that's meant to make us feel badly about who we are."

She stood up from the table. I thought she was about to leave, and I didn't want her to walk away offended.

Instead, she took a few steps away from the table, then approached us once more, extending her hand.

"How about we start over?" she suggested. "Hello, I'm Georgia, but all my friends call me Georgie." She handed me her resumé and we were happy to have the opportunity for a fresh start to the interview. And though we did act as though she had not just lectured us, that was a lesson that I would never forget.

We were all impressed with her work on behalf of women, including at the nearby Womyn's Center and at Planned Parenthood. She clearly had good connections and the ability to network, both highly desirable traits for the position as a member of our Board of Directors.

As I listened to her, I was also closely watching her. I think it's fair to say that many people will judge others, whether consciously or unconsciously, on a scale of masculinity or femininity. For example, an effeminate male might be judged as a 1 or 2 on a scale of 1 to 10, with 10 being the most macho masculine men. I wouldn't rate the "average" male as a 5, in the middle of the scale. My best guess would be that the average male would score as a 7 or 8 on that masculinity scale.

I think that women would be consciously judged on a femininity scale even more often than men would be on their scale. And not just by men. So as Georgie was telling us about her qualifications, I was silently judging her on her "feminine qualities."

It wasn't that I cared how masculine or feminine she was. It was just something that I did, and I assumed that everyone else did the same thing.

Her hair was cut short, with blonde streaks throughout the natural light brown. For the interview, Georgie was dressed in a tailored suit, with the arms of the jacket pushed up past her elbows, allowing her many bracelets to be seen. Although they were different colors, styles and materials, it was clear that they were of high quality and they looked good together. Her blouse resembled a man's dress shirt with a button-down collar, and she wore an expensive men's tie to complete the look. Her flat shoes showed her practical side.

Her manner was straightforward, firm, no nonsense, as she spoke in a voice that commanded attention. When she did break into a laugh, it was loud and hearty, not at all forced, like someone who might laugh at something they really didn't find all that funny.

As I continued to listen to her explain her commitment to gay and lesbian causes, I was so impressed with her determination and her goals for the future. Eventually, I totally forgot about assigning any number on a femininity scale to her. Instead, my impression was that as far as being a complete human being, she was a "10" in my book.

Eventually, our meeting came to an end. A few minutes before, I had asked Jando to run out for a fresh pack of cigs, as the restaurant didn't sell them. He purposely waited around the corner, as asking him to leave early was a pre-determined signal that a decision had already been made.

"Ok, Georgie, we'll be in touch after we discuss all the applicants," I said, as she rose to leave.

"Thanks, I really enjoyed meeting you and I'll look forward to hearing from you," she replied.

Georgie left the restaurant and started walking down 13th Street, which unfortunately was not the direction which would cause her to run into Jando. So, he actually had to chase after her. Hearing him running after her, Georgie went into defensive mode, but that changed when she saw who it was coming up behind her.

"Hey Georgie!" Jando panted, a little out of breath even from that short sprint. "Guess what...You're hired!"

"I know you're kidding me. Nobody makes a decision that fast!"

"No, really. We love you and we want to work with you. Come on back and Joey'll tell you."

Henry and I were grinning when Georgie and Jando returned to the restaurant. "Really? You already decided?"

"You bet we did," Henry answered. "It was a unanimous decision."

Georgie smiled back at us. "C'mon bitches," she said with a laugh, enjoying the irony of her language. "Let's go celebrate this deal with a drink."

The next two weeks flew by as our team worked together to not only run the club effectively, but to prepare for the grand openings of The Hole and Aphrodite's Lounge.

SIX

By 1980, Sanctuary was established as the leading gay club in Philly. I was there almost every night, along with the hundreds of gays, lesbians, and even some straights who were looking for a party. On the weekends, that number would swell to over a thousand.

As the owner, I got to know many of our patrons, although of course, there were plenty that I never met. Likewise, some of them knew me as the owner, while others never realized the role I played. Every person in the club had a story to tell, including how they ended up coming to Sanctuary. Many were regulars; others would show up once, never to be seen again.

If someone grabbed my attention, but I didn't know him or her, I developed the habit of giving them nicknames. Admittedly, I wasn't always kind with the names I gave to people. I never told any of them how I referred to them, since they were strangers. But I sometimes shared the names with my friends and we would laugh behind peoples' backs.

A few examples: Triple G would be a Gorgeous Gay Guy. His opposite would be an UGG. An Ugly Gay Guy. Or a troll, a worm.

The Stork was the guy with the skinny legs who wore skin tight pants that looked ridiculous to me.

The Raccoon had dark circles under his eyes. I wasn't sure if it was makeup that had been applied badly or if that was his natural look.

Bette and Joan were two friends who were always bickering with each other, just like the movie stars.

Anyone wearing oversize eyeglasses was FIG to me. A Freak in Glasses.

Fashion choices did not escape my attention. Polo shirts were very popular at the club, but if the shirt didn't have the collar properly starched, to stand straight up in the fashion style of the day, I called the guy Polio.

Sometimes, Henry would point someone out, asking my opinion whether we should invite him to join us. If I wasn't interested, all I had to say was "NMT." Not My Type. Or, spelling out the letters "N-O-T," for Not Our Type.

Sometimes, as my mind wandered, I would assign a trait to someone, for no particular reason, never knowing whether it was true or not.

"Look at Spanky over there," I'd say sarcastically, spanking my own ample butt when I saw a guy that I could imagine enjoyed a good hard spanking. Or, if I referred to someone as "Goldie," I wasn't referring to his golden blonde locks. Instead, I'd be making fun of him because someone may have told me that he enjoyed a certain fetish involving bodily fluids.

I was particularly hard on overweight guys. Fatty, Fatso, Hipster, Thunder Thighs, Gordo, Beached Whale, Elephant, were just a few of the names I would assign scornfully.

I know that this was cruel on my part. I'm not proud of it. I'm just explaining what I thought about some people in the crowd. I also want to point out that, as the years flew by, I learned to become much more accepting of people I might have scorned in the past. I do admit that I wasn't always as mature as I am now.

But the truth is that most of our customers were cool, fashionable, trendy. If anything, they were ahead of the trends, the trendsetters. You might see one guy wearing feathers clipped into his hair one week, only to see 10 guys copying the look the next week, and a few weeks later, the look would hit the straight clubs. Even people who hated us sometimes copied us.

And as quick as I was with a putdown, I could be equally quick with a compliment, a sincere compliment. Beautiful, Cutie, Handsome, Sexy, Lindo, were all titles I would assign liberally to lots of guys in the club.

I was definitely part of the crowd most of the time I spent clubbing. By that I mean that I was occupied with dancing, making out, taking drugs and drinking. Certain songs were like magic, drawing me to the dance floor, dancing in my own little world, without a care as to anything happening around me. Many nights just disappeared into the past, with me having no clear memory of anything that had happened, but always knowing that I had a good time.

Some nights, I'd hang out in The Hole, our separate bar designed for the leather crowd. I didn't always meet the requirements of the dress code, but of course, I was exempt. In here, there were no platform shoes, no polyester pants, no flowery print shirts, no crop tops. It was leather or denim or be banned.

Cody was the head bartender in The Hole. Or, more correctly, Sir Cody was the head bartender. He was the Alpha Male, without question. Even the other Doms recognized Cody's superiority; the subs were required to show their respect, or they would pay dearly.

One of the main attractions of The Hole was The Blackout Room. So dark, you couldn't even see your hand in front of your face. If I was in a court of law, under oath, I would swear that I couldn't see what went on in there. But of course, I knew. Everyone knew. Anonymous sex. With anybody. With everybody. Oral sex. Anal sex. Kinky sex. If you could imagine it, someone in there was doing it. The heavy scent of men having sweaty sex hung

102

in the air, making it impossible to miss what was happening in there.

Twinkie. I assigned that nickname to him the second I saw him. He was hanging out in The Hole, definitely interested in the Blackout Room, but not quite ready to enter what must have seemed like forbidden territory. Twinkie was dressed the part, wearing tight leather pants and a chain belt around his waist, black boots and a tight black latex tee shirt. A leather choker was worn tightly around his neck with a second leather band wrapped around his left bicep. But it was his body that made me wonder about him. Not your typical leather boy body. He was so skinny, no muscles whatsoever. He didn't look like he could handle the kind of sex the guys in here liked, which could get rough.

I didn't talk to him and I wasn't staring at him, but I did notice when he quickly downed a shot of whiskey and headed towards the opening to the Blackout Room.

An hour later, I was still there when he emerged from the darkness. I had to smile when I saw that his pants were stained with the cream from a few guys, his shirt was dripping wet and his hair was matted. Looked like Twinkie had a good time and had provided good service to a few of the men in the room.

Two weeks later, I was talking to Cody at the bar. He was telling me that his club, the Dark Angels, had adopted a new pup. To become a member of the Dark Angels, a guy had to prove himself worthy by engaging successfully in a hazing ritual. The dominant Angels dished out the hazing. The submissive ones, known as pups, had to survive sexual abuse from every member of the club. More than once. Lots of the guys who hung out at The Hole wanted to join the club, but few were accepted. Sir Cody had the ultimate say in who got in.

Cody motioned behind the bar so I took a look. There sat the new pup, a leash attached to his collar, with the leash tied to a hook on the bar. He sat in the same position as a dog sitting at attention. It was Twinkie. I smiled at him and his lips just barely curled into something that resembled the start of a smile. Before he lowered his eyes in a sign of submission, he winked at me. I knew he was just where he wanted to be.

"Nice catch," I told Cody.

"Let me know if you wanna join us sometime. That bad puppy likes to take it from all of us and a couple of my men'll use his ass twice in one night. He's a pro. Never saw one quite like him," Cody said approvingly. It was dark, so I couldn't be sure, but I thought I saw the hint of a blush on Twinkie's face when he heard Cody compliment him like that.

While I was talking about the pup with Cody, Tattoo Lou walked in and took his usual position against the wall across from Cody's bar. I had no idea what his real name was. I gave him the nickname Tattoo for the obvious reason. He had at least a dozen of them. I just picked Lou for the rhyme. Every time I saw him, he stood alone at that same spot, surveying the crowd. He wasn't ugly. He wasn't lonely. I had seen him get picked up or pick someone up plenty of times. It just seemed that he wasn't able to find the right guy, the one he would want to keep.

I don't know how many times I watched Lou go through his routine. Stand at the wall, drinking his beer, looking, looking, looking. But a few months later, I watched as his eyes lit up and he stood at attention. I had never seen him have a reaction like that to anyone, so I knew something special was up.

I thought he was looking at Dallas, who was known to everyone because he was the sports reporter on the most popular newscast in Philly. Leave it to Philly viewers to enjoy getting their sports report from a guy named Dallas. Of course, no one at the station knew that Dallas headed out to the gay clubs after his shift was over. They might be able to forgive his name, but his audience would never accept a gay man reporting on their beloved sports teams.

But he was actually looking past Dallas. I had to crane my neck to see who had captured Tattoo's attention like that.

As soon as I saw him, it was clear to me. Standing just past Dallas was a guy who clearly spent a ton of time at the gym. His musculature was intense. But that wasn't what Lou liked. It was his tatts. His back was toward us and he had the 7 chakras tattooed in a row down his spine. The colors were vivid and even from a distance I could see that the work was detailed nicely. He also had tattoos of huge angel wings spreading across the width of his back. This was an unusual sight, even for The Hole.

As he turned to face in my direction, I noticed the extensive tribal tattoos on his arms. These were dark and dramatic. His biceps and triceps were already of an impressive size, and those tribals just accentuated every inch and every angle. His chest was totally covered with another tattoo, one that looked to me like some sort of tribal mask. I thought that if I ever woke up to find that mask staring at me in my bed, I'd probably be scared to death.

He looked like a Pacific Islander, maybe from Hawaii or Samoa. I thought he looked exotic, with dark features, dark hair, dark eyes. His skin was a beautiful tone of golden brown.

I had to give him a nickname. My first thought was Tattoo Too. And in my imagination, I thought of how Tattoo Lou and Tattoo Too would make a perfect couple.

I watched as Lou walked over to Too and started a conversation. After that first night, every time I saw Lou at The Hole, Too was at his side. Lou's routine became completely different. He no longer arrived alone. He was with Too. He no longer stood against the wall like he was stalking prey. Instead, the two of them would play pool, shoot darts, or just engage in conversations and laughs with their newfound group of friends. They were regulars at The Hole, but their lives were transformed after that night they met. I even got to know their real names. Tattoo Lou was actually named Zak and Tattoo Too's real name was Fetu, and I had guessed correctly; he was born in Samoa. In his native language, his name means "God of the Night." What a perfect name for him!

Back in the main disco part of the club, there could be a hundred different love stories happening on any given night. Some of the stories were just beginning, as two guys met and found that something clicked between them. Others were in the middle, where things usually started to get complicated. Still others were at or near the end, sometimes accompanied by screaming matches, fits of jealousy, accusations and occasional physical violence.

Through it all, the music never missed a beat, the drinks never stopped being poured, and the drugs flowed freely.

Wilson and Shane were two guys in that middle part of their relationship. How could I possibly know that? Well, Wilson seemed to always be in the middle of a relationship. He would get heavily involved with a guy for 8, maybe 10 weeks, and then it would end, almost always badly. This happened over and over and over and over.

Wilson was well known in Philly's gay social circles. He was much older than most of the men who came to Sanctuary, already over 50. He always hung out at the back bar, where Lonnie and BJ worked. And he was always on the hunt for fresh young meat.

Yes, everyone knew that Wilson was a Sugar Daddy, a very rich Sugar Daddy. There seemed to be an endless parade of pretty young boys who were more than willing to provide Wilson with what he wanted, in return for money, clothing, jewelry or whatever else they could get out of Wilson before he inevitably tired of their company. Wilson didn't care if the guy who caught his interest was a hustler, a drug addict, a thug, or whatever. He had some bad experiences, including being robbed and even beaten up. But he was driven to look for these guys and use them for his pleasure. He would feel an intense desire for someone, but it burned out so quickly that he never gave anyone enough time to develop anything serious with him.

Shane was not a hustler, a drug addict or a thug. He was actually an innocent. Raised by a single mother, he craved attention from a father figure. He didn't know about Wilson's reputation, so he had hopes of having a long relationship with Wilson, whom he found to be attractive and comforting. Naturally, he also enjoyed the free drinks, the nice clothes and meals at fine restaurants that Wilson was happy to provide as he showed off his newest acquisition. He even convinced Wilson to dance with him at Sanctuary, which was not Wilson's normal style.

Given his history, Wilson would never trust any of the young men to have any real feelings for him. He loathed being the older man. He did everything in his power to look as young as possible, investing in plastic surgery, tons of skincare products and hair dye. He didn't realize he was actually attractive and he might have looked even better if he was psychologically able to accept the changes that come with increasing age. When his friends asked if he would ever consider settling down with one guy, his reply was, "Honey, they all come with an expiration date."

A few weeks later, after Wilson had dispensed with Shane, I noticed that Shane was also hanging out at the back bar, but now he was on the hunt for one of the older men who tended to congregate there. He was still looking for Daddy. Though Sanctuary wasn't necessarily the best bar to find a Daddy, Shane still enjoyed the place. He became friends with BJ, and they had fun trading stories about some of the older guys at the club.

Rainbow thought he might be at the start of a relationship the night he met Kelvin at the club. Rainbow had introduced himself to me as Rainbow, so I never really knew if that was his real name or if he had adopted it for himself. Always looking for attention, he would act as outlandishly as possible. He didn't care if the attention was positive or negative, as long as he was noticed by everyone.

For Rainbow, every night at the club was an opportunity to dress in some sort of costume. He might wear a sequined tube top with a multi-colored feather boa and drop earrings one night. The next time he might appear in a bunny rabbit costume. After that, dressed in formalwear. The idea was for people to notice him.

Plenty of people loved Rainbow. He was fun to be with and always carried on like a young, proud gay male. He had a tendency to flit from one guy to the next, but he always thought the next guy might be his forever love. That's why he thought that might be possible when Kelvin asked him to dance. Normally, Kelvin would not have approached Rainbow, because Kelvin really preferred men who were more masculine. By the end of the night, Kelvin and Rainbow made plans to go to Rainbow's place for the night.

Kelvin was a sex addict. Now some people might think all the guys in the club back then were sex addicts, and maybe that was true. But Kelvin was actually in therapy to address the problem.

Kelvin's therapist had suggested a method for him to learn how to say "No" to a proposal for sex. He told Kelvin to find someone that he was not attracted to, and then challenged him to spend the night with that person, without having sex.

That's why Kelvin asked Rainbow to dance. That night, Rainbow was in full makeup, with false eyelashes, heavy mascara and the reddest lipstick he could find. He wasn't trying to look like a woman. He wanted to look like a guy wearing makeup, so there was no wig, no dress. Rainbow and his friends loved the look, but Kelvin found it repulsive. However, he wanted to see if the advice from his therapist would help him, so he asked Rainbow to dance and soon after, they left the club.

When they arrived at Rainbow's place, Rainbow stripped completely naked and headed straight for the bed. Kelvin followed, completely dressed. As they were lying in bed, Rainbow started to undress his date, removing his shirt and pants.

"Hey man," Kelvin said, "I just wanna lay here with you. I wanna keep my underwear on, if that's alright."

"What? What do you mean?" Rainbow asked, not understanding what was going on.

Rainbow was clearly in an excited state and ready for action, while Kelvin remained soft.

"I just wanna sleep with you. I wanna keep on my underwear. I'm trying to learn how not to have sex, so my therapist suggested this."

Rainbow was incensed. He knew he wasn't everyone's type, but he never imagined that he would be used like this. He felt humiliated and couldn't believe that Kelvin had actually told him about this.

"You fuckin' asshole! Get the fuck outta here!" screamed Rainbow, getting up and tossing Kelvin's clothes at him. "Who the fuck do you think you are?"

Rainbow had the self-confidence to share this experience with his friends. They actually had fun plotting ways to seek their revenge on Kelvin, though they never carried any of them out.

Kelvin, on the other hand, only told his therapist about the experiment gone wrong. "Oh my God!" the therapist exclaimed, "You weren't supposed to tell him what you were doing. Put yourself in his place. How would you feel if someone did that to you and told you what they were doing?"

Kelvin understood but told the therapist he really didn't know what else to say to explain why he wanted to sleep in his clothes. So the two of them worked on practicing some lines he could use for his next non-sexual encounter, one that wouldn't be so clumsy and hurtful.

After Kelvin left that night, Rainbow felt like crying himself to sleep. Instead, he threw on some clothes and headed for the gay bathhouse, a short two blocks from his apartment. He spent the entire night having sex with anyone and everyone who even glanced in his direction. He had to feel wanted, so he accepted every offer he got that night.

After having as much sex as he could handle at the baths and then sleeping for about an hour, Rainbow started to walk back home. He felt sick to his stomach, was bleary-eyed, and walked at an unsteady gait, weaving a little as he navigated the deserted Center City streets. He wasn't really thinking clearly, so it didn't register that the air had a faint smell of smoke.

The sun was just coming up. As Rainbow reached his block, he suddenly became aware of the thick smoke rising into the morning air. His heart sank as he saw the fire trucks directly in front of his apartment building.

He sat on a stoop across the street, holding his head in his hands. The entire building was engulfed in flames. He didn't own much, but everything he had was in his apartment. A rush of adrenaline shot through his body as he thought about all his clothes and costumes. He wanted to rush inside the building to save what he could, but even in his confused state, he knew that would be useless.

As he was trying to think about what to do next, he saw that a message had been scrawled on the sidewalk in front of the building. In big, bold letters, the message proclaimed:

"God Hates Fags"

Rainbow lived on the second floor of the building, in a small studio. The third floor was vacant. The first floor was a storefront that had recently been rented by Reverend Greene, who was starting a ministry for gays and lesbians. It would later be determined by the fire department that the building had been fire-bombed, with the small church being the obvious target.

Anti-gay violence was becoming more prevalent, but the problem wasn't mentioned by the straight press. The gay papers covered this incident extensively, recognizing the need to inform and warn their readers of the increasing danger. The straight press, on the other hand, never used the word gay to describe anything about the fire. Newspapers just reported it as a fire at a small building located in a Center City alleyway. On the local TV news, they showed the firefighters leaving the building as they finished their work, never mentioning the arson, the gay church or the gay victim who lived upstairs who had lost everything.

Eventually, Rainbow gathered the strength to walk to his friend's apartment. He collapsed in tears when Vincent opened the door, unable to control his emotions. Vincent had been sleeping, so he had no idea what had happened. As Rainbow told his friend about everything that had happened the night before, it was Vincent who recognized that Kelvin had unintentionally done a huge favor for Rainbow. If things had gone differently, both Rainbow and Kelvin could have easily been victims in the fire.

They still hated what Kelvin had done, basically treating Rainbow as an object or as something sub-human, but they also had to acknowledge that his actions had possibly saved Rainbow's life.

Word travels fast in the gay community, especially when tragedy strikes one or more of our members. The Board of Directors of Sanctuary (Henry, Jando, Georgie and I) knew about the fire and its consequences for the community before the smoke had cleared.

Later that day, the same day as the fire, we met with Reverend Greene. Although we were committed to the gay club scene, we were also interested in being more than that. Providing a place for the Reverend to hold his services seemed like a good place to start with our efforts to become more community-focused. That was the start of Sunday Services at Sanctuary.

For the first few weeks, the services were held in the main disco area. Every Saturday night, after the last of the disco queens had left, the bar staff did a thorough cleaning, then set up folding chairs around the podium where Reverend Greene would preach his sermon. Eventually, we converted an area on the second floor, next to Aphrodite's Lounge, into a more permanent area for the preacher. Even later, that area would be used by various gay pride organizations that needed space for meetings.

I was reluctant at first, but Henry convinced me to start attending the services with him. More than anything, I wanted to be involved in all areas of Henry's life, and if that meant attending religious services, well, I was willing to go. I also started to find the Reverend's messages meaningful and uplifting, as they were mostly about how members of the gay community could love and support one another. Quite a change from the fire and brimstone messages I heard when my father dragged me to church as a boy.

Rainbow had to rebuild his life from scratch. But just like the church was able to not only survive, but also to thrive with the support they received from the gay community, Rainbow was able to do the same. He leaned on his friends for help as he worked to meet his goal of being self-sufficient again, and they didn't let him down. Before too long, he was back at Sanctuary, in costumes more grand than ever, searching for attention and enjoying his time in the limelight.

To the surprise of no one in the gay community, no arrests were ever made and no charges were ever filed in connection with that arson.

SEVEN

The A-List. The powerful. Sometimes beautiful, sometimes rich, some older, some young. Mostly white, though there could be a few exceptions. Whether they realized it or not, they had power, sometimes craving more of it and using it for their own purposes. Sometimes, those purposes benefited others, while other times, it benefited only themselves and their friends.

Of course, there's no actual list. But there are some people that, well, everybody knows their names.

Salvador is on the A-List. A son of the consul from Brazil, who was stationed at the embassy in Philly, he was instantly recognizable. Long, wavy black hair that was worn to his shoulders, big brown eyes with eyelashes that were the envy of every fashionable woman, broad, strong shoulders, slim waist and long legs. Every time I saw him, I thought of the song "The Girl from Ipanema," though of course I'd change the word "girl" to "boy."

Like a lot of gays and lesbians, Salvador, whose name means Savior in his native Portuguese, tried to live in two different worlds. And, like all those who try this, it put a tremendous strain on him.

Though you wouldn't know it to see him. His demeanor was always calm, a smooth talker who got along famously with everyone he encountered. But he was careful to not let anyone from the clubs get too close to him. So although he had many gay friends, he was never romantically involved with anyone in that world.

His family, highly conservative and religious, had expectations of him. They always talked about how Salvador would meet some beautiful Brazilian girl, get married, and have beautiful children. Maybe he would even become a diplomat.

114

At this point in his life, Salvador was working on developing an import/export business. He was finding success, using his many contacts back in Brazil along with the new people he was meeting in Philadelphia. Business was good, steady and profitable.

Every Wednesday and Sunday, Salvador had dinner with his family, consisting of his parents, two sisters and one brother. Salvador was the oldest child. And every Wednesday and Sunday, his parents would have a new young woman there to join them for dinner, hoping that one would eventually be found not just acceptable, but desirable by their first-born son. He was friendly with the young ladies during dinner, but he never followed up, not really showing any interest in dating, let alone marriage.

With each passing week, he felt increasing pressure, not just from his parents, but also from his siblings. Tradition dictated that the first-born son would be the first one to get married. Any talk of marriage by the younger children, who were all young adults, was viewed as premature by the parents.

He wouldn't even consider taking a guy home to meet his family. But he was drawn to the club scene, having recognized his gay feelings from an early age. He enjoyed the clubs, the friendships, and he liked to splurge, buying rounds of drinks for friends and strangers alike.

For someone who moved as gracefully as a feline, I never saw him on the dance floor. I always wanted to see him swaying to the music, that luscious hair blowing in the breeze, but he stayed on the sidelines, to my disappointment. Maybe, without even realizing why, he avoided the dance floor because he felt like he was always dancing, trying to keep his balance between two opposing worlds.

Of course, besides a longing for male companionship, Salvador had a strong sex drive. Rejecting the females constantly being paraded in front of him by his family, and not dating anyone from Sanctuary or any other club, I thought maybe he spent time at the baths.

But no, I was wrong in that assumption. Salvador had a secret way to get what he wanted, what he needed.

Managing his import/export business, Salvador had found that lots of men worked on the docks, which he visited often as imports and exports were being traded. In reality, he didn't have to be there, but he actually found it alluring. The men, the workers, strong and sweaty in their dirty jeans, work boots, grimy tee shirts. They fascinated him.

In many ways, they were the exact opposite of Salvador, who was highly educated, always impeccably dressed in the very latest fashionable attire, and well-groomed, including weekly haircuts, manicures and pedicures.

Having been taught his entire life that sex between men was a sin, a disgrace and something filthy, it turned him on to be with these men who took turns using him while they hid from view among the huge cargo containers on the docks.

He didn't know how long he could continue this balancing act between the gay and straight worlds. For now, it was working just fine. He assumed that eventually, he'd have to select a young woman to marry and follow the steps that were pre-ordained for him from birth. But for now, he just wasn't ready to take that step.

Lewis, the owner of Starry Nights Hair Salon, is another A-Lister, well known at Sanctuary and every other club in town. His business catered to wealthy women, many of whom lived in the Rittenhouse Square area, but of course, as word spread of his talent, women began to travel into the city from the suburbs, just to be pampered and styled by the very best. Only gay men were hired to work at Starry Nights, and Lewis himself decided which applicants would be accepted. To be a stylist, you had to know the art and science of hair care, including coloring and how to style hair in a way that enhanced the look of the client. Young men who showed promise as potential stylists were sometimes hired as shampooists, who would be mentored by Lewis in the hope that they would earn promotions.

The attitude of superiority that Lewis displayed at work was also evident in his social life. At Sanctuary, he only associated with other A-Listers. He'd walk through the club, basically with an entourage of adoring, fawning young stylists, often stopping to exchange air kisses and faux hugs with others he deemed as his equals.

I once heard him say, "Don't look at me," to some young man who just wanted to check out Lewis's fabulous fashions and accessories.

To Lewis's dismay, Sanctuary didn't have a VIP area. He would have liked to have a section roped apart, where the glitterati could mingle without being bothered by what he called "the common folk." He even suggested that to me.

I just laughed at the suggestion. One of my goals was to have a club where everyone felt welcome and safe, so I wasn't interested in segregating people according to their perceived class. But I also didn't lecture Lewis about his attitude of superiority. If that's how Lewis saw others, well, that was on him, in my opinion.

Everyone in Philly, not just in the gay clubs, knew Brianna. Formerly Ryan, she was not only positively gorgeous, but also the first person in Philly to undergo gender reassignment surgery. Of course, the surgery was neither the beginning nor the end of her story. She wasn't always as glamorous as she is today, but she worked to earn her status as one of the top A-Listers at Sanctuary, in the gay community and in the metropolitan area.

I never saw her dressed in anything other than a gown and heels. She wasn't shy with accessories, always shiny, brilliant and expensive-looking.

As cold as Lewis was to those whom he considered to be inferior to him, Brianna took the exact opposite approach. She was a friend to everyone, warmly welcoming people wherever she went.

I met her after she had transitioned, but I did see pictures of her as a youngster. She was a fairly large person, not too tall, but also not skinny. And though she now looked completely feminine, her voice was deeper than most who were born into female bodies.

When I saw her interact with others, I was impressed with her charm, graciousness and wisdom. I could imagine her working as a licensed therapist, but she wasn't interested in pursuing a formal education.

By the time I met her, she was already married to a wealthy man, who adored her and provided her with anything and everything she wanted.

Except for one thing. Brianna really wanted to become a mother, and the couple tried every adoption agency, always turned away without pity. So for Brianna, the young people who came to her for advice became her family, her children, and if anyone confided in her that they too felt out of place in their bodies, well, she would protect and nurture them as if they were her own.

On those nights when Brianna would appear at the door of Sanctuary, she was immediately recognized and greeted by any number of adoring fans. A true queen, she was at the very top of my A-List.

I never did any formal research on the subject, but it always seemed to me that many members of the artistic community were queers. The very best of them often found their way onto the A-List.

Jian had his own art studio in Old City Philadelphia and had exhibits in major museums, including the Philadelphia Museum of Art and the Whitney Museum of American Art in New York City. His specialty was sculptures and his work was breathtaking. He could literally sculpt anything, whether real or imaginary, his creativity unbounded by the real world. Mythical, mystical creatures would come alive in his art.

His parents had emigrated from China, settling in San Francisco, where Jian and two siblings were born and raised. Moving to New York for art school, he met and fell in love with another Chinese-American artist, named Chen, who specialized in paintings of Chinese landscapes as well as dragons. Chen had been offered a job as a curator at the Philadelphia Chinese Cultural Center and Jian agreed to move there with him. They became fixtures in the artistic and gay communities in Philly.

Being artists themselves, they fully understood the importance of supporting other artists. They were instrumental in forming a group called PAC - the Philly Arts Cooperative. They set up their headquarters in an abandoned factory two blocks from Jian's studio, which they were able to purchase for next to nothing. This was a step in the direction of forming a thriving community of artists in the area, which eventually transformed Old City into a highly desirable area to live in the city.

Through their work creating art, mentoring other artists and helping to run PAC, both Jian and Chen were highly visible, becoming ambassadors for the gay community. They were featured in newspapers, magazines and local TV shows, never trying to hide the nature of their relationship. They had an inherent understanding that many people would become more accepting of LGBTQ persons as they got to know some of them. They were welcomed and admired as premier members of the Sanctuary A-List.

Dallas was another member of that infamous group. He was the sports anchor at the Number 1 TV station in the Philadelphia metropolitan area. He couldn't afford to be openly gay, like Jian, Chen and many others. In the 1970s and 80s, having a sports reporter known to be gay would have been the death of that person's professional life. No gay man, or for that matter, no female, would ever be permitted access to a team's locker room. And without that access, the reporter would be useless.

So while Dallas had to hide his orientation at work, he was still a regular at the clubs, where of course, he was instantly recognized. How was that possible? How could the teams, the owners, even the fans not know about Dallas?

Well, the community wrapped its collective arms around Dallas, shielding him from exposure. It's as if everyone just knew instinctively that his secret had to be kept among us, with no outsiders to ever know the truth.

Dallas knew he was taking a chance. Just one phone call from someone who saw him at Sanctuary, particularly in the leather bar called The Hole, would have outed him, almost certainly ruining his career. And yet that never happened.

This isn't to say that everything was perfect or easy for Dallas. He still needed to present a certain face to the outside world. The gossip sections of the straight papers and magazines would regularly report that Dallas had been seen at some event with a beautiful young starlet at his side. There were constant rumors of his engagement to a stunningly beautiful woman. None of that was true, of course. But Dallas encouraged those stories, sometimes planting them in the press himself. Straight people almost always assume that everyone else is straight, so it wasn't all that difficult to convince his audience, especially with no evidence to the contrary.

I spent some time talking to Henry about the A-List. As he so often did, he offered a different perspective and suggested that I should think outside the box. He was good at that. However, my main argument about the list was that the members should be instantly recognizable to anyone and everyone in the community. If that wasn't the case, weren't they really on the B-List, or even lower?

Henry's response to my argument was to laugh. "Of course, you're right. You're talking about people who are well-known to just about everyone, and they all make some kind of positive contribution. Think about it. Try to expand your thinking. I agree that you're right about everyone you've named so far. But where do you go from here?"

I'll admit it; I was a little annoyed by Henry's comments. First, I was really just making conversation talking to him about the A-List. I wasn't actually writing down a list of names, and I had no purpose for such a list even if I did write it down.

But I also understood that Henry was always interested in what I was thinking and my method for making decisions. He was also interested in my personal growth, which is why he always encouraged me to think about various subjects in different ways.

So, who were the people I first included while I was thinking about the A-List? There was Salvador, aka The Boy from Ipanema. Next was Lewis, the somewhat arrogant hair stylist, followed by Brianna, the Queen of Transgenders, blazing a trail for others to follow. Jian and Chen, the artists, were next on the list, followed by Dallas, the TV sports anchor. At that point, I had only identified six people as being on the A-List, when in fact, there were easily a hundred that quickly came to my mind. So I didn't think I was on the wrong track at all. It was really that I was just getting started, with so many more people who could be added.

But I'm not here just to name names. That would be meaningless. The important part is to know the story behind the names, what stands out about these individuals that places them on gay society's A-List.

It crossed my mind that perhaps Henry thought that he, or we should be on the list. Well, I'm not going to deny that we are A-Listers, but I didn't think I had to actually say it. Several of us who worked at the club were clearly in that top tier: Me, Henry, Lonnie, and of course, DJ Thunder.

I did think of one A-Lister who perhaps fit the description of being outside the box. The first night that Sanctuary opened, a group of four guys set themselves up as the club's gogo dancers: Giuseppe, Matteo, Tito and Rocco. They were among the most popular boys in the club, but that didn't earn them a spot on the A-List. But their ambitions extended beyond dancing at the club, so they added a fifth member, Giovanni, and decided to form a gay boy band.

They had talent. All five of them could sing and dance. Their choreography was on point. People loved to watch them and listen to their songs.

To kick off their new careers, they wanted to perform at Sanctuary. A meeting was set up with the Board of Directors.

They were telling us their story, including how they came up with the name of the group. First, they thought about calling themselves The Pep Shot Boys. That was a combination of the Pep Boys auto store and a new singing group they had heard about called Pet Shop Boys. But they decided it sounded just too weird, so they axed that idea.

Their next choice was The BackAlley Boys, but that sounded too trashy. Years later, another boy band would have a similar idea. They would go on to become the worldwide phenomenon known as The Backstreet Boys.

Then they considered calling themselves The Villagers, trying to steal a little thunder from The Village People.

Henry kicked me under the table and whispered, "I hope their music is more original than their band names."

Rocco was getting to the end of the story about their name, telling us that they had made a final decision to call themselves The Diva Delites.

I smiled. I liked it. And anything, I mean anything, would be better than The Pep Shot Boys. And though I liked the name, I was a little worried that they would tell us that their first song was called D-I-V-A, sung to the tune of Y-M-C-A. Luckily, they hadn't thought of that.

Our meeting with the group was being held at Sanctuary. After telling us about themselves, they were set to perform. Jumping up on the dance floor, they gave the signal to DJ Thunder to begin, as we sat and watched.

They were good. Damn good. They had three songs ready, with catchy hooks, heavy beats and cool harmonies. Their dance routines were energetic, original, awesome. At the end of their first song, I jumped to my feel, clapping furiously. The rest of the Board looked at me like I was crazy. I sat back down, a little sheepishly, as the group went into their second song.

They never became a national hit, but they were very popular playing the gay circuit on the East Coast. We booked them for their first live show at Sanctuary. For a few weeks before that, DJ Thunder started regularly playing their songs, which were big club hits.

The night of their show, well, I had never seen the club so packed. Literally, it was impossible for anyone in the crowd to move, without causing the people near them to

123

sway in response to the movement. Watching from the DJ booth far above the crowd, I was struck by the support from the community for this new musical group. While they may not have been A-Listers individually, the group, The Diva Delites, earned their spot on the list, with their contributions to the gay music scene.

I mentioned before that there are too many people on the A-List to discuss all of them here. Many of them were heavily involved in the arts - musicians, dancers, craftspeople, actors, authors, etc. Others worked in professions such as medicine, law, psychiatry, education, even politics.

Though I can't describe the stories of every A-List individual, I would be remiss if I neglected to mention Kya. Her given name was Kyalamboka, but everyone knew her simply as Kya. She was Henry's cousin, bi-racial, lesbian and drop-dead gorgeous. Having the perfect body with a face to match, her early career was spent modeling, including runway, print and TV.

One could be forgiven for assuming that she was shallow, a beautiful outer shell with nothing on the inside. However, nothing could be further from the truth. Yes, she made her living by modeling, but she used her money, influence and power to help improve the lives of women everywhere. And yes, she had a special love for her lesbian sisters, but she also supported efforts to help all women become their most successful selves.

Her foundation, AWAKE, All Women Always Keeping Engaged, served as a resource for countless initiatives started by women, focusing on women's issues and causes, with a special emphasis on women's health issues.

Early in life, she considered herself to be too busy for romance. But by the age of 35, wildly successful, she began to miss the intimacy of having a special woman in her life. That's when she met Mona, who was a doctor, specializing in the treatment of women with breast cancer. The attraction between these two was mutual, intense and instantaneous. Totally in sync with each other, they described themselves to others as soul mates. Their relationship lasted for years, long enough for these two sweethearts to be among the first lesbian couples to marry legally in Pennsylvania, when same-sex marriages became legal on May 20, 2014.

Long before that time, Kya was celebrated as a significant, important, accomplished member of the LGBTQ A-List. I was proud to call her my friend then, and I continue to take pride in her up to this very day.

Henry gazed at me as I was telling him the stories of the people I considered to be on the A-List. Of course, he knew all of the same people, so I appreciated his patience as I told him about people he already knew.

"You know the best part about being part of Club Sanctuary?" he asked me.

"Is it all the opportunities we have for casual sex?" I teased.

"No, you know that isn't it. It's that we get to know all these amazingly cool people. Think about it. We'd never know half these people if we weren't at the club," Henry told me.

"I know, you're right," I told him. "And everybody at the club has a story," I said.

"And every story deserves to be told," Henry replied, smiling broadly.

EIGHT

"It's great to be at WGAE....and we know whyyyyyyyy!!"

"That's right, you're listening to WGAE, Gay Radio, 1111 on your AM dial."

"Our motto is: We're here, Queer, and have no fear!"

In the spring of 1980, three students in the Broadcast Journalism department at the PA Institute for Broadcasting approached the dean of the department with a request to start a gay radio program on the school's student-run station. They thought this was the right time for a creative, innovative program that would cater to the tastes of the many gay people living in Philly.

Demetrius, Taylor and Hunter had prepared a mission statement and a detailed plan for their proposal, asking for a 3-hour block of time every weeknight. Being immersed in the gay culture of the time, they knew that the right combination of music and talk would surely appeal to their intended audience. They even planned a dedication line, where members of the audience could call in to request a favorite song, and then publicly dedicate it to the ones they liked, loved, or admired secretly.

"This is a sure hit. 100% guaranteed!" Demetrius exclaimed at the end of their presentation, speaking in his bold baritone voice that was just perfect for a radio show.

The dean sat at his desk, looking intently at the three enthusiastic students. He hated to be the one to break the news that there was zero possibility that a state-funded school would ever allow an openly gay program to be aired on their radio station.

"We would immediately lose our funding. The legislature in Harrisburg would probably fire the entire staff if we ever tried anything like this. They might even shut down the Institute."

The three guys were disappointed, dejected, walking back to their apartment. Hunter, always the optimist, tried to bring back some of the excitement they had felt earlier in the day.

"Sing that jingle again, Taylor, please!"

"It's great to be at WGAE...and we know whyyyyyyyy!!" Taylor was a true tenor, and his voice filled the air as they continued walking.

Demetrius took the next line, using his baritone voice to full effect. He used his fist as a fake microphone as he intoned, "You're listening to WGAE, Gay Radio, 1111 on your AM dial."

Then the three friends joined together for the third line of the proposed theme for their program, starting to laugh as they chanted, "We're here, Queer, and have no fear!"

That broke some of the tension they were feeling. Before long, they were back at their off-campus apartment, ready to start preparing dinner.

Demetrius, Taylor and Hunter had met at school, taking some of the same classes, but they really connected after the three of them were at Sanctuary one night.

It was the spring of 1980 when the three friends made their proposal for that gay radio program at their school. They didn't have a back-up plan for their idea, so after they were turned down, they sort of expected that they would just continue with their classes, and maybe someday be able to find jobs in the broadcasting industry.

Taylor, the one with the golden voice, was the youngest of the three, at 19. His talent was undeniable and his real ambition was to sing. However, his family had convinced him to attend school to learn a trade, just in case his singing career never took off. Red hair, blue eyes and a crooked smile were his trademarks. Average height and weight, with pale skin that freckled in the sun, he loved to wear trendy clothes and could almost always be found singing one of the latest songs, putting his own spin on the tune. He was single, but actively looking for a boyfriend.

Demetrius, the baritone, looked like a linebacker, tall, large, strong. He loved to eat, loved to drink even more, and at the age of 20 had already developed a beer belly. He was African American, with dark skin, dark eyes and a thick goatee accentuating his high cheekbones. His voice commanded the attention of anyone he spoke to, making him a natural for radio or another job that required a distinctive voice. Very fussy about his hair, he went to the barber every week. At the club, he liked to wear bright colors to make him stand out from the crowd, though no one could ever miss him no matter what he was wearing. He was casually dating two guys, one Black and the other white. Not ready for a serious relationship, he was happy with his active sex life.

Hunter, eternally optimistic, looked like the classic science nerd. Tall, skinny, horn-rimmed glasses. Long, stringy hair, parted in the middle. When it came to sex, he liked things a little kinky, so he expressed that desire in his choice of jewelry and other accessories. For example, his favorite bracelet looked like barbed wire, and he often wore earrings in the shape of handcuffs, paddles or other kinky items. At the club, he made a point to wear tee shirts that expressed his desires, with sayings like "Spank Me Hard" or "I Drink From the Tap." He always wore a set of keys attached to the loop of his jeans on the right side, a signal that he enjoyed playing the submissive, masochistic role. At this time, he was unattached, always ready to have sex with anyone who also enjoyed the kinky side of things.

They weren't just roommates; they were also friends. To see the three of them walking together down the street, well, they each looked so totally different that you would wonder what they saw in one another. But in reality, they enjoyed being together, always talking, laughing and playing. And of course, they each had some degree of interest in broadcasting.

I met this threesome two nights after their proposal for the gay radio program had been rejected by their school. At Sanctuary, of course. I had seen them before, but had never met them. Being the owner, I tried to meet lots of the club patrons. Tonight, I joined the three of them on the dance floor, inviting myself into their group.

By the spring of 1980, Henry and I had been living together for a few years, and our relationship was going strong. And although I was devoted to him, our relationship was an open one, as we often played with others, both together and separately. As I danced with these three guys, I have to admit that my eye was drawn to the nerdy-looking one, who would shortly introduce himself to me as Hunter. He was wearing a tee shirt that read "R U HUNGry 4 a sub?" with a picture of a Wawa hoagie under the print. I pointed to it and laughed, then grabbed hold of one of his pointy nipples, wrapped my arm around his waist, and started to grind into him.

At that point, DJ Thunder switched to a new song with a totally different beat. The four of us left the dance floor and we headed over to one of the bars. I tagged along as if I was part of their group. I signaled to the bartender for a round of shots. I never paid for my drinks at the club, but I always tipped the bartenders. I introduced myself right after we all downed our shots, quickly ordering another round.

The alcohol was hitting me hard because I had already taken a Quaalude, like I did almost every time I was at the club. That familiar, welcome, numbing feeling was washing over me as I leaned into Hunter's body.

"You know, I am hung...hung...I mean I'm hung...oh hell, I'm trying to say that I am hungry for a sub tonight," I stammered. "But not for a hoagie, of course," I said, winking at this young guy who was looking sexier with every drink I poured down.

The group started talking about their idea for a gay radio station. Honestly, I couldn't concentrate and I wasn't really sure what they were trying to tell me. I waved to my partner, Henry, who was across the room, indicating that he should join us. I knew that Henry wouldn't be drunk or high; he took the work of managing the club much too seriously to get high during working hours. Of course, after work, that was a different story.

I tried to introduce the three guys to Henry, but I mistakenly called them Dennis, Tank and Harry. Of course, their names were actually Demetrius, Taylor and Hunter. To be honest, getting the first initial correct three times in a row was better than my usual average at remembering names the first time I met anyone.

I asked them to tell Henry what they were telling me about the radio program. He listened intently, while I was busy fantasizing about the sub boy. Henry handed his card to Demetrius and told him to call to set up an appointment to meet with our Board of Directors. Just then, there was a disturbance on the dance floor as three queens started shouting and one threw a fist right into the face of another queen. It quickly turned into a bitch-slap fight, before Henry and two members of the security team escorted them out the front door. Henry stayed out there with them, talking them down to control their emotions, until he knew that everyone would be safe.

He was still out in front of the club when I stumbled out the door, my arm wrapped tightly around the guy I was now calling My Subby. Henry laughed when he saw the two of us together. He knew me well, very well. He knew that I was submissive to him, always and completely. But he also knew that when I was high, I sometimes thought that I could be dominant with other guys, though it rarely worked successfully for me. Still, when I had the opportunity, I enjoyed trying out the dominant role. And My Subby Boy was clearly providing an opportunity for me to play the Top.

Henry came over to us to say goodnight. As we stood in a tight circle, I didn't even have to look to know that Henry was grabbing Hunter's ass, squeezing it and then trying to insert a finger into the boy's butt through his clothes. I knew because Henry was doing the exact same thing to me at the same time. Henry kissed me, then turned and kissed Hunter and told us to have fun. Then he kissed Hunter again, telling him that he hoped he'd still be in our bed when he got home later tonight. He pushed us on our way down the street, giving each of us a final, loud slap on our asses.

On the way to my place, which was actually mine and Henry's, the Sub started to talk to me. By this time, as high as I was, I couldn't remember his name at all. He was just "the Sub."

But Hunter wasn't high, not even drunk, so he was trying to have a real conversation. He told me that he was a Philly native, how much he loved the city and its rich history. He liked to hang out at Independence National Park, where the Liberty Bell and Independence Hall are located. He laughed when he described a conversation he recently had with a Benjamin Franklin impersonator.

I admitted that I had never even taken a tour or entered any of the buildings in the historic area of the city. A fleeting thought crossed my mind that I should ask Henry to show me more of the city. After all, I had been here for a few years now, but my focus had been on building Club Sanctuary into a successful business, and outside of that, my main focus was on having sex.

I wasn't sure if Hunter was trying to avoid talking about sex, or if he was really interested in talking about Old City Philadelphia. In my hazy state, I decided that it really didn't matter. I kept my arm around his shoulder as we walked along. He could talk about anything he liked. I was enjoying the scent of his cologne and the feel of his body against mine.

When we reached my building, I sat on the front stoop and patted the area next to me, inviting Subby to join me. He leaned his body into mine, lit two cigarettes, handing one to me. My high was starting to wear off just a bit, so I could finally concentrate on what Hunter was telling me.

We sat outside for a while, enjoying the feel of the cool air, when I was startled by the sound of two cats fighting in the back of the building. That sound went right through me every time I heard it. Hunter laughed at my reaction.

"Come on, let's go inside," he encouraged me, taking hold of my hand and helping me up from the stoop. Once inside, we both stripped naked and tumbled into bed. I loved the look and feel of his body, his scent, the look of anticipation in his eyes. But despite my excitement at the chance to show my dominant side, I fell asleep as soon as my head hit the pillow. I didn't feel anything as Hunter snuggled tightly next to me, wrapping my arm around him, as he relaxed into his own dreams.

While I was sleeping, and missing out on the opportunity for some fun, the party at Sanctuary was going strong. A group had gathered around Demetrius, in a far corner of the bar, watching him perform. He had this wonderfully deep baritone speaking voice that could capture the attention of anyone. He also had the ability to mimic other voices to perfection, and he memorized lines from movies, reciting them in voices that sounded like the stars themselves were speaking.

Just as Demetrius was ready to switch to a new routine, he saw that Isaac, the Black guy that he was dating, had finally arrived. Demetrius left his fans behind, heading to the dance floor to enjoy his time with Isaac.

Taylor, the third member of the broadcast journalism group, was busy scouring the club for an opportunity. He knew that lots of guys in the club had too much to drink or took too many drugs, and then they started to get sloppy with their money. There were plenty of times when he found money on the floor: ones, fives, tens, even the occasional twenty. Tonight, he noticed that a guy had just walked away from the bar, carelessly leaving a 20-dollar bill laying there. Obviously, that wasn't meant to be a tip, so Taylor quickly moved to that spot, covered the 20 with a one-dollar bill that he was holding, and ordered a drink, switching his one-dollar bill for the twenty. Taylor had learned early in life to feel no guilt about doing something like that. If someone wouldn't give him what he wanted, he really didn't mind just taking it.

When I awoke the next morning, Henry was quietly snoring in the bed with me. And with Hunter. My brain was still foggy and I was struggling to remember the events of the previous night.

"Coffee," was the only word that came to my mind. Not that coffee had anything to do with last night. I just needed some coffee to bring me back to Earth.

My body wasn't cooperating with my thoughts, so I just continued to lie there, wishing that somehow the damn coffee would just make itself. Just then, Hunter started stretching and let out a long, deep yawn. The noise and movement woke Henry, who was a notoriously light sleeper.

"Subby, you're still here. In that case, make yourself useful and go make us some fuckin' coffee," Henry said, not even bothering to lift his head from the pillow.

I thought it was strange that Henry called the boy "Subby." I thought that was my nickname for him. As Hunter got out of bed, I saw that his backside was red, bright red. Then I understood what had happened.

"Yeah, you're right, babe," I heard Henry say. "You were too high to take care of our little friend there, so I took care of him and gave him what he needed. Maybe I gave him a little too much, you think?"

I was laughing. "No, you probably gave him just the right amount, Henry."

He turned to look at me. "Yeah, I made the boy happy. But that could've been you giving him what he wanted. Maybe you should think about cutting back on the drugs a little."

"Yeah, you're probably right," I agreed.

A few days later, I found myself sitting at Denny's Deli, a popular place for lunch in the Gayborhood. Two tables had been pulled together to accommodate our party of seven, the four members of Sanctuary's Board of Directors and three handsome young men who were about to make a presentation about what could be the first openly gay radio station in Philadelphia, maybe even in the country. For the occasion, I had dressed in my favorite bright pink polo shirt, and yes, the collar had been properly starched. Henry was wearing a leather vest and leather pants. I remember thinking that I liked his new passion for leather fashions and accessories. I've tried, but I honestly can't remember what anyone else wore to the meeting that day.

"Okay, so I have a question," Jando said, after the three started by singing their proposed jingle about Radio Station WGAE. "Why don't you just call it WGAY, which is what I think you really want it to be."

Henry and I were nodding in agreement, and Georgie started to say, "I think it's because..."

She was interrupted by Demetrius, who told us, "The FCC regulates all the radio stations in the country. And they have rules...lots and lots of rules, including which call letters are permitted. So they have a long list of letters that cannot be used together, like WGAY, WFAG, WDIK, WQWN, WKOK. I think you get the idea."

"Oh," Georgie said. "I thought it was because you just wanted to be a little discreet."

"And what's wrong with WQWN?" I asked.

Henry rolled his eyes, saying "Honey, you're so cute. WQWN would be Queen Radio. Though it seems silly, I guess they're afraid that people listening to a station with those letters would turn into a bunch of queens."

The entire table laughed at that. I knew the FCC was conservative, never allowing anything even remotely positive about gays to be on TV, but I had never heard about these rules before.

"So we checked and WGAE isn't on the list of forbidden letters. I guess they missed that one," Taylor informed us.

"Demetrius and I would be the on-air talent, playing music, doing interviews, reading the news, whatever," Taylor went on to explain. "Hunter really knows the technical stuff, so he'll handle all the engineering."

"What exactly are you asking us for? Why do you need us?" Georgie asked.

"We need a studio and a place for a transmitter," Taylor answered. "You guys have a reputation, a good reputation, for doing things for the community. A gay radio station could be a really cool asset here. And our school refused to let us do it."

"And we were thinking that if you invested in us by paying the start-up costs, we could sell advertising to pay you back," Hunter added.

They started to sing their jingle again and surprisingly, everyone at the table joined in.

"It's great to be at WGAE....and we know whyyyyyyyy!!"

It seemed like everyone in the deli turned to look at us, as Demetrius used his booming voice to continue.

"That's right, you're listening to WGAE, Gay Radio, 1111 on your AM dial."

And then, in unison, the seven of us said, "Our motto is We're here, Queer, and have no fear!"

Personally, I was sold on the idea. The start-up costs weren't too much for us to handle, and the roof of Sanctuary would make a great place for the transmitting antenna. There was plenty of room inside the club building for a studio to be built.

The Board agreed with me and we approved the proposal. The guys quickly got to work setting up the station.

Some changes had to be made, of course. First, they discovered that approval from the FCC would take at least a year, so they decided to operate as a pirate station, pending FCC approval. They kept the call letters WGAE, just in case the FCC would eventually approve their operating license.

They also decided to use the FM band rather than AM, and 1111 on the FM dial wasn't a frequency that was actually available, since the range is from 88.1 to 107.9.

Less than three months later, the station was ready for broadcast. It was decided that the station would broadcast for 5 hours a night, from 8 PM to 1 AM, seven days a week. The first broadcast was scheduled for Wednesday,

October 1, 1980. And the very first words that were sent out were sung by Taylor, just as they had imagined it would be when they first started this adventure.

"It's great to be at WGAE....and we know whyyyyyyyy!!"

"That's right, you're listening to WGAE, Gay Radio, 89.9 on your FM dial."

"Our motto is We're here, Queer, and have no fear!"

Then Demetrius, who was working the first shift as DJ introduced their first song, "I'm Coming Out," sung by none other than the fabulous Ms. Diana Ross. For the first week, that song was played at the top of every hour, becoming a gay anthem of strength, power and solidarity.

I'm not sure what those three guys expected, but I was envisioning a gay media empire. After working so hard to make Club Sanctuary a success, I was used to thinking big. And I was certain that the gay community would not only embrace this idea, but they would also find it to be a useful, positive resource.

Demetrius and Taylor were naturally gifted as radio hosts, their voices soon becoming familiar to thousands of listeners. At first, Sanctuary was the main sponsor, running a lot of ads, but before too long, other gay businesses in the area started advertising on the station. I predicted to Henry that we'd recover our investment long before we had expected.

Everything at the station was running smoothly. About two months after their initial broadcast, Taylor told his friends/roommates/coworkers that he was going into work early. He had some ideas for new jingles and he wanted a chance to rehearse before sharing his ideas with Demetrius and Hunter.

When Taylor got to the club, the truck was already sitting outside, waiting for him. He quickly went inside and got to work.

Hours later, Hunter and Demetrius arrived, looking forward to hearing Taylor's new jingles for the station. Instead, they were shocked by the sight in front of them.

Everything was gone. EVERYTHING! All the studio equipment, including the furniture. Gone. Microphones, headphones, speakers, turntables. Gone.

They looked at each other, confused. Without a word, they both had the same thought at the same time and headed for the roof. "Oh no!" Demetrius moaned, when they saw that the transmitter was also missing.

There was no sign of Taylor. It took a minute for it to sink in. They had been betrayed. Robbed. By someone they trusted, not only as a friend but as a partner.

Hunter stood there, slowly shaking his head. "What the hell do we do now?"

A little later, Henry and I arrived at the club, finding the two friends sitting outside, afraid to tell us the bad news, but knowing they had to inform us.

I was furious when they described what had just occurred. Not only at Taylor, but at all of us. I started blaming everyone, including Henry, Demetrius and Hunter, including myself. Why? For being stupid. For being trusting. For thinking that we could make a difference in the community.

"Calm down," Henry implored me.

"I will not calm down!" I retorted, storming off like a child in the midst of a tantrum, needing to be alone for a bit. I walked a few blocks, wondering if Henry would follow me, but he wisely decided to give me some space.

Thirty minutes later, I had calmed down enough to return to the club, and though I was still angry, I offered my apologies for being so accusatory. After all, I really didn't even know any of the details of what had happened.

Or why.

I found Henry inside the club, talking with the two radio entrepreneurs. He filled me in on a few of the details. First, he assured me that the club had insurance that would cover our financial losses. However, that would require a police report, and Henry had waited to talk to me before calling the cops. I agreed that it was a necessary step, and gave him the okay to make the call.

For the time being, the radio station was off the air. We would have to decide later what to do about that.

Hunter and Demetrius headed home, angry and disappointed. They didn't realize that they could become even more angry, until they arrived back at their apartment only to find that Taylor had waited for them to leave the premises, then went in and took not only his own clothes, but all the electronics in the apartment. Two TVs, three radios, six speakers. Gone. And in this case, there was no insurance to pay for the stolen items.

A few weeks later, Demetrius and Hunter met with the Board of Directors of Sanctuary. The meeting could best be described as solemn.

"You guys, the three of you, had a great idea," Georgie was telling them. "The community could really use a voice like that. Too bad it got so fucked up."

"Do you want to try again?" Henry asked.

They both sat there silently.

Finally, after a wait that for me was unbearable, Hunter spoke. "No," he said, slowly shaking his head. Demetrius kept his head bowed, staring at the floor.

"I'm so fuckin' sorry about what happened," he finally said. "But like Hunter, I can't do it again.

"Sorry it turned out so badly," Georgie said, "But I totally understand."

I remained silent throughout the meeting, uncharacteristic of me. But I knew that if I started speaking, I would lose control, just like I did right after the theft. I just couldn't understand how anyone could betray not only their friends, but the cause they were working towards, which was to provide a valuable resource for the community. I asked myself a thousand times, "Why? Why? Why?"

All of us learned something from the experience and all of us were changed by it.

The Board decided to be much more cautious, never providing the opportunity for someone to steal from us again. We agreed that we thought we were taking precautions, but clearly, there was a lapse that we needed to avoid in the future.

I didn't like the change I saw in myself, becoming less trusting, more jaded, more suspicious. But I had to realize that not everyone in the world is good, kind, generous. Some people, even gay people, could be traitors.

Hunter, the one who already had a submissive streak, found himself searching for ways to punish himself for what he perceived as a weakness in his character, his easy way of trusting people. He didn't realize why he was doing it, but he found himself searching for sexual partners who would treat him badly, harshly, as a direct result of what Taylor had done.

Despite that, after graduating from the Institute, Hunter took a position as a recording engineer for one of the major TV stations in Philly. He hid his gay identity at work. His dream of a gay radio station died the day that Taylor stole their equipment.

Demetrius also changed, feeling depressed, without ambition, hopeless. He dropped out of the Institute. Despite that, his talent was enough to land him a job doing voice-overs for commercials and he later became the voice of a popular cartoon character on TV.

Occasionally, I would see them at the club. Never together. They had drifted apart; I think it was because they lost trust in each other as well. When I saw them, I would nod and wave, but I never had a real conversation with them after that last meeting with the Board.

Months later, I saw Demetrius talking to Henry at the club.

"Crystal meth. It was crystal meth," he told Henry, explaining that he had discovered that Taylor had developed an addiction, though he somehow managed to hide that fact from his friends.

"He threw it all away for some fuckin' drugs."

None of us ever saw Taylor again.

NINE

Peter and Paul, just like the saints in the Roman Catholic Church. I mean, the names were the same as the saints. That's where any similarity ended between these two friends and those saints.

They had been friends for years, meeting in the first few weeks of their college experience. If asked, neither one of them would remember clearly why they became friends. They started hanging out after class, talking and laughing together easily. Maybe it was their shared sense of humor that brought them together.

Both gay, they never had sex with each other. That was unlike Peter, who literally had sex with everybody he knew. But with his best friend, no.

Besides lots of casual sex, Peter always had a boyfriend. He wasn't faithful to anyone. To him, a boyfriend was someone handsome and sexy to show off at the clubs. His relationships never went any deeper than that.

During the times when Peter was between relationships, he counted on Paul to accompany him to the clubs, which were really the only things Peter considered important in life. He once dismissively described one of his friends to Paul saying, "Oh, he never made it at the club." Meaning, he wasn't a star, one of the desired ones, like Peter was.

Sometimes, Paul would have a boyfriend, but he would try to maintain his friendship with Peter, whether he was involved with someone or not. Peter didn't return the favor. He would happily cut Paul off while he was having fun with his current fling.

This went on for years. I guess it just became a habit for them, because they didn't seem to realize the cyclical nature of their friendship. Or, they were both tolerant of the situation, getting what they wanted from each other.

Despite this odd arrangement, they did actually have fun when they spent time together. You know how your best friend knows everything that's going on in your life? That's how it was for these two. It's just that Peter always had a lot of action in his life, while Paul's life was, well, more boring.

They were both the same age and this year, they would both would turn 30. Neither one of them were looking forward to that. The joke when they turned 25 was that they were a quarter-century old, but they knew that was just a joke. Thirty struck them as no laughing matter.

Paul, to be honest, was jealous of Peter's successful social life. Just like Peter, Paul defined success in that area as being able to attract lots and lots of sex partners.

In the same way, Peter was jealous of Paul's successful professional life. Peter made enough money to get by, but he hated his work and dreaded the trip to the office every weekday morning.

Paul had put more effort into his education and chose a field that he enjoyed and that made him financially secure. He loved going into his law office every day, working for corporate clients that paid handsomely for his work.

I saw them at Sanctuary all the time. They practically lived there on the weekends, showing up on Friday and Saturday nights, and usually coming to Tea Dance, held on Sunday afternoons, as well.

For the past year, Peter's success at picking up new guys was starting to wear thin. A little older, a little more flabby in the stomach, he was losing the ability to have his pick of anyone he wanted. So he was spending more time with Paul, which he enjoyed, but he was also getting frustrated.

Paul was starting to have more success with guys than Peter, annoying Peter immensely. It wasn't that Paul had suddenly become more attractive; he just happened to have what a lot of young, pretty boys were looking for. Cash. Lots of it. And he was willing to spend it.

He didn't like to pay anyone directly for sex. Both Peter and Paul had spent years keeping clear of the many hustlers who could always be found in any club. If it looked like a guy couldn't afford to buy his own drink, well, they both warned each other to watch out for those types.

But they were about to be the dreaded 30. So there would surely be changes to make, and Paul was in a better position to afford those changes.

Carlos and Freddie had moved to Philly a few months before. They had decided they had to get away from their dismal lives in Oklahoma City. Both young, both Black, but without much of a plan, they randomly picked Philly as a place to try to build new lives.

They imagined that they would be stars, easily finding jobs and acceptance in the community. That fantasy was met with the harsh reality that Philly, like anywhere, can be a cold, unwelcoming place. Only a few weeks after arriving, Freddie had already given up and gone back home, moving back in with his mother.

Carlos was on the verge of making the same decision. He had already purchased a bus ticket back home. His one suitcase was packed, along with one cardboard box filled with a few books and other personal belongings. He went out for one last night, hoping to have a little fun. And that's when he met Paul.

Carlos couldn't afford a drink. He was wearing an old tee shirt that actually said "CREEP" on it. Peter immediately recognized both of these as glaring red warning signs. He even pointed out the person he perceived as a loser to Paul, discreetly pointing in his direction and shaking his head "No."

144

But Carlos knew how to cruise, how to let someone know that he was interested. And he was cute. That was enough to make Paul ignore Peter's warning and he bought Carlos a drink. Before long, they were out on the dance floor.

Peter wasn't used to this. Usually, he would be the one to find someone to hook up with, leaving Paul to fend for himself. So Peter sat, sulking at the bar, watching his friend go through that familiar gay mating ritual. Dance. Drink. Dance some more. Drink some more. Make out. Maybe head to the bathrooms in the back looking to score some drugs. Dance a little more before heading out of the club. Everybody there had seen and done the exact same thing, many, many times. Or so it seemed to Peter.

He tried one more time to send a warning message, but Paul ignored his friend. He was having fun, not worried about any potential problems.

When they got to Paul's place, Carlos sensed an opportunity. But that part would come later. For the first night, he just wanted to please Paul, so he was on his best behavior, in the sense of doing his best to be sure that Paul had a good time, a happy ending, as it were.

The next morning, Carlos sat up in bed, ready to set his plan into action. The size of Paul's bedroom was twice the size of the apartment where Carlos had stayed for the last two weeks. The corner apartment, in one of the newer apartment buildings located in the area called Society Hill, offered views of the Delaware River to the east and all of South Philly from the southern-facing floor-to-ceiling windows. "This will do just fine," Carlos thought to himself.

Paul invited Carlos to stay for breakfast, not really expecting anything more than that. As they ate, Carlos explained his situation to Paul. Recent transplant to Philly. Unable to find a job. Living with a friend, but having worn out his welcome there, Carlos was planning to leave, returning to Oklahoma City, that very night. He showed Paul his bus ticket.

Or, maybe those plans could change.

He told Paul that if he could just have a few more weeks in Philly, he could certainly find a job and start a new life here. But he'd need a place to stay. He kept his gaze fixed on Paul's eyes as he told his tale of woe.

Paul listened intently. He wasn't the impulsive type. He had been warned for years to stay away from anyone who might just be hustling. But sometimes, Paul felt tired of his conservative, careful ways. How bad could it be if he took a chance on this guy? And he did find Carlos attractive, very attractive.

On the downside, the sex the night before really wasn't all that great. Paul was usually the bottom guy, but Carlos had assumed that position last night. Paul did what was expected of him, but it didn't really feel natural to him. Maybe they could work that out later, he thought, as Carlos continued with his story.

Paul had very little experience with relationships that lasted longer than a few dates. He had zero experience with having a live-in boyfriend. As he considered his options, he knew what it would be like if he just let Carlos walk out the door. He'd go back to what he always had. A beautiful apartment, with no one to share it with. A life without love. A life with one best friend who, he had to admit, couldn't really be counted on for much.

He didn't really think things through. There was no plan. No rules were set. No timetable, in case things went wrong, like a trial period. Paul simply made the offer to let Carlos stay with him.

That afternoon, Paul drove to the Greyhound station, where Carlos had left his suitcase and one cardboard box in a locker, then returned to the apartment.

Problems started almost immediately. First, there was the matter of their schedules. Paul had one. Carlos did not. He didn't really consider that on Monday morning, when Paul would be leaving for work, Carlos wouldn't be leaving. Late Sunday night, after spending an awkward afternoon together, Paul suddenly got nervous at the prospect of Carlos being in the house without Paul being present.

Paul told Carlos that they had to talk, deciding that he needed to take some precautions. So he told Carlos, as gingerly as possible, that he'd have to spend the day outside, somewhere away from the apartment, while Paul was at work.

Paul didn't realize that Carlos had already been in this position and had already had these types of conversations. So Carlos was, in Paul's estimation, more understanding than expected. He told Paul that he'd spend the day out looking for a job.

Though he told Paul what he wanted to hear, it wasn't really what Carlos had hoped for. When he and Freddie had left Oklahoma, they had heard stories of young, cute guys becoming houseboys for rich, sometimes famous gay men. They didn't really know what a houseboy did. They imagined a life of providing sex on demand, and that was as far as their imaginations took them. They never considered that maybe a houseboy had responsibilities or had to do any actual work.

For the first week, Carlos left the house every morning, carrying a bag containing a book and a few copies of his resumé. But it was a rare day when Carlos actually filled out any applications. He had already decided that Paul wasn't the guy that he was looking for.

What he really wanted was an A-List gay man. He had to be rich, of course. Famous would be nice, but that was of secondary importance. What he needed was a guy with

147

connections in gay society. Someone who would take him to parties. Like, every night. That's how he imagined Paul lived when he first met him, but in reality, Paul's life was quiet and mostly lonely. After work, Paul would generally want to spend some quiet time at home, reading a book, watching some TV, relaxing before bedtime, then heading back to work the following day. This had become Paul's routine. By allowing Carlos to stay with him, he thought maybe he could get out of that dull existence.

The reality is that neither one of them were what the other one expected or wanted.

Every Thursday afternoon, Peter and Paul would meet for lunch. Except, of course, when Peter would cancel. That would be whenever Peter was too busy with whatever guy he was currently seeing. But this week, they met as planned.

Always at the same place, same time, same menu. This routine had developed over the course of many years, and for both of them, it was comfortable and familiar.

They sat at the back booth at Cafe Coco. As soon as they entered, they simply told the waitress, "We'll have the usual, honey!"

In a few minutes, Peter would be presented with a grilled cheese on rye, a side of fries and a Coke. Before eating, the sandwich and fries would be sprinkled liberally with salt.

Paul had the turkey club, extra mayo on the side, with macaroni salad and a ginger ale.

They spent this time catching up and Peter was anxious to know how things were going with the new boy, though he tried to hide the fact that he was very, very curious.

Paul had nothing to hide. He was used to telling Peter everything. He often counted on Peter for advice, though he didn't always follow what Peter thought he should do.

148

But he valued his opinion and welcomed the opportunity to hear what someone else thought.

That particular Thursday, Henry and I were having lunch at the same place. For us, it was a spur of the moment decision, just stopping in for a quick lunch before heading out on a shopping trip. We knew Peter and Paul casually, not really friends, but we knew them as regulars at the club. I smiled and waved when I saw them.

After spending a few minutes speaking about how their days were going, Peter got to the point. "So how's your new boytoy?"

Paul sighed. "It's not what I expected. First, the sex isn't any good."

"Oh, I thought he looked like a bottom," Peter sneered. "Am I right?"

"Yep," Paul admitted. "So neither one of us are getting what we want."

"What else?"

"We don't have anything in common, nothing to talk about. And all he really wants to do is go out and get high all the time."

"So what're you gonna do about it?"

"I don't know," Paul said. "I really just don't know."

"Would it help if he had a job? Something to do?"

"Maybe. I think so."

Peter told Paul that he had an idea. He stood up so he could see the booth where Henry and I were sitting, getting my attention and waving for us to join them.

After talking to the two guys whom I usually referred to as The Two Saints, for obvious reasons, I had agreed to meet with a guy they knew who might be a good candidate for a job at Sanctuary. Maybe a barback. Henry gave The Two Saints our business card, writing on the back a date and time for the guy to come in for an interview.

To be honest, we didn't have high standards for employees at the barback level. I mean, all they have to do is show up and work to keep the bartenders stocked with supplies, occasionally cleaning up a few messes. Turnover was constant, so we hired Carlos on the spot.

Paul was still thinking of Carlos as a boyfriend. So although he thought it would help if Carlos had a job and a regular schedule, this particular job just added to Paul's misery. Now, Carlos would leave for work late at night and stay out all night long. He'd sleep while Paul was at work, and vice versa. Having opposite schedules did nothing to help what Paul saw as a chance to have a boyfriend. Besides that, Paul had to allow Carlos to stay in the apartment to sleep during the day, and he didn't fully trust that arrangement.

Carlos hated the job. Although it provided opportunities to meet new men, possibly someone who might actually want a houseboy, he wanted to be at the club as a customer, not as an employee. But at this stage, he couldn't afford to be picky.

During the second week of working at Sanctuary, Carlos felt like he hit the jackpot when he met a man named Klaus. He didn't go back to Paul's apartment that night. Instead, he spent the night in a mini-mansion across the river in New Jersey, with Klaus, who was not only a top, but he was actually interested in having a houseboy, not a boyfriend.

The next day, when Paul came home from work, he found Carlos sitting with his suitcase and cardboard box, the same items he had when he first moved in.

"This just isn't working out," he told Paul, then giving him a quick hug and walking out the door.

Carlos didn't bother going to Sanctuary for work that night. But he did show up there the following Friday to collect his last paycheck. We weren't really surprised by his actions. That sort of thing happened all the time. Like I said before, constant turnover.

For Paul, it wasn't that easy. He was faced one more time with an empty apartment, feeling that his life was equally empty. But he took heart in knowing that he had tried, and maybe he would have a little more confidence the next time. At the very least, he would know to set some ground rules before letting someone just move in with him. Lesson learned.

TEN

"I'm so sick of being poor." Finn was talking to his friend Travis as they sat at one of the bars at Sanctuary, nursing their drinks.

"Tell me about it. It's still early and I'm already outta money. C'mon, let's dance," Travis replied.

Finn and Travis showed up at Sanctuary every weekend, whether they had money for drinks or not. They were both recent college graduates. Finn had a B.A. in History. Travis had a degree in Anthropology. They both found after graduation that they had no marketable skills. In other words, they couldn't find a decent job, certainly nothing in their respective fields of study.

Right after graduation, Travis was desperate for work because he refused to move back home with his parents. He had living expenses, of course, but he also had student loans to repay. "No ads in the paper for anthropologists today," he joked to Finn, though in reality, it wasn't a joke to him.

"Yeah, I didn't see any ads for historians today, either," Finn said, as they danced, trying to forget their predicaments.

Despite the lack of funds, both of them were still young, proud gay men. They wanted to be part of the community. They wanted to have fun. That's why they were regulars at the club.

Some of the fashion divas looked down on people like Finn and Travis, who simply couldn't afford the latest fashion trends. Not that they didn't try to look good, but they had to look good on a budget. A severe budget.

Most Saturday afternoons were spent visiting the thrift stores on South Street, searching for something decent to wear that night. Tonight, Finn was wearing a used Scout uniform shirt he found in the $1 bin. He added a neckerchief to complete the look. Travis had found an old bowling team shirt that someone had donated to the store. He liked the colors, red and white, and he liked the style, despite the fact that the name "Boris" had been embroidered over the chest pocket. On the back, "Nicetown Brewery Boys" was written in a bold script, obviously the name of the bowling team.

Both of them loved to dance. Some nights, they spent hours on the dance floor. Their feet moved effortlessly, and they had even developed a few dance routines. For certain songs, they would start a line dance and they would soon have most of the dance floor following their lead.

On this particular night, during a short break from dancing, the bartender brought each of them a drink, indicating that they were sent by a guy who was seated at the other end of the bar. Neither of them recognized the man, who looked to be in his late 20s and was dressed in a silk collarless shirt, two gold chains and an expensive-looking watch. That was all they could see from where they were sitting.

Travis and Finn each blew a kiss in the direction of the handsome stranger. They started to walk towards him to offer their thanks for the drinks and to see what, if anything, the man wanted. But it was crowded so it took a few minutes for them to make their way around the bar and by the time they rounded the corner, the man was already gone.

Travis needed money, so after fruitlessly looking for a job for several weeks, he decided that he had to take some drastic action. He had seen some ads placed in the gay papers where guys offered massages. He took a chance and placed an ad, though he wasn't quite sure about taking this step. First, he didn't really know anything about giving a real massage. Second, he wasn't sure if anyone who answered the ad would even be interested in getting a real massage. He suspected that these ads were really offers of sex for pay.

It didn't take long for Travis to get his first call from someone looking for an appointment. He had hesitated to give his phone number in the ad, but he really didn't have time to wait for contacts through PO Boxes. He was cautious enough to use an alias, so the caller addressed him as Bill, which was the name he gave in the ad.

The man on the other end of the call identified himself as Matthew. He was breathing heavily throughout the call, making Travis wonder if he was possibly masturbating. Phone sex wasn't going to make any money for Travis, so he was prepared to steer the conversation away from any sex talk, if necessary.

"Matthew" told "Bill" what he was looking for. He explained that he would be nude during the massage and that he expected the same from the masseur. "And of course, you don't leave until I get my happy ending."

Travis sighed quietly when he heard that. Still, the man was offering $50 in cash, money that Travis badly needed. So, he agreed to the terms and set out for his first appointment.

It couldn't be said that Travis enjoyed the experience. The man who called himself Matthew was older and more hairy than Travis would have liked, and it took him longer than most to reach his ending. Still, nothing horrible had happened, so Travis felt relieved when he left the man's apartment with $50.

Finn was working at the only job he had been able to find, making fries at a fast-food restaurant on Broad Street. He was humiliated, after earning a degree, to find himself working mostly with kids who were still in high

154

school. Still, he needed the paycheck, so he swallowed his pride and went into work every day he was scheduled.

The next Saturday, Finn and Travis were back on South Street, scouring the bargain bins at the thrift store for tonight's outfits. Travis found a pin-striped Phillies shirt that he considered, but after talking about it with his friend, he put it back in the bin. They kept looking, but sometimes it was hard to find anything they would want to wear out to the club.

"Look at this!" Travis was holding a silk collarless shirt. much like the one worn by the strange man the week before. Holding it in front of him, Travis giggled, since this shirt was size Large while Travis was skinny and usually wore size Small. "Should I try it on?"

Finn laughed even harder. "Dude, you already know."

Finn was getting tired of looking, not finding anything he liked in the men's section. He wandered over to the women's side of the store, pausing at a bin filled with bras. He reached in and grabbed a gigantic bra, held it in front of his chest, saying, "Imagine the lady who wore this!" He started twirling it over his head, but then quietly placed it back when he saw an older lady staring at him.

Travis was almost beside himself with laughter. "You're really worried about offending her?"

Just then, Finn noticed a very bright, very cute shirt hanging on a nearby rack. Checking the tag, "Size Small, perfect!" he told Travis.

"That's a woman's size Small," Travis cautioned, as they both laughed. Finn held it up against him, thinking it might be a tight squeeze, but decided it was worth the cheap price.

Since it didn't take too long to find their outfits for that night, they had time to go to the gym. Recently, they had joined the Downtown Y, which was free to join, and they were starting to see some results. Their workouts consisted mainly of exercising their upper bodies with free weights, to build some muscle. They didn't think they needed cardio, since both of them were very active, including those hours of moving on the dance floor. Their legs were strong, if a little on the skinny side.

Of course, they also enjoyed the sights at the gym. Plenty of guys in the pool, on the treadmills and bikes, and using the weights. Plenty of guys in the locker room and showers, too. An hour or two spent at the gym went by very quickly for these two.

All sorts of people patronized this Y. A mix of straight and gay, but due to its location, there were enough gay people to make Finn and Travis feel safe enough to act like themselves. Like them, most of the people here couldn't afford to join one of the many private gyms in the Gayborhood, though some of them chose the Y simply because of its convenient location.

After some time using the weights, they usually took a few laps in the pool. Today, Finn had forgotten his swim trunks, so he decided just to swim in his bikini underwear. "What's the difference, right?' he asked Travis.

After finishing the laps, they spent some time just horsing around in the pool, pushing and splashing each other, like a couple of kids just having fun. Finally, they were ready to head to the showers, when Finn reached for the side of the pool to lift himself out of the water.

He looked back when he heard Travis screaming with laughter.

"Oh, honey, you really can't wear those in here again. I can see EVERYTHING!"

Finn looked down and saw that the water had made his white bikini briefs almost transparent. In the front, he could see everything he had. So he knew what Travis had been laughing about when he saw Finn from the back, climbing out of the pool.

Laughing and laughing, they headed for the showers. They both knew that all eyes were on Finn as they passed guys along the way, some of them snickering while others looked at him with interest.

Most people would probably wrap their towel around their waist in a situation like this, but Finn wasn't like most people. He wrapped his towel around his head like a turban as he and Travis pranced their way to the shower room. That made them laugh even more, enjoying the attention they were getting from the guys there.

Later that night, Travis was getting dressed for the club. He loved the way the oversized silk shirt hung on his body, billowing with every movement. He decided to wear it unbuttoned, with an athletic shirt underneath. He figured that would provide a more dramatic look when he was dancing.

Finn ran into a problem when he was getting dressed. His new small shirt was very tight, so tight that a seam ripped under the left arm while he was putting it on. "Oh shit!"

He checked himself in the mirror, wondering if he could get away with wearing a torn shirt. He started to dance, lifted his arms, and saw that no, it was just too noticeable. But then he had an idea. One tear was a fashion disaster, but multiple tears would be a fashion statement. So he went to work with his scissors, making slices and tears in various areas of the shirt. It was almost in shreds when he figured it was just right, smiling at the result as he checked out his image.

"You look fabuloso!" was the first thing Travis said when he saw Finn wearing his shredded shirt.

"Oh honey, you're looking ultra fabuloso!" Finn replied, admiring Travis's outfit.

That was their word of the week. Everything they liked was now "fabuloso." Next week, they'd have some new word to describe whatever it was they found to their liking. Grabbing hands, they headed to the dance floor for a night of fun.

Travis and Finn each enjoyed their time on the dance floor more than anything. When they heard a song with a certain beat and rhythm, they went into their line dance routine, thrilled to see that everyone on the floor joined in with them. Their friend Ramón joined the two leaders at the head of the line, adding some Latino flair to the dance. He was wearing a backward baseball cap, a tee shirt with a graphic of the Puerto Rico flag, loose, baggy jeans and white sneakers that were immaculately clean. He loved to dance while waving and snapping two fans that also featured Puerto Rican designs.

When the dance was done, Finn and Travis headed to the bar for a short break. "That was fabuloso!" they both exclaimed.

Much like their word of the week, the two friends regularly switched their favorite drinks. This month, they were drinking Harvey Wallbangers, as many as they could afford during their nights at Sanctuary. They were pleased when they found the bartender with their drinks ready for them, thinking it was the bartender's treat. But the bartender nodded towards the back of the bar, where they saw the handsome stranger from last week smiling and nodding at them.

Without hesitation, they both headed in his direction, sipping those delicious drinks as they walked. They agreed that they tasted even better when they were free.

Klaus introduced himself to the pair, explaining that he had been checking them out. "I have a proposition for the two of you," he said, putting his arms around them.

These weren't the first two young guys to be propositioned by Klaus. As a matter of fact, this was a regular occurrence for him. Klaus was always looking for young guys who seemed vulnerable, who looked like they needed some fast cash.

"I produce videos," he told them. "And I'm looking for a few new guys. I like your look and I think you would both be great. Whaddya think?"

Neither Finn nor Travis had ever been in this situation before.

"You're talking about X-rated videos, right? Gay porn?"

Klaus admitted that was exactly what he was talking about.

"My actors get a flat $500 fee for one day's work. Of course, you have to perform to get paid."

Travis and Finn looked at each other. They both needed the money, but working in porn was never in their plans. Klaus handed each of them his business card.

"Listen guys, it's up to you, of course. But I don't make this offer twice. It's take it or leave it. But I don't need an answer right now. My van will be picking up the other actors for tomorrow's shoot at 3 o'clock in Rittenhouse Square. If you want the job, be there and show the driver these cards."

Travis and Finn were speechless. "Uh, thanks, we'll think about it," Travis finally managed to reply.

"Oh, one more thing. Besides the video shoot, it's also a pool party tomorrow. At my private pool, of course. So be sure to bring your swim trunks, unless you like to swim nude," he said, laughing.

That made both Finn and Travis giggle hysterically, as they remembered the incident at the pool earlier that day.

"I can't promise, but we're probably gonna be there for you tomorrow," Travis said, shaking hands with Klaus before they walked away and headed back to the dance floor.

Klaus was fairly confident, based on previous experiences with other guys, that his offer would be accepted. Those two would make his quota for the number of actors he would need tomorrow, so he left the club and drove back to his luxurious home in Jersey. The porn business was very lucrative for Klaus.

At 3 PM the next day, Travis and Finn were waiting at the Walnut Street entrance to Rittenhouse Square, along with 10 other young guys. They had spent the rest of the night at the club talking about their encounter with Klaus, wondering if the offer was legitimate or if it was just too dangerous to take the chance. But the offer of a quick $500 was just too appealing for them to turn down. When they saw the van with the same business logo as the one on their business card invitations, they eagerly got in the vehicle.

It didn't take long to cross the bridge to Jersey and for the van to arrive at Klaus's home. During the trip, a few of the guys explained that they had worked for Klaus before, assuring them that he always paid the same day as the shoot, and in cash.

The driver escorted the passengers to the back of the house, where the pool was located and Klaus was waiting. Finn and Travis were very impressed with the huge house, gigantic yard and Olympic-sized swimming pool. Various areas had been set up with video cameras, lights and furnishings such as air mattresses, hammocks, sofas, etc., to accommodate the actors.

Klaus would be directing four scenes all at the same time, each with three actors. He divided the large group into the smaller groups that would be working together. Finn and Travis were both relieved that they were in different groups. As they split up, Finn assured Travis,

"Don't worry, honey; we got this. It's gonna be fabuloso!" Travis laughed as he walked over to meet his partners for the scene.

Finn found himself in a group with TJ and Elvis, who both told Finn that those were their stage names. They explained that no real names would be used in the video credits while they all signed the forms verifying that they were of legal age. Finn told the cameraman he didn't have a stage name, as he stripped off his clothes. "No problem, you're clearly Dickie," the cameraman laughed, eyeing Finn's larger than average penis.

Klaus walked over to Finn's group. "Ok guys, nothing too fancy here. A simple 3-way 69. Everybody sucking and getting sucked at the same time. No fucking in this scene; let's keep it to sucking. If you really like the guy you're with, maybe a little finger action. Any questions?"

Finn's group got onto a couple of air mattresses as the scene began with the cameras rolling.

Klaus then turned his attention to Travis's group, which also included Bucky and Lucky, who often worked together. "I guess that makes you Chucky," Klaus said with a laugh to Travis.

"In this scene, it's a classic Tag Team position. Lucky, you fuck Bucky while our new guy Chucky sits on top of Bucky and gets sucked off. And Chucky, try to control yourself and don't finish too fast. Sometimes, that's a problem with new guys. Y'all ready?"

Bucky laid on his back and opened his legs while Chucky positioned himself over Bucky's chest, ready to penetrate his mouth.

The filming only took about an hour, which included re-takes with some groups whenever there was a technical glitch or someone came too quickly. After that, all the guys relaxed around the pool, drinking, smoking, eating and chatting. Klaus was a good host, making sure that

Carlos, his houseboy, served the group of guys whatever they wanted. They stayed for about two more hours before Klaus handed each one an envelope with $500 in cash and sending the van back to Philly.

It was still early when the van dropped them off, so Travis and Finn decided to hang out in the park for a bit. They sat on a bench, smoking, thinking about what had just happened.

"That really wasn't bad," Finn started.

"Not at all. It was easier than I thought it would be," Travis replied, bringing them both to a fit of laughter.

"One thing bothers me, though," Finn said. "Klaus just spent $6,000 to pay each of us $500. And that's all we get, no matter how much money the video makes. And think about it. He's definitely making more than $6,000, maybe way more than that. He could make $100,000 and we'll never get an extra nickel."

"You're right," Travis answered. "It was great to make $500 that fast, but did you see that house? Did you notice his car in the parking lot? And that pool, wow! That guy must be loaded."

They started talking about the difference between acting in a video and actually producing the videos. These were two smart guys, both college graduates, who unfortunately didn't get good jobs after college. But that didn't mean they couldn't figure something out.

They started to think they could do something similar. Klaus had four video recorders, cameramen, lighting techs and actors. They didn't need all that; they could start something on a smaller scale. But what about content? They actually thought that the porn business probably carried a lot of risks and they also thought the competition was probably fierce.

"You know what we're both good at? Dancing," Finn said. "And you know how we always say we don't have to do cardio at the gym, because we dance so much."

"I know. If we put our money together, I bet we could buy a video cam and put on a show ourselves. And you know that Ramón knows how to edit video. He probably knows how to use the camera too. Then we'll just need one of those machines to make copies."

Both Travis and Finn grew excited about the possibilities for this project. They walked over to Ramón's apartment and were glad to find him home. By the end of the night, the three of them had agreed to work as equal partners, producing and selling dance exercise videos.

"We do need a catchy name, but I don't know..." Travis said, as they were reaching their final terms of agreement.

"Well, we're doing exercises by dancing, but if we want to appeal to a gay audience, we need to incorporate sex somehow," Ramón said. "How about if we call it Sexercising?"

"Fabuloso!" Travis and Finn both agreed.

It didn't take long for them to get to work on their first video, called "Sexercising With FTR Volume 1." Of course, FTR were the initials of the stars/producers: Finn, Travis and Ramón. It was an instant hit, not only with gay audiences, but also with straights. Volume 2 was titled "Sexercising for the FuTuRe," again incorporating their initials into the title. As producers and actors, the three friends made a fortune in profits.

Of course, they still went to Sanctuary every Saturday night, but it wasn't long before they were buying their club outfits at the big department stores and later at the fancy clothing boutiques instead of the thrift stores.

They never could have imagined that a chance meeting with a porn producer would change their lives for the better so dramatically.

ELEVEN

Philadelphia, Pennsylvania, not really known as a party town, right?

Okay, I can already hear the boys from Philly and the surrounding area complaining about that statement. But let me explain.

Think about events that are known nationally. For example, New Year's Eve. What city comes to mind? New York, right?

Mardi Gras? New Orleans.

Thanksgiving? Wherever your hometown happens to be.

The Fourth of July? Now that one should belong to Philly, but it doesn't. If you're watching fireworks on TV that night, chances are they're being broadcast from Washington, D.C.

Name one nationally known event that takes place in Philly. Did I hear someone say the Mummer's Parade? Hmmm. If you're not from the Philly area, right now you're probably wondering, "What's a Mummer?" My point, exactly.

So Philly is stuck with this perception of being a place where nothing ever happens, which is unfortunate, because nothing could be further from the truth.

As a matter of fact, the good people of Philadelphia actually celebrate everything. They just do it on a scale that doesn't garner national attention.

I mean, can you name another city that has parades on New Year's Day, Lunar New Year, St. Patrick's Day, Easter Day, Memorial Day, the Fourth of July, Labor Day, Puerto Rican Day, Von Steuben Day (German culture), Kosciuszko Day (Polish culture), Thanksgiving Day, and a parade in honor of African American culture?

And on those rare occasions when a local sports team wins a championship? Well, watch out! They go wild here.

Which brings me to my point. Even with all those parades and celebrations, for some people, that wasn't enough. And no, I'm not talking about a Gay Pride Parade. Back in the 1970s and 1980s, that celebration in Philly was extraordinarily small. Happily, things are different now.

But I'm talking about a made-up for no real reason celebration called Super Sunday. On the second Sunday in October, for a few years from the mid-70s to the mid-80s, Philly threw a gigantic block party on the Ben Franklin Parkway, for no apparent reason other than to have a party.

The Parkway stretches from City Hall to the steps of the Philadelphia Museum of Art, and I'll admit, it's a beautiful sight. To see hundreds of thousands of people jammed onto that one street was amazing, especially because there were never any reports of violence or crime. All of the cultural institutions along the Parkway were open for people to explore.

Amusement rides and food vendors lined the street as well, making for a carnival atmosphere. On Super Sunday 1980, Henry and I were among the thousands of attendees. I was amazed not only by the sheer number of people, but also by how many of them I knew because they were regulars at our club. Good to see the gay community out and about, sometimes blending in, but sometimes proudly showing their gay selves.

I was thinking about that when I first noticed an unmistakable scent, the smell of cotton candy from a street vendor. Wow, that brought back the happiest of memories, when that boy Drizz had given me my first real kiss. It really wasn't that long ago, but so much had

166

happened in my life since then that it seemed like it happened in a different lifetime.

I stopped in my tracks, closed my eyes, and let that delicious smell waft over me. Henry looked at me like I was crazy. I filled him in on the story.

"Oh, that's why you keep that little kangaroo in the car!"

"Well, it's actually a joey," I corrected him, making him laugh.

"That's a cool memory, but I'm not sure I like the idea of you thinking about some other dude every time you smell cotton candy or see a stuffed animal," he said, only half joking.

"No worries," I assured him.

He grabbed me by the hand, making our way through the crowd to a carnival game. "I wanna win something for you, babe." We were standing in front of a game where you had to throw a baseball and knock over some bottles to win a prize.

Henry handed a buck to the guy running the game, grabbed a baseball and in an instant, he had knocked over the pyramid of bottles. I was amazed. I had never seen him do anything like that.

"Did I ever tell you I was the star pitcher on my high school baseball team?"

With that one pitch, Henry was eligible for any prize offered at the stand. "I'll take that one," he said, pointing to a purple stuffed snake that was about ten feet long.

He took it and placed it around my neck. "Well, maybe that guy gave you a joey, but I'll always be the guy that gave you the biggest snake ever!"

I was laughing so hard, having such a good time. Henry really knew how to give me just the right amount of attention, without being overbearing or too possessive.

It was estimated that 300,000 people attended the Super Sunday block party that year. As we meandered through the ever-growing crowds, we started to run into people we knew, and we ended up traveling up and down the Parkway with a group totaling about ten guys, including us. Ten gay guys, of course.

Javier was among them. He's the nurse who had taken care of Henry in the hospital, who then turned down a position on the Board of Directors, recommending Alejandro, aka Jando, instead. Not surprisingly, Jando was there with Javier.

After a few hours of eating, drinking, smoking, playing carnival games and going on rides, I was getting tired. It was an unusually warm day for mid-October. I actually think that's why the party was held at this time of year, to take advantage of the waning days of Indian Summer, with much cooler weather ahead as we got closer to the start of the winter season.

"Why don't we all head back to our place and party a little?" Henry asked the entire group. I gave him a look of concern. Did he really want to bring eight guys back to our apartment? Was he looking for an all-out orgy?

Sensing my discomfort, Henry looked me directly in the eye, then glanced around at all the other guys. "Just one rule," he added. "No sex. Just fun. Dancing, drinking, smoking, eating, whatever. But no sex. Just hanging out as friends. Agreed?"

Maybe some of them were expecting an orgy, maybe that's what they really wanted, but everyone agreed to Henry's terms. A block from the Parkway, we were really lucky to find a bus that was nearly empty, and we headed back to our apartment to continue the fun.

This was unusual for us. When we invited anyone to our place, it was almost always to join us in a sex session. But it was a nice change just having friends over to enjoy each other's company. As he so often did, Henry found a way to make me happy and to expand our social opportunities.

I wasn't the life of the party that night. Sunburned, a little drunk and tired, I was more of a spectator. Although they were guests, Blake and DeeDee basically took over the hosting duties. They kept the conversation going, as they both never tired of talking about what was going on in the world, including the worlds of fashion, entertainment, music, gossip, and of course, gay society. Pouring drinks, lighting and passing blunts, even barbecuing food that tasted even more delicious since we were all heavily into smoking weed. Luckily, there was no lack of food and drink in the house, but of course, what's a party without a delivery from the closest pizza shop with a couple of pizzas, calzones, cheesesteaks and fries? This group had no problem finding room for all that.

The only real drama of the night? That would be when DeeDee, who adored makeup and fashion, convinced Willie to let him paint his nails. Willie was already effeminate, so it wasn't the actual nail painting that caused the drama. Instead, it was when DeeDee accidentally knocked over the small bottle of polish, leaving a bright red stain of gel on Willie's pants.

Willie shrieked in horror at the spill, but quickly relaxed, thanks to the calming effects of the weed he'd been smoking. And though his pants had been ruined, he had to admit that his nails looked fabulous. He was even more happy when Henry appeared, tossing a pair of my pants that he had grabbed from my closet, to him. Leave it to Henry to be thorough. He had made sure that the pants he selected matched Willie's shirt. We all made a scene, fussing over Willie's beautifully done nails when he emerged from the bathroom wearing my pants, which fit him perfectly.

When you're having fun, time passes by so quickly. So many conversations, singing along to our favorite songs being played on the cassette tape player, line dancing, and even more eating and drinking. DeeDee managed to convince all of us to get our nails painted, all in wild, bright colors. No more accidents, no more spills.

By 1 AM, the party was about to wrap. The eight guests all decided to head over to Sanctuary, ready to keep the party going. But first, they'd each head home for a quick change of clothes. Shorts and tee shirts were fine for Super Sunday, but most of this group preferred clothes a little classier for hitting the club.

Going their separate ways, they agreed to meet at the club in about half an hour. Willie didn't need to change, since he was wearing a new outfit for him, so he headed directly for Sanctuary. He didn't usually walk in that area alone. It was much safer to be with a group, or at least one other person. Remember, Sanctuary wasn't located in the best area of Center City. It was in the warehouse district, with very few residences and most of the businesses were closed late at night. In a word, the area was mostly deserted by that time, especially on a Sunday.

He wasn't worried when he saw a small figure approaching him as he walked up an alleyway, taking a shortcut to his destination. After all, there was a club nearby, so you would expect to see some foot traffic. But as the guy got closer, he saw the glint of something metallic catching the light from a nearby street lamp. Willie froze. First considering running, he changed his mind when he decided that he really was too drunk to run very fast.

When the man got closer, Willie realized that he recognized him. A street hustler. Willie saw him sometimes, standing outside of a nearby 7-11, begging for coins. Young, unwashed, straggly hair. Though Willie

170

felt a little sorry for the guy, that didn't mean that he thought it was all right that he was about to be robbed.

But that's exactly what happened. The guy held his knife in a threatening manner, telling Willie that he'd have no problem stabbing him unless Willie handed over his cash. His hands shaking, Willie reached for his wallet, about to take out a few bills.

"No man, all of it," the guy said, waving the knife in Willie's direction.

The guy took all his cash, but luckily for Willie, he left behind the wallet, containing his ID, credit cards and his bank card.

Willie was a tough little guy. He had spent his youth defending himself against the taunts of the neighborhood bullies. In the gay world, he always put on a brave face when he was teased for being too effeminate. His life wasn't easy, but he was determined to always make the best of things and have a good time.

Naturally, he was upset about what happened. There were lots of ways that he could react. He could call the cops; he could run home and cry; he could chase the guy and try to fight him for his money. But Willie did none of those things.

He headed for the closest ATM and withdrew enough cash to ensure that he could continue having a good time when he met his friends at the club. He walked back to Sanctuary, avoiding the alley where he had just been mugged, went inside and met his friends. He told absolutely no one what had happened. No one ever had a clue.

Back home, Henry and I decided that cleaning up after the party could wait until the next day. I knew I'd regret that decision later, but I was ready to call it a night. We climbed into bed, naked as always. I felt his arousal against me.

"Did you like that snake I gave you today?" he asked me. "I got another one right here for ya."

He didn't have to see my face to know that I was smiling.

TWELVE

Wednesday, October 1, 1980. Henry woke me up that morning, or actually, that afternoon, pestering me with questions. "What're we gonna be this year? Have you made any decisions?"

Of course, I already knew what he was talking about. Halloween was just 30 days away, and now was the time to begin planning in earnest. Last year, we didn't really put much thought or planning into the process, and unfortunately, it showed. We were out-costumed by just about everybody in the club and I had to agree with Henry's assessment. It was a little bit embarrassing.

Many years later, Halloween would become a major holiday for most of American society - gay and straight. But in 1980, it was a holiday that straight people thought was mostly for kids. For those involved in the gay culture, Halloween was a time for celebration - to be who you really were, or whomever you wanted to be.

Closeted gays sometimes used the opportunity to dress up in ways that made them unrecognizable, and that was their one time during the year they would dare to walk into a gay club. Openly gay guys often used Halloween as a chance to go against their regular image. For example, a chiffon queen might butch it up in leather, and a leather queen might be in heels, dress and wig. Or, you could just take your regular identity to a new extreme. Whatever costume might be chosen, the point was to have fun.

We not only had to think about our own costumes, but we also had to choose decorations for the club. Sir Cody convinced us that he and his pups could transform The Hole into a vision of a living hell. We encouraged him to go with that idea, with the freedom to make his own decisions about the specifics.

173

At our Board meeting, which basically consisted of the four of us gathering somewhere to eat and talk, Georgie was sharing some ideas from the staff at Aphrodite's Lounge. Georgie was in favor of having the main theme as witches and witchcraft. She described witches as being strong, powerful, mystical women who were in tune with the natural world. "Ok," I said, "But how do you get that message across without falling into the modern stereotypes of cackling witches riding around on broomsticks creating mischief with their witchery?"

"Don't worry," she assured me. "We'll make it cool and modern, but we also want it to be fun."

The other idea from the bartenders in the lesbian bar was to turn the club into an Amazon Queendom, with the club staff dressed in Wonder Woman type costumes, but with no clear idea on how to decorate the club to resemble Amazonia. Georgie suggested the witchcraft theme as more practical and well-thought-out. "Maybe we can do the Amazon idea next year," she suggested.

The main disco would be decorated in classic Halloween style. Lots of jack-o-lanterns, skeletons, ghouls, ghosts, cobwebs, etc. Each bar area would have additional decorations designed by the bartenders. This was an all-inclusive event! Lonnie and BJ, for example, wanted to dress as sexy pirates, with lots of torn clothing, eye patches, big hoop earrings and tons of makeup. They fashioned their tip jars into models of crow's nests, like the lookout on a pirate ship. Small versions of the pirate flag, the Jolly Roger, were strewn along the length of the bar and were also worn as kerchiefs around their necks. Of course, they made sure that their trousers were torn in such a way as to show off their jockstraps, which had crude skeletons drawn on the pouches.

The three bartenders at the main bar chose a futuristic theme, with spaceships, flying cars and robots. Their costumes were skintight bodysuits, with no underwear, showing every curve of their luscious bodies and demonstrating how we had chosen a well-hung crew to work in this area. Covering their faces were masks that were totally devoid of any expression, with glassy eyes to make it look like they wore a vacant stare. When I saw them, I found it a little unnerving to see those handsome faces, usually so enthusiastic and joyful, looking so blank.

The third bar, off to the left side, chose slutty drag as their theme. The decorations were hilarious, with male blow-up dolls in all sorts of sexual poses. These bartenders were very masculine, so dressing in drag was funny for them. For Halloween, they decided to be as glamorous as they could possibly be, with the highest high heels you've ever seen, fishnet pantyhose, garter belts, micro miniskirts, and extra extra large bras stuffed to the point of no return. They wore wigs shaped as huge bouffants, gigantic fake eyelashes, more rouge and eye shadow than on most queens, and tons of cheap jewelry to finish the look.

October 31, 1980. Friday night. All I really wanted was for the club to be packed with an assortment of costumed queers having the time of their lives. I would not be disappointed.

We had an open bar until midnight, to encourage our patrons to arrive early. Wearing a costume earned you a bracelet that would extend the open bar until 1 AM. These ideas had been suggested by Georgie, who was a bit of a marketing genius.

As the club was filling up, I took a walk outside, just to see the costumes of the people who were waiting in line. I had to admire the creativity that I saw out there on the street.

My personal favorites were the costumes that were totally outrageous and flamboyant. I called them the Peacocks. They weren't impersonating anyone or dressing in a costume bought from a store. These guys created their own designs, sometimes masculine, sometimes feminine, sometimes androgynous and sometimes simply indescribable in terms of sexuality. I knew I could count on the Peacocks to party until dawn. We were extending our usual 4 AM closing time to 6 AM. Of course, we couldn't legally serve any alcohol past 3:30 AM, but we had a plan to work around that.

Besides the Peacocks sporting their original awe-inspiring designs, there were plenty of other costumes. As I walked along the line, I saw a couple of clowns: funny, circus-type clowns, sad clowns, even killer clowns.

I stopped to talk to one of the clowns. "Ah, Monsieur Pierrot, how nice to see you. Such a sad clown. I actually have a figurine of you back home."

His make-up was impressive, making him look just like the famed Pierrot, with the white face paint, rosy cheeks, dark, sad eyes, and jet-black hair. The frilly collar of the white clown suit, with oversized black buttons and black shoes, completed the look.

"Merci, Monsieur!" the clown replied, and then somehow made his face look even more sad, before turning back to continue talking with his friends.

The line included a lot of sports figures: football players, hockey players, baseball and basketball players, etc. My guess was that many of those guys had never played in an actual game their entire lives. So Halloween allowed them to pretend to be athletes for a night. Of course, some of them could have been reliving their glory days. If you believe that gay people can't be good at athletics, well, that's clearly a stereotype that doesn't reflect reality.

Then there were those dressed in religious garb. Priests, monks, nuns, especially the nuns. Modern habits, old-fashioned habits, even habits that were modified to make them especially sexy. Nothing was off-limits.

"Good evening, Sisters," I said to two nuns who caught my attention, folding my hands as if in prayer and bowing my head slightly. When I looked more closely, I saw that the two nuns were Peter and Paul, the guys I always called The Saints.

"Hello, my son," one of them answered. "I'm Sister Tina."

"And I'm Sister Angel Dust," the other one said, as the three of us burst out laughing at the drug references.

They were dressed like the star of that TV show, "The Flying Nun," with huge hats that allowed the nun on TV to literally fly through the air on a windy day.

"Don't let the wind take you too high," I cautioned.

"Oh honey, we're already flying. You can be sure of that," Sister Tina assured me.

Next, I stopped to chat with two of the Peacocks. Kaos and Rainbow were chatting as they waited in line, with about 25 people ahead of them. Kaos looked like a star, literally like a star in the sky. The illusion was achieved with a mixture of materials, including a base constructed of wood and metal and flowing fabrics that made it appear that he was in mid-flight when even the slightest breeze caught the material. Shimmering glitter, rhinestones and glow-in-the-dark paint were used to make his handsome face resemble the most glamorous girl on the planet.

"Look at me, Joey, I'm a fuckin' STAR!" he shrieked when he saw me approaching.

"Honey, I knew that long before tonight," I answered, attempting to hug him but not really succeeding because of the costume. Instead, he took me by my shoulders, held me tight, and kissed me hard on the lips. That might have been inappropriate if I didn't already know Kaos. But he was one of those sexy boys that I liked and he had spent more than one night with me and Henry. I remember thinking that I loved the costume, but didn't like the way it kept Kaos's hot, tight body from view.

"And I'm the Queen of the Fuckin' Universe!" Rainbow shouted at me.

"Holy shit, baby, you never looked more beautiful than you do tonight," I replied. Rainbow truly lived up to his name with tonight's costume. He had incorporated every color of the Rainbow Flag into his design.

In the design of the original Gay Pride flag, there were 7 colors, each with its own meaning. The Pink stripe was at the top, representing Sexuality. The rest of the colors, in descending order were: Red (Life), Orange (Healing), Yellow (Sun), Green (Nature), Royal Blue (Harmony) and Violet (Spirit).

Personally, that was my favorite version of the flag, because the pink stripe was deleted in later versions and I thought removing the pink took away an important part of its message.

Rainbow was shouting at me because he was wearing platform shoes that had the highest platforms I had ever seen. "Darling, wherever did you get those?" I asked, trying not to sound jealous of the shoes. It seemed to me that they added at least a foot to Rainbow's height.

"Honey, you know you can get anything in New York City," he answered proudly. Shopping trips to NYC were high on Rainbow's list of weekend activities.

I called to the bouncer to let these two beaming Peacocks go to the head of the line, and I watched, giggling just a little, as Rainbow walked gingerly to the door of the club, doing his best not to fall.

More people arriving, a never-ending surprise of colorful, comical, glamorous, sexy, and sometimes ridiculous costumes. I was glad to see that so far, no one was dressed the same as Henry and me.

It would have been impossible for anyone to duplicate our costumes, but I was a little worried that someone might have a similar idea. A few weeks before Halloween, Henry and I had been shopping on South Street, when we stopped into an art studio owned by our friend, Gio. He had just hung a new painting on the wall, a beautiful work of abstract art. Bright reds, greens, yellows and blues dominated the canvas. I loved it the moment I first saw it. I liked the combination of what appeared to be random splashes, dots and drips of the paint as the colors intermingled in places. And while the placements seemed random, I knew that in reality they were not. I had seen Gio in action, working on his art, and admired the care and intensity of his artistry. And I was well aware that if I tried to place random splashes, dots and drips of paint on a canvas, my results would not be anything like what Gio achieved. I purchased the painting on the spot.

As we talked with Gio, I had what I considered to be a great idea. I asked him if he'd be interested in creating a work of living art, painting the bodies of me and Henry for our Halloween costumes. Always up for a challenge, Gio readily agreed, quickly coming up with a few ideas about how best to achieve a dramatic look.

He actually drew a few sketches for us to consider, only asking us to let him know our choice a few days before Halloween. He also told us that we would have to completely shave our bodies, and he emphasized that there was to be no hair anywhere except on the top of our heads. I was laughing as I thought about what that actually meant.

179

Early in the afternoon, Henry walked out of the bathroom and into the bedroom, where I was still sleeping. He had already finished shaving his body and I was amazed at the transformation, fixated on his private areas as he stood proudly before me. His body was mostly smooth naturally, but of course, I had never seen him with no pubic hairs at all, no hair under his arms, smooth as silk dick and balls. Somehow, I thought his dick looked even bigger without its surrounding dark and curly hairs.

He was stiffening while standing there in front of me, and he began to stroke himself slowly and sensually. "You fuckin' hairy Yeti," he snarled at me. "I'm saving this for you till your ass is as smooth as my cock!"

Now I wasn't very hairy, either, so I was hardly a Yeti. But I got his point. I hurried into the bathroom and shaved my body as quickly as I could. Henry didn't allow me any privacy. He wanted to watch; he even wanted to be the one who shaved my balls. He didn't ask for permission. He didn't have to. He knew that he was always in charge.

"Turn around, you know what comes next," he commanded, laughing quietly to himself, as he then proceeded to remove every hair from that most delicate area. By the time I was smooth as silk, Henry's hardon was about to explode on its own. He couldn't wait to take me back to the bedroom. He thrust himself into me right there in the bathroom, pumping furiously until his seed flooded me. It felt funny when I started to stroke my own dick, since there was no hair in the area, and I was feeling immense pleasure. But Henry would not allow it. "Not yet, bitch. I want you to save that for later tonight." I would not and could not voice any complaint about Henry's command. I loved him and I loved being under his control.

While he was calming down, but before he disengaged from me, Henry placed his mouth next to my ear and whispered hoarsely, "I like you like this, baby. So smooth! I want you to keep yourself this way for me. Promise me, okay?"

And of course, I complied.

When Gio arrived later that afternoon to start work on the painting, he told us that he liked the design we had selected, but he also said that he would probably improvise in some places, so we should not expect an exact match to the sketch. We both assured him that would be no problem.

We were told to strip naked. As we did so, I asked Gio what we were supposed to wear for clothes. "Even in my own club, I can't walk around totally naked," I joked.

"No worries. You'll both be wearing these. Only these. Except for sandals. You can wear sandals, ok?"

With that, he handed each of us a posing strap, which is basically a small pouch to cover the dick and balls, held up only by a waistband. No leg straps, like a jockstrap would have. "I want as much of the art as possible to be seen," he said, smiling.

He also gave us two cotton hospital gowns that could be worn when necessary, such as when I took my walk along the line waiting to get into the club. But he urged us to use these as little as possible, to decrease the chance of smears and smudges.

It seemed to take forever while Gio worked on us, but the results were amazing and I was thrilled. We really did look like a walking, talking work of modern art. The designs on our bodies were similar, but not exact copies. We were two sides of one painting.

While most of the painting was done in the abstract manner, Gio did place two identical designs on us. I had a yin-yang on my chest, surrounding my left nipple, and

181

Henry had an identical yin-yang on his chest, around his right nipple. Other than that, there were swirls, twirls, lines, drips and drops, in multiple colors. both fashionable and dramatic.

Gio asked if he could take a few photos. Of course, we agreed. Gio promised that the nude photos would be part of his private collection, but those with the posing straps might later be showcased in his studio. I considered that to be an honor.

And we were a huge hit at the club that night!

Hundreds of people, hundreds of costumes, gays and lesbians drinking, dancing, taking drugs, carousing, cruising, making out, hooking up. On Halloween night, anything goes.

Georgie and her girlfriend walked into Aphrodite's Lounge, which had been transformed into a witch's castle. There were steaming cauldrons of witch's brew, ancient runes painted on the walls, moons, wands, symbols for goddesses, pentagrams, anything associated with witchcraft had been incorporated into the design. Georgie was elegantly dressed as the Bride of Satan and her lover, Paloma, was dressed as Satan Herself. After all, no particular gender could really claim Satan to be his/her own, right?

The club that night was a sea of women, flirting, dancing, having fun. But networking was also taking place. Parties like this presented opportunities for like-minded women to find one another. It was also an opportunity to inform the community about events and resources, which is why Georgie had placed stacks of handouts at the door, providing the names and phone numbers of various women's resource centers. Georgie never missed an opportunity to reach out to women who might be in need of some help.

With all the activity happening on Halloween night, it was easy to lose sight of some of the highlights. For me, the main event was the Parade on the Catwalk, when the drag queens really had a chance to be showcased in all their glory. Not everyone in the gay community appreciated the divas, but I had a special fondness for them. That's why the parade was held at 3 AM, to expose the ladies to as many fans as possible. DJ Thunder organized the parade, introducing each of the queens as they sashayed down the catwalk, stating their names and playing a special song selected by each diva to accompany them during their moment in the spotlight.

Not everyone dressed in drag that night participated in the parade. That was lucky for us, due to the sheer number of guys who chose to dress in their best feminine attire. But we had 15 to 20 who signed up to participate, with the chance to win one of the titles and a cash prize.

A panel of judges, including our A-Listers Brianna, Lewis and Kya, watched closely as each of the queens made their way down the walk. The audience was loud and boisterous, giving their drunken opinions of the effort put forth by each of the contestants.

The prize for Most Comical went to a newbie with the unlikely name of The Mink I Stole. As DJ Thunder explained as she walked, her outfit consisted of all the mink she could steal from the various women's stores downtown. She was wearing a mink hat and a mink stole; at least, it gave the appearance of mink from a distance when seen through the bleary eyes of the drunken judges. She wore fur-covered boots up to her thighs, though the fur was fake and dyed pink, and her dress was a super-mini, also in hot pink. Her wig was short and also pink. No surprise there. I would have called her the Pink Mink, but then, I wasn't in charge of naming her. In the eyes of the judges, what set her apart from the others was a contraption that she had devised that made it appear that she was taking a group of mink out for a walk. Furry little somethings were somehow attached to leashes and they wiggled and twirled as she made her way along the catwalk. They weren't real, but the magic was in the illusion.

Most Fabulous was won by Ms. Kitty Kat, who knew how to design and sew clothing like a pro. Her outfit featured shimmering gold lamé, the metallic fibers gleaming in the glare of the lights. Her hips and breasts were padded to be super-large, and her makeup was flawless. She wore an oversized hat at an angle that just screamed sluttiness, and she walked as though she were a streetwalker on the prowl. Fabulous was the perfect word to describe her.

The title of the Queen of Halloween 1980 went to none other than BaeBae herself, the same queen I had tipped that night long ago at Sharkey's Club in North Philly. I found out later that she was also in the show at Sharkey's earlier in the evening, where she had won the coveted title of Ms. Sharkey's of the Sea. In our show, she was absolutely stunning, in a long black curly wig that reached midway down her back. She wore a gown that was slim in the waist, but featured oversize padded shoulders. She walked like the elegant queen that she knew herself to be, a vision in black and white with every detail done to perfection. The colors of the outfit were offset by the thick gold chain around her neck, with a huge purple gemstone dangling just above her breasts. The crowd roared its approval as she was presented with her tiara and a check for $1000.00.

As the Drag Extravaganza was taking place, the men who had chosen to spend Halloween in The Hole were missing the whole thing. But they were also being treated to a show, as Sir Cody had arranged for the members of his club to show off their "pups." Some of them had quite literally been turned into puppies, wearing masks that made them look like dogs, with collars and leashes, and even some with butt plug tails. Other pups were being publicly emasculated in other ways, such as being forced to wear chastity devices, nipple clamps, and harnesses. Still others were forced to wear pink panties and bras in a show of forced feminization. Twinkie had begged Cody to let him wear leather, but Cody kept telling him he'd be wearing women's lingerie. Though in the end, Cody gave his pup what he wanted, parading him around in a brand new, studded outfit made of genuine leather. Twinkie loved it!

The fourth member of our Board of Directors, Jando, had decided to spend Halloween in The Hole. He didn't really know where he fit into this lifestyle, but he knew it appealed to him. He didn't go all out for a costume. He was wearing combat boots, camouflage pants and a tight white athletic shirt, looking like a young military recruit. His face and arms were adorned with camouflage paint, as if he was ready to stalk an enemy in the midst of a jungle.

Jando found out that plenty of guys there were attracted both to him and to his costume. But then, guys were always attracted to Jando. He had a look that plenty of guys wished they had; some would call it a baby face. Undeniably attractive, smooth, and looking even younger than his age. When Jando looked in the mirror, he had to admit that he knew he was attractive, but he wished that he looked more masculine, more rough. He had spent the last year working out at the gym regularly, developing muscles he didn't even know he had. Despite those muscles making him think he looked more masculine, he still thought that his face made him look too much like a boy. Or maybe even like a girl.

185

That's one of the reasons he went for the military look for his costume. Guys always assumed that when it came to sex, Jando would be the bottom, the passive one. Jando wanted to change that perception.

Despite being out as gay for several years, he didn't think that he had really found his place in the community. Of course, he was on the Board of Directors at the hottest club in Philly, so he had made plenty of contacts in the gay world and he felt that he was making a positive impact. But that wasn't the part that bothered him. He didn't feel that he was successful in making truly personal connections with any of the men he met. Sure, he had a good friend in Javier, the nurse, but that was different.

Lots of one-night stands. Plenty of group sex scenes. Sometimes, sleeping alone in his bed and wondering why. And when he saw successful couples, such as Joey and Henry, he couldn't help but feel a little jealous and wonder why he couldn't find something similar in his life.

As he looked around at the guys in The Hole, he saw plenty of attractive faces and sexy bodies. He thought that Halloween probably wasn't the best night to sulk in a club and wish for a meaningful relationship. So he downed his drink, ordered a fresh one, and headed towards the Blackout Room. Another night of anonymous, meaningless sex. It would have to do for now.

At 3:30 AM, the parties in all the bars at Sanctuary were still going strong. Legally, we were required to stop serving alcohol, but the club was staying open till 6 AM. At exactly 3:30, all the bartenders left their posts and headed for the storage rooms. From there, they wheeled out carts that had been filled with everything a person might need to make their own drinks. Plastic cups, ice, mixers, bottles of alcohol, all free for the taking until 6 AM. Coolers filled with ice containing various brands of beer were also set out for the crowd. We wanted to keep the party going and for our Halloween party to be one that would be remembered for a long time.

By the time Henry and I got home, our "costumes" were a wet, dripping mess of colors. We hopped into the shower to finish removing the body paint. I washed Henry's body, enjoying the look and the feel of his beautiful dark brown skin. He stood there with his sturdy legs spread apart, watching me wash his throbbing manhood. He told me to stroke him until he was ready to cum for the third time in less than 24 hours, then ordered me to open my mouth to receive a gift from my King.

He told me to also stroke myself, and I did so gladly, almost desperate for that rush of sexual release. As Henry filled my mouth with his precious liquid, my own splattered on the shower floor, washing away down the drain.

As we slept, Henry kept one of his legs over my body, making me feel secure, but also reminding me that he was the Dominant one in our lives.

THIRTEEN

Although I was immersed in gay life, I was also blind to certain aspects of it. My world revolved around my club and the customers we served 7 nights a week. Most, though not all of us, led lives that were fairly privileged. Not that we didn't have problems, facing hatred and discrimination, because we did. But I didn't have to worry about money. I had plenty. I didn't have to fight loneliness. I was constantly surrounded by friends. I used drugs, but I was never an addict. I drank too much, but I wasn't an alcoholic. And when I faced problems, I had the love and support of my partner, Henry, to help me work through whatever troubles I encountered.

I had a tendency to think of gay people as fabulous, fashionable, trendy, cutting-edge individuals. And sure, some of us are.

But did you ever think that a homeless person you pass on the street could be LGBTQ? If you attended a meeting for recovering addicts or alcoholics, do you just assume that everyone there is straight?

Lonnie, the bartender at Sanctuary, spent a few nights in a homeless shelter, after he was kicked out of his home by his mother, following being outed by the press. He was not only horrified to be homeless, but also terrified. Sleeping in a room filled with strangers. Who knew what might happen? Why were these people homeless? He didn't know the answers, and that filled him with dread. Luckily, he was able to escape that system after just a few nights.

Most are not that lucky. The cycles of homelessness, alcoholism and drug addiction can be relentless. The struggle to escape can seem endless, hopeless. Some never make it out.

After spending a few nights watching the crowds at Sanctuary come and go, Shorty worked up the courage to ask someone to sponsor him as a guest for the night. He felt out of place in his shoddy clothes and unstyled hair. But at least he had been able to take a shower earlier that day, so he didn't stink, like he did most days.

Not really knowing how to act, he found one spot in the club and just stood there, frozen, watching, waiting. He didn't really know what to expect, either. From habit, he tried to not draw any attention to himself. He knew he was at risk of being ejected from the club. After all, he'd been kicked out of plenty of places before.

It hadn't always been like that for Shorty. Earlier in life, back when he was in school, he was attentive, eager to learn, always ready with his homework neatly completed. Craving attention from his teachers, he did his best to be a good student. It was important for him to feel like he was welcome somewhere; he never got that feeling at home.

No one is destined to become an addict, but everything in Shorty's life pointed him in that direction. His father was sent upstate for dealing and he wouldn't find freedom for many years. His mother was an occasional user, but she wasn't really there for her children. Trapped in poverty, unable to find a job that she could hold onto for any length of time, she did what she had to do to survive the madness her life had become.

He was exposed to drug abuse and sex much earlier in life than anyone should be.

He never personally witnessed anyone having a healthy adult relationship, though he was influenced by what he saw on TV. Those shows were so far removed from his own reality, that he could only assume that they were entirely fictional, with no basis in anyone's experience. It was a mystery to him how people developed relationships.

Those thoughts were far from his mind as he stood there, watching the circus of people at Sanctuary. He'd had what was for him a good day, scoring a trick and being invited to spend a few hours at the guy's house, encouraged to take a shower before leaving, and stealing over $200 from the man before quickly making his getaway. That was on top of the $80 the guy had given him for providing certain services.

He bought himself a beer, grabbing his change without leaving a tip, and made his way out to the dance floor. An hour later, he was still dancing by himself, occasionally trying to act like he was dancing with someone, but never making any connections. He didn't spend much on alcohol; that wasn't his thing. And he knew that the night would get much more expensive later. His drugs didn't come cheaply.

His plan to dance until closing was ruined when he spotted one of his old dealers. Funny, he thought that guy was still locked up, but here he was, and in a gay club, no less. Shorty didn't look in his direction, hoping he wouldn't be seen. He owed that guy money. And though he had cash on him, he already had plans for that. He slid away as discreetly as he could.

An hour later, he was slumping forward, his chin resting on his chest, in a place best described as a flophouse. A dozen other addicts were scattered about, in various stages of drug-induced ecstasy. He felt no regret, but the drugs didn't really make him happy, either. At best, he felt the numbness that started in his limbs, working its way to envelop him completely.

When he awoke, he found that he had crawled close to Terrence, a friend with whom he often spent time running the streets. Uncomfortably close. Because Shorty liked Terrence, possibly more than Terrence would appreciate. So he was glad that Terrence was still passed out, giving him time to move to a safe distance, not wanting to raise any suspicions.

His first thoughts in the morning were always the same, how to make enough money to feed his drug habit. That's the life of an addict. Never thinking too far ahead. Never dwelling too much on the past. Just how to provide for your needs that day.

Last night, he had close to $300. Like he did every morning, he woke with empty pockets. Every night, he would spend every dollar he had, in a desperate bid to satisfy his cravings.

He watched Terrence stir in his sleep, gradually awakening to another bleak day of existence. They couldn't sleep too late, or they'd miss the breakfast being served at the nearby men's shelter. They felt no shame standing in line with 50 other homeless men. They had long ago lost their sense of dignity. And besides that, they were hungry and the food being served was hot and satisfying.

Shorty had met Terrence when they were both in the city jail, awaiting trial, unable to make the small cash bail to be released. They were actually from the same neighborhood, a small white enclave in the middle of a Black neighborhood in South Philly. They went to the same school, but Terrence was a few years ahead, so they never really connected there.

After breakfast, they headed to Center City, deciding to boost some clothes from a store they knew as lacking adequate security, making them a fairly easy target for shoplifters. They already had a connection who would gladly pay cash for anything they could steal.

They had it down to a routine, switching roles every other time. One of them would cause a commotion, distracting as many people as possible, including security.

The other would grab as much merchandise as he could, as discreetly as possible, and head quickly for the exit.

Unfortunately for Shorty and Terrence, the store they chose to hit today had recently upgraded their security system. The store had been experiencing too many losses, so action had to be taken.

They always knew they were taking a chance, but it's always a shock when you get caught. It was Shorty's turn to grab the merchandise, and he was caught red-handed. No one could prove that Terrence had anything to do with the theft, so he was allowed to leave. He felt badly about it, but there was nothing he could do to help his friend, so Terrence just left the store.

Shorty's hands were cuffed behind his back as he was led out to the police car. He hated going to jail, but even more, he dreaded the withdrawal he'd be facing tonight with no drugs in his system.

Expecting a short ride to the closest police precinct, Shorty was surprised when the officer drove him to a secluded area along the Delaware River, just north of Center City. Still cuffed, Shorty was pulled from the car and stood facing the cop.

"You know I can make all this go away," the cop said, staring at Shorty.

He knew the cop wanted something, but he wasn't quite sure if it was sex or drugs. When he saw the officer reach to draw down his zipper, he knew what to expect next.

Although Shorty was gay, the cop didn't know it. This was abuse of power. It was sexual assault. It was wrong.

But Shorty was so accustomed to transactional sex and drugs that he barely gave it a thought. He was just happy to be released after providing the cop with a quickie. As soon as the cuffs were removed, he bolted away as fast as he could.

Shorty was no longer in custody, but he wasn't free. An addict is never free, until they free themselves of their addiction. And being released by the police would only hurt anyone's reputation on the streets. Being suspected of snitching made people extra cautious, and now Shorty would have that additional hurdle to face. If he explained that oral sex had been his ticket to freedom, he faced ridicule and hatred, possibly even more than if he had snitched. Terrence decided he couldn't trust Shorty anymore, so he refused to spend any more time with him.

I got to know Shorty when I saw him sitting at the Food Court at the Gallery Mall early one morning, all alone at a table, quietly crying. He looked so pathetic, that I was moved to buy him a cup of coffee and see if maybe I could do something to help.

He started rambling about his problems, almost incoherently, jumping from one story to the next, not making a lot of sense, but it was clear that he was in a state of distress. I bought him some solid food, which he gulped down while staring at me, wondering how I was going to use him, like everybody else did.

But I had no intention or desire to use Shorty in any way. He was rightfully suspicious, given his history, so I tried to reassure him, but trust wouldn't be developed that quickly. After eating, he stood and thanked me, quickly walking away.

I saw Shorty a few more times after that, on the nights he was drawn back to the club, feeling that desire to be surrounded by gay people, even if he didn't feel like he really belonged there. I don't know the details of how he survived on a daily basis, but there he was, dancing all alone, eyes closed, maybe imagining a different life, maybe just being lost in the sensations of the lights, music, male company, and probably feeling the effects of drugs and alcohol as well.

He disappeared for a while and then one morning, I saw him again at the Food Court, early in the morning, still alone, and crying again. He saw me from a distance and gave me a cautious wave. I think I scared him a little, though he never told me that. I quickly bought two coffees from the nearest booth and headed towards his table.

Now I knew he was gay. To me, that made him a brother, in a way. Not that I loved him, or understood his entire journey, but at least I understood part of his struggle.

Sipping the coffee, he asked if he could get a meal. I handed him a twenty-dollar bill and told him to go get whatever he wanted. He could have walked away with the money, but he returned a few minutes later with breakfast for both of us. It struck me that he wanted to share a meal, not just use the money for himself.

After taking a few bites, he swallowed hard and looked at me. "Can I tell you something?" he asked.

"Sure."

"I never thought I'd say this, but I need help. I gotta get into a program," he confided to me. I saw the tears welling up in his eyes as he looked away, avoiding eye contact.

By that time in my life, I had plenty of contacts in the city. I told him that I could help. But I had one question.

"Are you sure?"

"Yeah, I gotta do it. I can't take this anymore."

Right now, maybe you're thinking that every story has a happy ending and you're settling back, ready to see how this one plays out. Shorty would go into rehab, come out totally clean, ready to join the priesthood or go to medical school and eventually find the cure for cancer.

But you know that wouldn't be real. Rehab was a struggle for Shorty. He went into a residential program, but staying there made him claustrophobic and paranoid. He left after two nights, finding himself right back at the houses where his fellow addicts spent their nights.

In and out of jails. In and out of programs. Endlessly struggling.

I still see Shorty from time to time. I feel sorry for him, even a little guilty, but I can't cure him of his problems. Every once in a while, I give him some money, or buy him a meal. But I won't buy him a drink at the club, or share my drugs with him. I don't want to contribute to his problems. And I'm thankful that I have my drug use under control. When I see Shorty, I'm reminded how intensely drugs can take control of a person's life, and I don't want to ever fall into that trap.

And as long as he's alive, there's still hope. People do recover from addictions. So far, Shorty hasn't been able to do it. But I still have hope. I hope that he does, too.

***

James thought he had a fairly secure life, with a steady job where he had already been working for 25 years, an apartment of his own, and a gay best friend. He didn't think it was important to develop a circle of friends, preferring to know one person really well, having a trusted friend he could count on for support when needed. From the outside, it appeared that he was successful, but so much of what people saw was really a front, a sham. Like many people, James lived beyond his means, drowning in debt, with no savings, no backup plan.

Six months ago, his best friend, the one he expected to help him in times of need, was killed in a motorcycle accident. And today, his employer informed the entire office staff that the company was being bought by a foreign conglomerate, and all operations would be consolidated at the new headquarters in Houston, Texas. No one would be transferred. Every position was eliminated; everyone was out of a job.

That's how James, at the age of 45, a single, gay white male, found himself applying for unemployment insurance, which would pay him less than a third of his normal take home pay. Discovering that, he didn't know how to make up the difference, especially since he was already deep in debt. Maybe, he hoped, he'd be able to find a new job quickly. After all, he had experience and was good at his job as a customer service rep.

One week went by quickly, then two, three, four. It seemed like no time before it was the first of the month, and all those bills were coming due.

During that first week without work, James found it kind of nice to not have to deal with any work-related stress. He didn't know how concerned he should be about finding a new job; maybe one would come easily.

So, he decided to enjoy the time off, at least at the beginning. James didn't have much experience going to gay clubs, but he certainly knew about them. Deciding to explore that life in closer detail, he started going out, finding himself at the clubs more often as each week passed.

When he was younger, gay clubs were secret affairs. The openness of the clubs, and the people inside, fascinated and delighted him. Before long, he found himself buying a membership to Sanctuary, which quickly became his favorite hangout.

That caused problems. James had never really invested in club clothes, so he was self-conscious when he wore business attire, and felt unfashionable when he wore his casual clothes. Buying appropriate fashions for the club was an unexpected added expense.

Another problem was the amount of money he was spending in the clubs. If he met a young guy, he quickly discovered that he was expected to pay for drinks. Same thing if he invited one of those young beauties out for dinner. James paid. So while he was having fun, for the first time in a long time, it was fun that was basically unsustainable.

He tried to use credit cards to cover these extra expenses, but after one or two missed payments, his cards started to be declined.

After three months of being unemployed, James was in a tight spot. The unemployment checks basically paid for food and drink, including drinks at Sanctuary and the other clubs in Philly. He knew he shouldn't spend money there, but it started to get out of his control. Meanwhile, unpaid bills piled up, his credit was in ruins, and while he did spend time looking for a job, he wasn't getting anywhere.

One Sunday, he was down to his last $5, with no money coming until his next benefit check the following Friday. He sighed, went out and spent the last $5 on lottery tickets. Scratch, scratch, scratch. Nothing. Scratch, scratch, scratch. Nothing. Five tickets. Five losers. Damn!

He had a date that night to meet Simon, a handsome young man he had recently met at the club. Penniless, he stood Simon up, unable to figure out any way to fake his way through a date that night.

The next morning, loud knocking on his apartment door woke him up earlier than usual. When he answered the door, he saw an eviction notice hanging there. He had until 8 PM that night to remove his belongings. After that, the locks would be changed.

Panic attack. Heart pounding. Head throbbing. Unable to think.

He realized that he really didn't have anyone to ask for help. At least, no one in Philly. More desperate than ever, he went out to a phone booth and made a collect call to his closest relative, his brother, who lived in Pittsburgh, clear across the state. As he placed the call, he thought it had been maybe 15 years since he had any contact with his brother. They had never been close, and James never felt the need to maintain close contact with anyone other than that one friend, the one who had died.

He listened to the recording coming over the phone, informing him that the number he was calling had been disconnected. Dejected, he just left the phone hanging, not even bothering to place it back in the receiver, before he walked slowly away.

Returning to his apartment, he packed as much as he could, completely filling the trunk of his car, which was old and rundown, but paid for, so not subject to being repossessed. After packing, he sat in the front seat, ready to drive away, but he became confused. He honestly couldn't think of anywhere to go.

For the next three weeks, James lived out of his car, trying to pretend that life was normal. He kept applying for jobs, but he was forced to give the number of a payphone on applications. There was no guarantee he would even know if he was offered a job.

His benefit checks were now being sent to a PO Box, but he was nearing the end of those.

Still, he didn't want anyone to know how desperate he was becoming. The crowds at Sanctuary had no clue that when James left, he would be sleeping in his car, parked in the lot of a nearby abandoned factory. It's easy for us to assume that everybody else is doing okay. And that's what James wanted people to think. He didn't want pity. He didn't want to be humiliated, discovered to be poor, unemployed, homeless. He wanted to hold on to his dignity.

I'm sure that James wasn't the only desperate man at Sanctuary that night. It's impossible to know everyone's story. And when everyone is trying to give the best possible impression, that just makes it even more difficult.

Weeks later, James picked up his final unemployment check. After cashing it, he considered his options, which he saw as extremely limited. Getting into the car, sighing deeply, he headed to I-95. He knew that he could get to Florida, just by driving south on that one highway. He filled the tank of his car, ready to leave Philly for good. He said a quiet prayer that Florida would somehow provide new opportunities for him and began his journey.

Halfway through Delaware, on his way to Florida, James saw a young man, long hair flying in the wind, only partially controlled by the bandanna he was wearing, hitchhiking on the side of the road. He held a sign indicating that he was headed to Orlando.

James only had a minute to make a decision, pulling over and opening the door, smiling as the young man ran towards his car, then sliding into the passenger seat. James had a good feeling about this. Maybe Orlando was the right spot for him.

FOURTEEN

Thanksgiving Day, Thursday, November 27, 1980. The night before was the biggest club night of the year, due to a combination of college students returning to visit family for the holiday feast and the desire of people to get out of the house and do something before the weather turned much colder.

The weather that day was unseasonably warm, and Henry and I woke in the early afternoon to an unusually bright day as we were heading into the Winter season. I had no obligation nor desire to visit with family members for any occasion, especially not Thanksgiving. Henry assured me that no one would miss him at the large family gathering which would be taking place at his Mom's house. He joked that he was the "Black black sheep."

He told me to pack a bag for the weekend, explaining that he had already made arrangements for Georgie and Jando to handle anything that might come up at the club. He had booked us a room at one of the new casino hotels in Atlantic City. "Stash some cash in there," he said, as I finished packing. "I'm feelin' lucky so I wanna hit the blackjack tables. And if you're a good boy, I might let you play some of the slot machines with the little old ladies," he joked.

Since it was late autumn, the summer crowds at the shore were long gone. Still, I was surprised at the number of people at the casino, especially considering it was Thanksgiving. More people than I expected seemed to be happy with a free buffet at a casino for their Thanksgiving feast.

Henry and I were walking along the boardwalk at close to 11 PM. Most of the tourist shops were closed, and there was very little foot traffic. Most people seemed to be in a hurry to get from one casino to another, with only a few stopping at the pizza shops that stayed open after Labor Day. The wind was picking up, and I was glad that we had dressed warmly. Henry took hold of my hand as we walked along, If anyone noticed or cared that two young men were walking arm-in-arm down the length of the boardwalk, well, we didn't notice them. I was enjoying being with a man who made me supremely happy.

Wrapping his arm around my waist, Henry guided me towards the beach. We simply ignored the signs warning that the beach was closed after 10 PM. We both took off our shoes and felt the cool sand under our feet as we headed towards the ocean. The tide was going out, so we knew we could safely sit at the high-water mark. Henry pulled a blanket out of his backpack and spread it on the sand. We sat down and started to cuddle, both for warmth and partly out of habit.

The almost full moon was glowing brightly above us in the cloudless sky, its image shimmering on the dark waters below. The sound of the waves crashing, the scent of the salty air and the warmth of the man I loved combined to provide me with a feeling of peace that I wished could last forever. I watched as a couple of seagulls strolled by, completely oblivious to the human intruders on their beach.

We both let out a sigh, spontaneously and in unison. I laughed, thinking how much in tune with each other we were. Henry reached into the backpack, pulling out a bottle of champagne and two glasses. "What's all this?" I asked him.

"Do you ever think about the future?" Henry asked.

"Sure," I replied. "I'm already thinking about what kind of party we should have at the club for New Year's."

"No, babe. Not that kind of future. I mean, the real future, our future. Do you ever think about that?"

I was feeling hot inside and my face was turning red, though Henry couldn't see it. Of course, I was always thinking about what I wanted with Henry. I loved him, like I had never loved anyone. In my dreams, we would stay together forever. But I was also well aware that gay culture wasn't accepted by mainstream society, and while all couples faced hurdles in maintaining a relationship, there were even more obstacles placed in the way of gay couples.

Pop! The champagne was open and Henry was filling the glasses.

"I've been thinking about our future since the first day we met," Henry was saying. "Here's to all the good times we've had so far," he continued. We lightly tapped our glasses together and sipped.

He turned and looked directly at me. "I swear to God, you've made me the happiest man in the world every day we've been together. I love you so much it hurts. I've done my best to make you happy. I want to dedicate my life to your happiness."

I was close to the point of tears. I didn't know what to think or to say, except to nod my agreement.

"Babe, will you make me happy? Will you marry me?"

He pulled a small box from the pocket of his jacket. I was breathless. He opened the box, showing me the most beautiful diamond engagement ring I had ever seen. I recognized quality when I saw it, and this ring was exquisite. A two carat round cut diamond solitaire set in a 14 K white gold engagement ring. I held out my hand and he slipped it onto my finger. My heart was pounding as I watched, my hand was trembling, and I know that the sparkle of that diamond was reflected in my eyes.

I hugged him more tightly than I ever had and didn't want to let go. Sobbing with joy, at first I thought I should try to hide my emotions. But with a sudden insight, I understood that I could freely show this man what I was feeling. He understood me. He accepted me. He loved me.

I pulled back a little so Henry could see the tears streaming down my face. He brushed my face with his fingers, a delicate caress.

"Henry, I love you. I want you to know that. I'm totally and madly in love with you. And yes, I will marry you."

We started caressing and kissing again, more passionately than before. Henry was nibbling on my ear, and I heard him whisper, "You wanna have some Sex on the Beach to seal the deal?"

"You got the vodka and the mixers in your bag over there?" I joked.

"Nah," he said, guiding my hand towards his hardness. "I want the real thing."

Later that night, we went out to continue the celebration. Every gay club in Atlantic City was closed after the summer season except for one, that could best be described as a dive bar. We weren't concerned about the lack of ambiance. We wanted to celebrate our engagement with other gay people.

I'm not really a super feminine guy, but that night, I was fluttering around that little club like a social butterfly, showing off that beautiful ring to everyone in the place. We found a mostly supportive audience there, as guys came up to us to offer their congratulations as word spread among the crowd.

We were seated at a table and at one point, an aging drag diva came over to sit with us. She eyed the ring suspiciously. "Is that really real?" Henry assured her that it was indeed real, and that we were going to get married.

"You know it ain't gonna be legal," she sneered, looking at me with a mixture of resentment and envy.

"Very true," Henry answered her. "But just 'cause it isn't legal, that doesn't mean it ain't the right the thing to do. And we're gonna do it. We don't need permission from anybody, including you."

The diva stood up and walked off in a huff, muttering under her breath, "Stupid ass faggots. Two men can't get married. That shit ain't natural." I wanted to chase after her and confront her, but Henry held my arm and waved her off.

"Don't let her get to you, babe. At least she had the balls to say what a whole lotta people are gonna be thinking."

I felt suddenly depressed. "Do you think it'll ever be legal?"

Henry stopped and thought for a minute. "No, I don't," he said. He pulled me up from my seat and we started slow dancing on the tiny dance floor, even though the song was an upbeat fast-paced disco hit. "But don't worry. I'm gonna spend my life protecting you. Protecting us. I swear to God."

Back in Philly, the Thanksgiving holiday was being held with the usual festivities. A big parade, featuring the appearance of Santa Claus at the conclusion. Large family gatherings. Huge meals featuring the special dishes of individual families. Football games on TV. Combing through the special edition of the newspapers, with hundreds of ads for Black Friday deals to be found the following morning, if you could get to the stores early enough.

Ruby and Rosetta spent the afternoon checking out those ads. Money was tight, so they needed to find the best deals if they wanted to find some decent Christmas gifts. "Oh honey, look at these gold bracelets!" Rosetta exclaimed, eyeing the circular featuring the jewelry department at Kmart.

Ruby was equally excited. "These are my favorites!" she said, pointing to a gold-plated bracelet with synthetic amethysts and a charm bracelet featuring tiny animal charms.

"You got a good eye, girl," Rosetta said, pointing out a few that she also liked. "I know how much you like anything with a panda on it!"

They both broke out laughing. They weren't stupid. They knew that cheap costume jewelry was just that, fake, a costume, not real. These girls were really wonderful, caring people, who were caught in a set of unfortunate circumstances. They identified themselves as "ghetto fabulous," doing their best to look and play the part of people who had much more than they currently were able to afford. Although they were poor, they didn't want that fact to control their lives. They strived for more and if they had to fake it for now, well, so be it.

"Mmmm, that smells good!" Ruby was referring to the Cornish hens that were baking in the oven, the main dish for today's Thanksgiving meal. Rosetta had stolen them from a supermarket downtown. There were no supermarkets in their own neighborhood. The mac and cheese, green beans and stove top stuffing had all been purchased from a small neighborhood store, and Ruby had everything she needed for her signature sweet potato pie. They were looking forward to enjoying a good dinner together.

It seemed like they had been best friends forever, though they had actually met just 5 years ago. They attended the same neighborhood public high school and soon found that they had a lot in common. They both looked and acted more like girls than boys. They were both ridiculed, bullied and snubbed. At least that was true until the boys in school were looking for a blowjob. If a girl wouldn't do it for them, they would often turn to Ruby or Rosetta, who at that point in their lives were known as Damon and Tremont. There were even some boys in the school who seemed to enjoy the mouths of the boys even more than those of any girl, and they liked to gossip about those boys, wondering what their stories were.

Damon and Tremont were soon spending lots of time together, playing dress up and practicing wearing makeup. They weren't interested in each other sexually. They considered themselves to be best girlfriends, sometimes getting in trouble together, but each one always being protective of the other. Eventually, they shared their biggest secrets, that each of them wanted to have sex change surgery. It seemed like an impossible dream, but it was their dream.

Now they were 19 years old, sharing a tiny apartment, working towards fulfilling their life dreams. It was far from easy, but both of them managed to maintain their positive attitudes. It was especially difficult to find jobs. They were young, uneducated, having both dropped out of high school, effeminate and perceived as gay. Most employers wouldn't give them a chance.

A few weeks before, Rosetta got hired at a company that conducted public opinion polls by telephone. It was shift work, minimum wage, $3.10 an hour. No guarantee how many hours would be worked each week. No benefits, no security. But it was a job.

Ruby kept applying, but so far, no job would take her. She wanted to attend Beauty School, but she had no way to pay for the classes.

Although they knew it was dangerous, they survived by working as sex workers. Prostitutes. They both hated that word. But like many oppressed minorities, they knew that by embracing words meant to hurt, they took ownership and power away from the oppressors.

"We ain't pros, we hoes!" became their catchphrase.

They didn't hang out in the Gayborhood. That area was mostly for guys searching for other guys. For Ruby and Rosetta, they tried to look and sound as much like "real women" as possible. Some of their johns might be looking for a real woman. Others knew what they were getting when they hooked up with one of them. That was what they wanted. A secret desire. A shemale. A chick with a dick. Some of their customers would even use those words to make it more exciting for them during their encounters. The feeling of a powerful masculine male taking advantage of and using what they considered to be an inferior feminine male.

Ruby and Rosetta enjoyed their simple, tasty meal together. They laughed and joked, just like you would expect best friends to act with one another. They gave thanks for what they had, including each other. There was no mention of their families, who were more than happy when the girls left home.

After dinner, they cleaned up thoroughly. Their apartment was small, but it was also immaculate. You would never find a speck of dust in their home. Unwashed dishes were unthinkable. Anytime a cockroach would make the unfortunate decision to invade their space, it was met with a ferocity that ensured the roach and any companions wouldn't last long.

Before taking their naps after dinner, which were necessary because a long night's work awaited them, they spent some time looking through their favorite fashion magazines. It was fun for them to imagine how they would look in those glamorous gowns and fancy, expensive outfits. They studied the makeup on the models, often using them as examples for their own stylings.

Rosetta shared her fantasy about how her strong Black King would come along one day soon, a straight man who would be happy to pay for her surgery, would marry her, and together they would live a fairy-tale life. Ruby always listened, always encouraging her dear friend, her sister, in her aspirations for a glamorous life. Ruby wasn't so sure about what she wanted in her life. She knew she wanted to be loved for her real true self, but she couldn't imagine how to make that happen. For the time being, she would be happy just to go out on dates, real dates, not the kind of date where she found herself crawling into some stranger's car for a quickie. She didn't feel that she was ready to settle down, but she did feel that she deserved better than what she was getting right now.

"Wake up, girl. It's time to get ready." Ruby felt Rosetta poking her in the ribs, which turned into tickling, which then turned into gales of laughter from the two of them. As they applied their makeup, wigs, and paddings, they continued to gossip about all the kinds of things girls talk about. Recently, they had gone to see the movie "The Blue Lagoon," and they were imagining what man they would like to be stranded with on a desert island. Oh, the possibilities!

They expected the night to be cool, but they had to dress seductively. Well, really, they had to dress like sluts. That was the only way to get the attention they needed from the men who would be on the prowl for sex later that night.

Rosetta was wearing bright yellow hot pants with a matching bikini top, fishnet stockings and bright green high heels. Big hooped earrings. No jewelry around the neck. That would be too easy for someone to grab. A gigantic Afro wig completed the look.

Ruby was feeling cute in her long blonde wig with bangs. She wore her lucky earrings, the ones with the little pandas dangling below her ears. Her tight vinyl red dress was so short that you could see her lacey pink panties. Black stockings with red heels completed the look.

"Mouthwash?"

"Check."

"Lipstick?"

"Check."

"Pepper spray?"

"Check."

These were the essential items they made sure to carry in the small purses they wore strapped across their bodies, resting against their hips. They knew their work was dangerous, and they wanted to be prepared for any emergency. Rosetta went to her drawer and pulled out two small switchblade knives. "Here," she said, handing one to Ruby. "It's a holiday. We better be extra careful tonight."

Most people on the street ignored the two young ladies as they walked to the bus stop. Sometimes, they would be subjected to catcalls or even have objects thrown at them, but not tonight. The streets were mostly deserted, since most people in the neighborhood would spend the night at home with their families.

They didn't even have to discuss where they were headed. The bus took them directly to Belmont Plateau, known simply as The Plateau to the locals. It was a good sign when they saw all the cars driving slowly through the area. They knew that these were the men who were out looking to party tonight, and it looked like a good night for making the money they needed for their Black Friday shopping spree.

The goals were always the same. Get invited into as many cars as possible. Once inside, do as little as possible. No kissing. Never. Find out what the john wanted and settle on a price. Set the price as high as possible. Close your eyes, swallow your pride and do what had to be done. Take the money and get out of the car as fast as you could.

They had some regular customers. That always felt safer. But they always reminded each other to never let your guard down. Any guy could turn on you in an instant, for any reason, or for no reason at all.

There were plenty of customers tonight, but there was also competition. Other girls were out on The Plateau tonight. Some were real girls. But there were also plenty of others like Ruby and Rosetta. When they saw the others, they would greet each other with air kisses and fake, enthusiastic hugs. Although they were competitors, it couldn't hurt to have a few friends to help if needed.

In and out. In and out. There was plenty of work tonight. During a slight lull, Ruby and Rosetta stood together, smoking, when Ruby suddenly tensed up. "There he is," she whispered. They both watched as a brand new 1981 Corvette drove slowly by. Beautiful car. Ugly guy. Ugly personality, that is. Both Ruby and Rosetta had had bad experiences with the man in that car. He was rough. Too rough. Rough to the point of scaring the girls that he might go too far and actually hurt them, or worse. They watched as another girl leaned into the car, talking with the man, then she walked around to the passenger side and got in. Without saying a word, they both hoped the girl would survive the experience.

Ruby's mood brightened when she saw what she was looking for, a 1978 Lincoln Mark V. She had a secret crush on the man in that car, who had told her that his name was Dominick. Ruby suspected that the name was fake, but she understood. He was probably married, maybe even with kids. He was nice-looking, approaching middle age, but it wasn't his looks that she found appealing. It was the way he treated her. With respect. She didn't get much of that from the guys in the other cars. So Dominick stood out among the pack.

She spent more time in the Lincoln than she would spend in other cars. She also let Dominick do whatever he wanted with her. Truthfully, he didn't want too much, but he did always ask Ruby to remove the duct tape that kept her small penis tucked between her legs. He wanted to look at it, to touch it, while Ruby worked on him. His smooth voice was comforting to Ruby, even as she brought him to his climax.

"I see how much you like me," he whispered as he put himself away, still looking at her small stiffness.

"Don't let that fool ya, honey," she kidded. She waited a minute to get soft again and re-applied the duct tape. As she got ready to leave the car, he handed her a few bills, her regular fee plus a Thanksgiving holiday bonus.

"Buy yourself a nice gift from me," he told her, smiling.

It was getting close to dawn and most of the cars had disappeared, the men returning to their regular, drab lives after the excitement of the evening. Ruby and Rosetta headed towards the bus stop, planning to go home and rest a little before their Black Friday shopping trip.

Without warning, a large black sedan screeched to a halt a few yards behind them. A few seconds later, another large sedan was blocking the path in front of them. "Oh no!" Rosetta muttered. Four young white guys jumped out of each car, each one armed with a baseball bat. They wasted no time, charging at the girls at full speed, screaming obscenities about killing faggots.

Rosetta tried to reach in her purse for her weapons, but she felt the crack of a bat hard against her arm before she could open the purse. The second blow was to the back of her knees, and she felt herself falling to the ground. She tried to reach for Ruby, for support, but she hit the ground hard as the young males kept beating her. Blow after blow after blow. A vicious hit caught the back of her head, splitting it open, and she was gone in an instant.

There was no time for Ruby to react. She wanted to help her sister, but she was met with baseball bats battering her from all sides. The blows forced her to the ground and she ended up on top of Rosetta. She was lying on her back and she closed her eyes tightly as she saw the bat coming towards her face. That was the last thing she ever saw.

CLUBBED. TO. DEATH.

The attack only lasted a minute or two. That short amount of time for two beautiful young lives to be so cruelly ended. Why?

Eventually, the two bodies were found, and the police were called to the scene. Their lack of concern was appalling. There was never any real intention to investigate. Lost gay lives were low priority. Murders of young Black transsexuals? Simply ignored.

The news outlets weren't much better. No screaming headlines. No outrage. No warnings to the community.

There was a small article that could easily have been missed in one of the mainstream, straight papers, describing two men dressed in women's clothing who were found dead in the park. They didn't even bother to mention that "the men" had been attacked and beaten to death.

Luckily, there were several gay newspapers that reported on the crime and served as a warning to the gay and trans communities.

What lessons were learned by those young men who had attacked Ruby and Rosetta? Quite simply, that they could easily get away with murder by choosing targets who were not valued by society. Not one of them was ever questioned about the matter and they went on with their lives as if their victims had never even existed.

I wish I could say that the gay community in Philly had an outpouring of emotional outrage for these two victims. But sadly, that wasn't the case. Reverend Greene held a memorial service a week later, which was sparsely attended, mostly by other young Black transgenders who knew Ruby and Rosetta. They understood the pain and the horror. But for the majority of the mostly white, educated, employed gays in the city, the story of Ruby and Rosetta was seen as sad, but far removed from their own lives.

Henry and I attended the memorial service. Henry even spoke, encouraging the attendees to find a way to unify our community, not just for the sake of safety, but also because it would be the right thing to do. While calling for unity, he also called for strength and standing up for our rights. Listening to his words only made me love him even more.

But looking at the number who attended, and knowing that not even one family member of Ruby or Rosetta was there, it impressed on me that our community still had a lot of work to do.

When Henry finished speaking, he walked up to each person in attendance and handed each one a card, a lifetime membership card to Club Sanctuary. We wanted every person there to know that, as long as the club was open, they would have a place where they would be welcome.

FIFTEEN

The month of December was always a lot of fun at the club. 1980 was no exception. There were lots of relationships that blossomed in December, only to die a quick death in January, after the parties had been attended with the new partner, the gifts had been exchanged on Christmas Day, and the kisses had been given at midnight on New Year's Eve. For me, it was fun to watch who hooked up with whom.

Stephen was a new face at Sanctuary. He stood out, for all the right reasons. Taller than average, slim-built with muscles in all the right places. Six pack. Military style haircut. Always dressed in fashionable outfits. I don't think I ever saw him wear the same pair of shoes twice. And that face. Oh, what a face!

Everything about his face was perfect. A 12 on a scale of 10. Bright eyes, gleaming smile. The look of an angel. Every time I saw him smile, I was captivated. The same could be said for every other guy who was lucky enough to have Stephen smile at him.

Stephen seemed to have a goal of sleeping his way through the club. Every time I saw him, he was with a different guy, or meeting a new guy for the first time. I joked to Henry that Stephen had a different guy for every pair of shoes he owned. We wondered if anyone would be able to get Stephen as their "December date," or if Stephen would just continue to sleep around.

I kept a close eye on him. I found him intriguing. He didn't seem to have a preference for any particular body type. Some of the guys I saw him with were skinny, some had muscles, some were even heavy. The only similarity was that they were all pretty. He was definitely picky about that. They didn't have to be gorgeous, but they needed that pretty face to have any chance with Stephen.

He also had a secret that I would discover later. That military style haircut? There was a reason for that. Stephen was a military man. A naval officer, to be more precise. He had graduated near the top of his class from the Naval Academy a few years ago. The Navy was his chosen career, so he had to be careful. Being discovered as gay would ruin his plans, and he would end up with a dishonorable discharge, maybe even a court martial. The U.S. military made it very clear. No gays allowed.

That was the main reason that Stephen wasn't looking for any long-term relationships. He wanted sex, needed sex; he craved the company of other men. But his career was his top priority.

He decided to take the chance to visit the local gay clubs starting in a different city, where he was stationed before being assigned to Philly. On the rare occasion when he saw another military guy in a club, whether they knew each other or not, he figured that they were both in the same predicament. If the other guy told, he would have to explain how he knew. And no one wanted to be subjected to that line of questioning from their superiors in the military. And it wasn't like he wore his uniform to the clubs. The other person would have to have already known that Stephen was a member of the military.

By the middle of the month, no one had managed to become Stephen's December date. I would continue to watch for any interesting developments.

"Do you want to go shopping for your wedding gown today?" Henry asked me, laughing.

"Yes, honey," I replied sweetly, cocking my head to one side and waving my wrist limply as I blew him a kiss.

I knew that he was kidding. We had already rented our tuxes. His was black; mine was white. We would both

215

wear pink cummerbunds and bow ties. After all, this was going to be a gay wedding. The clothing had been selected, but we had to go order the wedding bands today. We would get matching gold bands, but we would keep the inscriptions a secret until the rings were actually exchanged during the ceremony.

During the walk to Jeweler's Row, we walked closely together, but we didn't hold hands. Even in 1980, when we were feeling somewhat free to express ourselves in public, we knew we had to be careful. Henry led us to the same shop where he had purchased my engagement ring. We were buzzed in, since store security was tight in this part of the city, where dozens of jewelry shops were located on this one block.

Recognizing Henry, who had recently made a major purchase, the manager came over to us immediately. With a wide smile, he firmly shook Henry's hand, then reached for mine, with a slightly quizzical look on his face. That's when he saw the engagement ring on my hand. He froze. The look on his face changed instantly from warm and friendly to cold hate.

"I didn't know I was selling that ring to a faggot," he said, talking to us like we were some lower form of life. "Get outta here. Now," he commanded, buzzing the door so we could leave.

Henry hesitated. He wanted to argue, but that would be pointless. A bigot is a bigot is a bigot. No words would convince this man that our love was real and should be valued. He didn't hate us for anything that we did. He hated us for whom we were.

I pushed the door open and held it open with my foot as I pulled Henry towards me. "Let's try that store right down the street," I managed to say, though I was shaking with emotion. Right there in the door of the shop, I grabbed Henry tightly against me and kissed him passionately. That kiss drained away all the negative energy we had just encountered.

I wish I could say that we were greeted warmly at the next shop, and found the perfect rings, but it didn't happen that way. To my amazement and disappointment, we were turned away from the next three shops that we tried.

Henry asked me if I wanted to take off the engagement ring before we approached the fifth jewelry store of the day. "Fuck no," I told him. "If we can't buy our rings openly, fuck 'em all. We'll keep looking until we find what we want from a jeweler who accepts us as we are."

"Hey! Hey you!" An older man was waving at us from the doorway of a shop half a block away. We walked in that direction, not quite sure if the greeting was friendly or not. "I heard about the problems you've been having. News travels fast around here," he said. "What is it that you're looking for?"

What a relief to see a friendly face and hear a friendly voice. "We're interested in wedding bands. We have a ceremony coming up soon. And we need them engraved," I told him.

He held the door wide open for us. "I've got beautiful wedding bands here. Let me show you a few."

Pulling a tray of wedding bands from the display case, he smiled and winked at me. "There's some real assholes working in some of the shops around here, don't ya think?" he asked.

The bands on this tray were simple. Elegant, but too simple for our tastes. They were plain bands, some made from gold, others from silver, even titanium. I was hoping for something a little more flashy.

"Not to worry," he said, returning the tray to its place. "Let me show you something that might be more to your liking."

217

My eyes lit up when I saw one particular ring on the second tray. The band was made of white gold, with complementary stripes of rose gold. Embedded in the center were stunningly beautiful black diamonds. "Ooh, look, Henry!"

"That's the same one I was gonna pick," he said, and we knew we had found the perfect rings to serve as symbols of our love.

"You have excellent taste," the man said. "I'm sorry, let me introduce myself. I'm Bernard," he said, offering his hand. "I'm so happy for the two of you. When's the happy day?"

We explained that our ceremony would be on Christmas Day, so we were in a hurry to get the rings inscribed. "No problem," he assured us.

"You know, my husband and I were together for 34 years." I saw that he was getting emotional, his eyes welling up with tears. "We never had a ceremony. We couldn't."

He told us about his husband, Franklin, who had passed away just over a year ago. It happened suddenly, from a heart attack. Bernard was still mourning him. That would continue for the rest of Bernard's life.

I couldn't help myself. I took hold of Bernard in an embrace and just held him, feeling his body shake as he tried to control his emotions. After a moment, he regained control of himself.

"I'm so sorry. You must think I'm a silly old man."

"No," Henry assured him. "We understand. I can't even imagine how hard it must be for you right now."

Bernard took a handkerchief from his pocket and dried his eyes. He sighed deeply, then turned to me.

"Have you decided on the inscriptions?"

I had already changed my mind a thousand times about what words to have engraved on the inside of Henry's ring. "We're keeping these secret until the wedding, so don't show him," I said, handing a small piece of paper to Bernard.

On the paper, I had written: "You are my Sanctuary" followed by a drawing of two hearts melded together into one. The initial "H" was inside the first heart, with "J" inside the second.

Henry also handed a piece of paper to Bernard. On it, he had written: "Henry and Joey: We Are Family Dec. 25, 1980"

Bernard smiled as he read the inscriptions. "For you two, there's no charge for the engraving. Consider that my wedding gift to you. This is the first time I ever had two guys buying wedding rings. It's a special occasion for me too."

"Maybe one day, it'll be legal for us to get married, and you'll have all kinds of gay couples in here buying rings," Henry said, as he handed Bernard the credit card to pay for our rings. We all laughed at that, not even able to imagine a world where two men could ever get married legally.

As we passed the other shops on our way back home, the shops that had refused to serve us, I held my head as high as possible. I felt proud, walking along the street with the man that I loved, the man I would soon marry, and my heart was soaring as I thought about those beautiful rings. I took hold of Henry's hand. "Dammit, if we can buy wedding bands, we sure as hell can walk down the street holding onto each other," I thought.

The days and nights were speeding by. It was getting closer to Christmas. At the club, more and more guys and gals were hooking up for the holidays. With just a week to go, I was surprised to see Stephen, the Naval officer, hanging out at the back bar. I didn't think of him as someone interested in older guys, yet there he was.

"Oh," I thought, smiling to myself. "Now I see what's up. He's after Lonnie."

I could easily understand why Stephen was interested in Lonnie, who was just about as cute as anyone. I already knew that Stephen liked them cute. But I had to wonder why Lonnie would be interested in Stephen. Lonnie was always with young, feminine guys and that did not describe Stephen. Maybe Lonnie was more versatile than I thought. Maybe Lonnie would be a submissive bottom for Stephen. That thought made me smile. Any guy lucky enough to ride Lonnie's sweet ass would be sure to have a great time. Or maybe Stephen had a submissive side that I had somehow failed to notice.

In any case, every night that week, I saw Lonnie and Stephen together. They made a beautiful couple and they clearly enjoyed each other's company. Stephen was content to sit at the bar while Lonnie served his customers and anytime Lonnie wasn't busy, I could see them talking and laughing together. Oh, and occasionally making out too.

While Henry and I were very busy, running the club, preparing for our wedding ceremony, and just living our lives, we faced an unpleasant task. Through Alejandro, our beloved fellow Board member at Sanctuary, we had kept in contact with Javier, the nurse who had cared for Henry while he was in the hospital with anaplasmosis. Although he had declined to become a Board member at Sanctuary, Javier was definitely a party boy, showing up at the club on a regular basis, always partying till dawn.

One night, while walking home with a guy who was destined to be Javi's trick for the night, they both stopped in a dark alley because Javi just had to pee at that very instant. Unzipping himself, Javi let loose with a strong stream, splattering against the wall of an abandoned building. "Oh, fuck!" he muttered when he heard the sirens behind him, accompanied by the flashing lights of the police car. Unable to stop the stream, Javi stood there as Mr. Trick for the Night disappeared into the darkness.

Months later, Javi's case came up for trial, where he was sentenced to three months in the city jail for indecent exposure.

Henry and I woke up very early that morning, since we were going to visit Javi at Curran-Fromhold Correctional Facility, better known as CFCF, located on State Road. Although visits didn't begin until 10 AM, we had to be at the facility before 8 AM, to be among the first in line. Those arriving later would basically spend the entire day at CFCF, waiting for hours until it was their turn, for a visit that lasted one hour.

I couldn't believe what I saw when Javi came out to the visiting room. First, it was shocking to see him clad in an orange prison jumpsuit instead of his usual nurse's uniform. Instead of his normal gleaming smile, he looked somber. I thought he was probably feeling humiliated to be seen in such an unfortunate circumstance.

At first, Javier was hesitant to look at either Henry or me directly, instead choosing to stare at the table placed between us. Inmates were not permitted any physical contact during visits, except for a brief hug at the start and end of the visit, so the tables were actually used as obstacles, preventing human contact. For the first five minutes, Javi's eyes were filled with tears as he shared his fears of what would happen to him. He was not only afraid of the other prisoners, but also the guards. He had heard many stories of the abuse that happened all too frequently in penal institutions.

"But what scares me the most is what's probably gonna happen after I get out of here. I have a record now. How am I gonna be able to get another nursing position?"

221

The three of us shared our concerns, and both Henry and I were determined to do anything in our power to help Javi. But we weren't sure how much, if any, we'd be able to help. However, we promised to be there for him when he was released.

"There's just one good thing that's happened since I got here," he confided to us. He subtly pointed in the direction of another inmate who was also having a visit. "That's Gabriel. He's from Puerto Rico, too, and he's been looking out for me. I'm not sure what would happen to me if he wasn't helping me out."

Henry and I both looked over at Gabriel, who returned our gaze, smiling and nodding slightly and giving a small wave of his hand.

"Yeah, we're cellies, and we even...well, we've been having what some people might call an affair."

I wondered if that was a wise thing to do, but I wasn't about to criticize Javier for seeking comfort in these horrible conditions.

"To be honest, the only problem we have is that he sweats like a pig at night. I mean, the sheets on the bunk are completely soaked. You ever hear of such a thing?"

Later on, we would indeed hear of gay men suffering from night sweats, along with other ailments.

***

Christmas Eve 1980. Wednesday night. Traditionally, one of the slowest nights for clubbing. Understandably, many people chose to spend that night with friends and/or family. For some people, that night and the following day might be the only time they got to spend with their families all year.

Henry and I didn't go to the club that night. We were excited about the wedding, set for 6 PM on Christmas

Day. We decided to have the ceremony in the evening, to accommodate any guests who would be spending the day elsewhere.

The entire main disco area of the club was being transformed for the wedding. Rows of folding chairs were assembled where the guests would be seated. Of course, the decorations for Christmas remained in the club, but they were complemented with beautiful, romantic decorations that were more akin to those for Valentine's Day. We would keep the club closed on Christmas. Only the invited guests, numbering 350, would be allowed inside. The plan was to have a short ceremony, somewhat similar to a straight wedding, followed by a party/reception inside the club.

When I was a youngster, knowing I was different before I had any idea what it meant to be gay, I had never envisioned myself getting married. Even now, it didn't quite seem possible. But in just a few hours, I'd be walking down that aisle in front of all those people, ready to make a public commitment to a man I loved deeply.

We knew that our union wouldn't be recognized legally. Most of society would ignore what we were doing. Some people would try to destroy us if they could.

When we had purchased our wedding bands, Bernard had advised us to seek legal resources. He explained that without a will, he would have had no legal right to any of the property that was in his husband's name at the time of his death. He told us that one of Franklin's relatives had even tried to get his will declared invalid, based on Franklin living what the relative called "an insane, illegal, and un-Christian life as a gay man." That claim rejected, because the lawyer who had drawn up the will was an expert, who knew what he was doing. But the fact that someone could even try to deny Bernard his rights served as a warning of what might happen.

The butterflies in my stomach got more active the closer we got to the time of the wedding. At 4 PM on Christmas Day, Henry and I both went to the club for a final check on the arrangements. The decorations looked perfect to me. Behind the podium where Reverend Greene would stand, screens had been placed to hide the sight of the bar in the back area. Lacey red and white hearts, intertwined with the "twin" signs of Gemini, decorated the screens. Vases filled with red and white carnations, mixed with red and white roses, added a beautiful look and scent to the room that normally smelled of stale beer and cigarettes.

Shortly before 6 PM, the room was filling quickly with guests. Staff from the club had offered to act as ushers, escorting our excited friends to their seats. Maybe it was silly, but Henry and I got dressed in separate rooms. It isn't like we hadn't already seen each other's tuxes, but somehow, it just struck us as romantic to dress separately.

Henry took his place at the front of the room, standing next to Reverend Greene. At 6:00 PM, the cellist began playing "Canon in D Major" by Johann Pachelbel. I knew that was my signal to appear.

I had asked Bernard from the jewelry store to escort me down the aisle. He looked perfect in top hat and tails. He was forced to use a cane to help him keep his balance, as a recent foot injury hadn't fully healed. That walking stick actually made his overall appearance even more perfect, I thought.

Bernard and I walked slowly out to the aisle, where he would then accompany me to my future life. The cellist continued playing as we walked down the aisle. I could barely see the smiling guests through my misty eyes, but I did notice that Lonnie and Stephen were together, holding hands. When we reached the end of the aisle, Bernard took my hand and placed it into Henry's, who looked more handsome than I had ever seen him.

We stood facing each other, holding hands, as Reverend Greene greeted the guests, reminding them of what a special event they were about to witness. A gay wedding. Practically unheard of. Illegal. And yet, it was going to happen despite the obstacles in our way.

With a deep breath, Henry began to speak, saying his vows slowly, deeply, emotionally.

"Joey, you are my angel. When I look into your eyes, I know that I want to be with you forever. I treasure you. I promise to always love and respect you, to support you in anything and everything you want in life. I will be your devoted husband forever."

Reverend Greene nodded to me, indicating it was now my turn.

My heart was beating fast and I could feel myself trembling.

"Henry, before I met you, I wasn't sure if love was possible for me. You taught me that I can love and be loved. I promise to share all of life's adventures with you, loving you every step of the way. I will be your devoted husband forever."

"And now the rings," Reverend Greene said.

Bernard stood and handed a ring to each of us. My heart was melting as Henry slid the ring onto my finger, and then I did the same for him.

"And now the best part, the kiss," said the Reverend.

Henry and I held each other tight, embracing there in front of all our friends, publicly declaring our love as we kissed, kissed, and kissed a little longer.

Reverend Greene placed a hand gently on each of our shoulders when we finished, turning us towards the assembled crowd. "I now present to you, Henry and Joey, forever joined as one. But before you walk away, we have one little surprise for you."

At that, a few of the club's bartenders stood and walked up to the screens that were behind us. They turned them around, showing gigantic photos of the two of us in our Halloween costumes, the photos of us in our posing straps, living pieces of modern art.

There was a loud mixture of laughter, applause, cheering and a few sobs coming from the audience. At the sight of the surprise photos, Henry and I were both giggling, a perfect way to begin our married life. With that, DJ Thunder cranked up the music as we made our way back up the aisle. Then we turned, facing our guests, as Henry shouted, "Let's get this party started, bitches!"

SIXTEEN

The party was still going on when we left for the airport, on our way for a short honeymoon in Key West. The warmth of the sun, the beaches, the overall gay atmosphere, all added to the joy of being on vacation with my husband. We stayed in a small, gay-owned and gay-friendly guest house, one block from the beach. Our days were spent sunbathing, boating, relaxing and enjoying the food at the small cafes and restaurants that always seemed to be crowded with friendly gay couples and groups. Everywhere we went, people asked us about our rings, and we happily described our wedding ceremony. I saw the gleam in the eyes of some of the people we talked with, and I wondered, and secretly hoped, that we might inspire some other gay people to take the same step. To marry.

We knew that the club was in good hands while we were in Florida, but we did want to return in time for the big party on New Year's Eve.

On Tuesday, December 30, we flew back to Philly. Lonnie had agreed to pick us up at the airport to give us a ride home. I had to smile when we saw him at the baggage pick-up area, because guess who was right there with him? Yes, it was Stephen.

As he drove us back to Center City, Lonnie told us that he had a surprise announcement. "You two are getting married?" I asked kiddingly.

"No," Stephen laughed.

"One of you is pregnant?" was Henry's guess as we roared with laughter.

Lonnie's demeanor turned serious. Henry and I got quiet in the back seat of the car, wondering what was going on.

"I'm getting transferred out West, to California," Stephen told us. "And I asked Lonnie to come with me."

"And I agreed," Lonnie added. "I think I wanna go out there and see if I can get an acting job."

"Wow, that sounds great!" Henry exclaimed.

"I know it seems fast," Stephen said. "We haven't really been together for very long. But we have fun together, we like each other, and if we want to see if maybe something will come of this, well, I want us to stick together and give it a shot."

I reached forward and placed one hand on each of their shoulders. "I never would've guessed it," I admitted. "But I'm all for it. There's nothing wrong with taking chances in life. Look at me and Henry, and how things worked out for us."

Lonnie told us that New Year's would be his last night working at the club, since they would be leaving for L.A. a few days later.

"Los Angeles," I sighed. "That sounds so fabulous."

Later that night, back at Sanctuary, DJ Thunder had a friend up in the booth with him. "This is Jock," Thunder told us. "My buddy from San Francisco. He's visiting for the week."

There were groups of gay guys, particularly in the early 1980s, who were disparagingly known as "clones." They all looked alike, dressed alike, went to the same hangouts, drank the same drinks, took the same drugs, well, you get the idea. Jock was an anti-clone. He thought for himself, had a mind of his own. He wore what he wanted to wear, what he liked. I understood why Thunder would be friends with him.

Even after all this time, Thunder was still having trouble with Charlie, the guy who had first followed Thunder home long ago. Charlie had never given up on his quest to become one of Thunder's boys. But Thunder wasn't interested, so Charlie remained frustrated.

Charlie still went to the club, a lot. He still stood by the dance floor, getting drunk and high, swaying to the music, waiting to be asked to dance. Thunder pointed him out to Jock, telling him what a pain it was to have Charlie always trying to get Thunder's attention. Jock actually found that interesting. Besides that, Jock never really cared about the opinions of others. He wasn't trying to impress anyone. He felt no peer pressure about anything.

So without giving it a second thought, Jock went over to Charlie, took him by the hand, and led him onto the dance floor. They danced all night, both of them high on alcohol and drugs, both of them feeling the music and having a good time.

"You gonna be here tomorrow night? Maybe around midnight?" Jock asked Charlie, who couldn't believe his good luck. Spending the night dancing with a good-looking, sexy guy from San Francisco was more than Charlie could have hoped for. To be asked to meet him again the following night, on New Year's Eve at midnight, well, Charlie was excited and of course, he agreed.

"Just one thing," Jock told him. I don't care what you wear tomorrow, but I want you to wear a jockstrap under your clothes. I like to fuck a guy wearing a jock and I wanna be fuckin' you tomorrow."

Charlie spent all day New Year's Eve worrying that he'd be stood up. He tried to prepare himself to be disappointed, but he also couldn't deny that he was excited at the prospect of finally having a good time on New Year's.

I wanted to wear our wedding outfits to the club for New Year's, but Henry wouldn't allow it, claiming it would be tacky. I disagreed, telling Henry that I didn't want those beautiful clothes to end up in the back of the closet, wrapped in plastic, protected with mothballs.

Henry laughed at that, but also gave me a look that said his mind was set.

"Let's glam it up tonight, baby," he said.

"You know that glamorous is my middle name," was my smiling reply.

We had a few hours to shop, so that's what we did. One of my favorite activities. I found skin tight gold capri pants in the ladies' section and paired those with a flowing black and gold metallic silk blouse. Glittering gold makeup with gold hoop earrings would complete the look. Except for the shoes. "I need shoes," I implored Henry.

"Nothing you own will go with that outfit," he agreed, and we headed to a shoe store for women. I was happy when we found glittering gold shoes with a small heel in my size.

For Henry, the outfit was all black. Black silk shirt, black necktie. Black trousers with a gold stripe down the side. Black dress shoes with an extremely pointed toe. "Nice, but a little plain, don't ya think?"

"Don't worry, babe. This isn't the complete look for tonight. Let's stop at the craft store." That's where we purchased glitter glue and gold glitter. By the time we finished adding glitter to Henry's clothes, well, he glittered like a golden god.

I was excited about the start of a new year. After all, 1980 had been nothing short of fabulous. Think about it. I had actually gotten married, to a man I loved deeply, that year. I had high hopes for our first year of marriage, and equally high hopes for the future of the gay community. To me, it felt like we were making progress in spite of the many obstacles that confronted us.

Not that I had forgotten the bad times. The worst day of the year for me was the day we held the memorial service for Ruby and Rosetta. Still, I was happy to see that the membership cards we handed out at the service were being used, and we always made an attempt to make our trans friends feel welcome at the club.

Most of the people in the club before midnight had entered as couples. I noticed and I understood. Some people didn't want to be standing alone at the stroke of midnight, when they would be surrounded by couples celebrating the new year with their first kiss.

As the moment approached, Henry and I were dancing. I noticed some of the couples dancing around us.

There was Georgie, with her new girlfriend, Maddie, both dressed beautifully for the occasion. Maddie was stunning in a flowery dress and white heels; Georgie dressed in an expensively-tailored suit and her signature tie.

Salvador, the Boy from Ipanema, was dancing with someone I had never seen before. It was good to see them enjoying themselves as they got acquainted with one another. And I was happy that someone finally convinced Salvador to show his moves. In the past, he had been shy about getting up and dancing.

Dennis and Lance had their eyes locked together as they were grinding their hips to the beat.

Drew and Edward, two members of the gay deaf community, looked to me like they had found true love with each other.

Bennett and Sammy were already so high that they were hanging onto each other for support.

The Two Saints, Peter and Paul, were there, still best friends, alone together, meaning that neither one of them had a current boyfriend. Somehow, they seemed happier when they were together. Watching them dance together

231

that New Year's, I couldn't possibly predict what would soon happen to them.

Above the sound of the music, I heard someone screaming behind me, "Happy Exiversary, sweetie!" Still dancing, I turned to see what was going on. The two tallest queens in the club, Vinny and Mikey, were air kissing each other and doing one of those fake hugs. I was laughing, watching them greet each other, clearly drama queens. Actually, I already knew them quite well. They were the very best of frenemies.

When people think about frenemies, they usually think of people who act like friends, but who really hate each other. Vinny and Mikey were the opposite.

A few years ago, they had been lovers, but that burned out quickly. And since they had first met on New Year's Eve, it was technically their anniversary. But they called it their exiversary, since they were now exes. Though they were the best of friends, they often fought like enemies. If you didn't know them, you might think they hated each other. But that was just part of their act, the way they played off each other. They immediately jumped up on the dance floor and danced as they chatted incessantly, always gossiping about anyone and everyone.

About ten minutes before the start of the new year, I saw Charlie, alone, looking a bit nervous at his usual spot close to the dance floor, drinking even faster than he normally did. I thought about grabbing his hand and inviting him to dance with me and Henry, but before I could decide, I saw Jock walk up to Charlie and grab his ass from behind. Charlie jumped, startled, turned around and to his relief saw that Jock actually did show up.

Jock wasn't the type to just ask Charlie to dance, or to just lead him to the dance floor. Instead, he pulled out a pair of handcuffs, placed one around his left wrist and attached the other one to Charlie's right wrist. "I'm not giving you a chance to escape tonight, boy," Jock told him sternly. "You got that, boy?"

"Yes Sir," Charlie replied, with a joy in his heart that he didn't even know he could feel.

Throughout the night, Jock paraded Charlie around like he was his personal property. Some guys saw Charlie in a new light, as maybe someone who deserved their attention. But Jock had Charlie's total attention, so he never noticed anyone looking at him differently.

By 1 AM, Jock waved to Thunder, indicating that he was taking his new boy over to The Hole for the rest of the night. Over there, Jock continued to treat Charlie just the way he had always craved being treated, like an obedient submissive whose loyalty was demanded and required. Before they left at 3 AM, both Jock and Charlie had consumed enough drugs and alcohol to make it worthy of a memorable New Year's celebration.

Jock insisted that they remain cuffed together even during the walk back to Charlie's apartment. Jock understood that Charlie craved humiliation, even public humiliation. It was the best New Year's that Charlie had ever had.

Jock spent the next few hours enjoying his control over the obedient Charlie, who took orders like a pro. He was hungry to please this new man, the first man who had paid any attention to him in such a very long time. And while this was a new and exciting experience for Charlie, it was not a new experience for Jock, who was used to being adored, worshipped, obeyed. Still, Jock enjoyed it immensely and treated Charlie to three of his huge orgasms. Charlie took every drop willingly, wishing the night would never end.

But of course, the night did end. They always do. Charlie was ready to be disappointed when they woke up later on New Year's.

"Wanna hit the parade and then go bar-hopping with me?" Charlie could hardly believe it. Those words were exactly what he wanted to hear. So Charlie's new year got off to the best possible start, spending the entire day with Jock taking him to all the bars and clubs, making it clear that Charlie was his and his alone. At least, for now.

When Jock flew back to San Francisco on January 2, Charlie was upset, but he had to admit that Jock had given him the best couple of days ever. Maybe his luck had changed. Maybe he would get some attention in Philly. And Jock even promised to keep in touch and come back for another visit sometime soon.

For me, 1981 was shaping up to be a banner year. I felt like I loved Henry more every day that we were together. And every night, when he made love to me, I felt secure and comforted, even in the heat of our passions.

The club was having its best year ever. More and more people purchased memberships and we were THE place to visit for tourists. A visit to Sanctuary seemed to be on the to-do list of every queer who heard of us.

Every Sunday afternoon, Jock would call Charlie from San Francisco. They'd talk for a few minutes, and then the conversation would always end up as a phone sex session. Jock had as much fun controlling Charlie as Charlie had being submissive to Jock's commands. Jock even promised to come back to Philadelphia for a visit, assuring Charlie that Jock wanted to re-create the scenes from New Year's.

On Sunday, March 15, 1981, Jock called Charlie at the usual time, but Charlie didn't answer the phone. Jock was a little annoyed. Actually, he was quite annoyed. Charlie was supposed to be an obedient boy, and here he was, ignoring a call from his Master.

Jock called back on Sunday, March 22. This time, there was a recording that the phone had been disconnected.

Jock wondered what had happened. This didn't seem like anything that Charlie would do.

Jock didn't know it, but on Monday morning, March 9, Charlie woke up with a bad cough and a fever. He felt progressively worse throughout the day and by the next morning, he was having trouble breathing. Like most people, Charlie assumed he had caught the flu or something similar, and he decided to just treat himself at home. When he woke up on Wednesday, his bed was soaked with sweat and he could barely control his cough.

He called a cab and used all his strength to get himself to the closest emergency room. He had to wait several hours before anyone at the hospital would see him. But once the attending physician saw his symptoms, he was admitted immediately for tests.

The doctor didn't return until the next day, a look of concern on his face. He told Charlie that he had pneumonia. But that wasn't all. This was a rare type of pneumonia, usually only seen in elderly patients. The doctor couldn't explain why or how Charlie had contracted this particular strain.

Charlie heard the words, but he really didn't understand. "Pneumocystis carinii pneumonia."

"Pneumo what?"

"It's called Pneumocystis carinii pneumonia. PCP. We're putting you on antibiotics. Should clear up in a few days," the doctor said, patting his shoulder.

But the antibiotics didn't help. Charlie's condition continued to grow worse. His second night in the hospital, he woke up in a panic. Again, he was soaked in sweat and gasping for breath. He stared at the ceiling and whispered a little prayer. He didn't know why this was happening to him. With a sudden jerk, he took hold of the guardrails on the side of the bed, taking the deepest breath that he could. He struggled to get up out of the bed, though he didn't really even know why he wanted to get up or where he wanted to go. He fell back heavily onto the bed. And at that moment, he passed away.

Alone. Afraid. And now, dead.

Jock never found out what happened to Charlie. Though as time went on, Jock would eventually assume the worst.

To be honest, no one at Sanctuary ever realized that Charlie wasn't there anymore. DJ Thunder might have given him a passing thought, but only to think that the guy who used to stalk him seemed to have finally moved on to some other pursuit.

The party continued at Club Sanctuary. Guys met, fell in love or in lust, started and ended relationships, simply enjoying their lives.

On Saturday night, May 16, 1981, BJ was working at the bar, and like always, he would take occasional breaks, giving blowjobs to his regulars in the men's room. BJ was on his knees, working his magic on Tracey, who was getting close to climax. Tracey reached down and inside BJ's shirt, wanting to massage BJ's back as he sucked.

"What the hell is that?" Tracey pulled his hands back. BJ had no idea what he was talking about. "Man, you have a big bruise or something on your back."

BJ took off his shirt and turned to look at his back in the mirror. He didn't remember hurting himself, but he did see what looked like a large purplish-black bruise on his back. He wasn't really alarmed, so he put his shirt back on and went back to serving drinks at the bar.

The bruise didn't heal. Two weeks later, more bruises appeared on BJ's legs and his neck. That worried him, so he decided to go to the free clinic, where he would usually get the meds he always needed for the various STDs that he always seemed to catch. At the clinic, they jokingly called him the Syphilis Queen, but this was clearly something different. The clinic nurse suggested that he go to the hospital. Maybe someone there would be able to help.

Sometime during the first week of June, 1981, Stephen called me from Los Angeles. He told me that Lonnie had been in the hospital for a few days and had been diagnosed with cancer. "They called it Kaposi's Sarcoma," he told me. "I never heard of it. I don't know what they're going to do."

That same week, BJ got the word that he had the exact same diagnosis, Kaposi's Sarcoma. What the hell was going on? None of this made any sense.

Meanwhile, Peter and Paul, the two whom I always referred to as the Two Saints, were experiencing difficulties. They had their usual bouts of being best friends, only to have Peter, the more popular one, end up ignoring his best friend whenever he had a boyfriend. This summer, Peter went through a string of boyfriends, more quickly than usual. It was like he had become insatiable in his desire to feel wanted, which basically meant that he would fuck with anybody who was at least decent-looking.

During a brief period of time between boyfriends, he and Paul met up for their usual lunch at Cafe Coco. Afterwards, instead of going their separate ways, they decided to celebrate their renewed friendship with a few drinks. For some unknown reason, the drinks hit Peter unusually hard, so Paul basically had to help carry Peter back home. Once there, Peter collapsed into bed, immediately falling into a deep sleep.

Paul hung around for a while, since he was comfortable being in his friend's apartment. He watched some TV, flipped through some magazines, checking out the latest fashions on the hot boy models, as the afternoon slipped by. He thought it was strange that Peter would sleep for so long.

Peter didn't wake up until 8 PM, and even though he had just slept for six hours, he awoke feeling even more exhausted than when his nap started. Paul, ever the good and helpful friend, made some soup and watched as his friend slowly sipped on the warmed-up canned chicken noodle soup.

"I don't know. I think I'm ready to go back to bed," were the only words Peter said during the entire meal.

Paul ended up staying the night at Peter's apartment, sleeping soundly on the sofa in the living room. It was around 2 AM when he woke up, softly walking into Peter's bedroom, shocked at what he saw. Peter's bed was literally soaked in a pool of sweat. Peter himself was drenched. Paul couldn't understand, since the room was actually a little chilly with the air conditioning set at full blast.

From that night on, Peter suffered with night sweats, but the suffering didn't stop there. He was another victim afflicted with the dreaded Kaposi's Sarcoma, this mysterious disease that was striking at the heart of the gay community. No one knew what was causing it, but it struck fear into the hearts of gay men everywhere.

Peter had always prided himself on his ability to attract plenty of men for sex, mostly because of his attractive facial features. Those beautiful green eyes that pierced right through anyone he gazed upon, his perfect nose, high cheekbones and lips that any gay guy would want to kiss with passionate abandon.

Some of our friends and acquaintances with this rare type of cancer found lesions on their bodies, in places where they could easily be covered. Peter had the misfortune to have lesions growing on his face. Eventually, no amount of concealing makeup could hide the fact that Peter was deathly ill. That beautiful face turned into something monstrous, with the lesions multiplying incessantly. Then, whatever was causing this illness, took aim at Peter's eyes, first dimming his eyesight and eventually causing him to go completely blind.

All of Peter's friends, his many lovers and ex-boyfriends, abandoned him in horror. They were too afraid that they might catch something from him, since no one had identified the cause of this mysterious disease. And not only were many gay men getting sick, but they were dying...at an alarmingly fast pace.

Paul, however, remained true to his friend. Was he worried? Yes, of course. But as frightened as he was, he recognized that Peter needed to be comforted, and Paul was determined to stay by his side until he recovered, or...

***

On Thursday, July 2, 1981, I woke up and immediately thought of my father. Exactly five years had gone by since my father died in that car accident. So much had changed in those five years. I was openly gay. I owned a gay club. I was married to a wonderful, sexy man. I was financially successful. I was happy.

On the following day, July 3, Henry was reading the New York Times when I came to the table for breakfast. "Look at this," he told me, pointing to an article.

The headline:

"RARE CANCER SEEN IN 41 HOMOSEXUALS"

A sense of alarm grew in me as I read the article, which described a new gay cancer that was reported to be spreading among gay men for no apparent reason.

This is how the epidemic, the pandemic, started for me. First, it was called the gay cancer. Then GRID: Gay-

Related Immune Deficiency. Finally, AIDS: Acquired Immunodeficiency Syndrome.

Nothing could protect our community from this. No club could provide a safe space, a sanctuary. We needed help, but it would be a long, long time before help would arrive.

As a community, we would have to unite and fight. Fight ignorance. Fight prejudice. Fight hatred.

We thought we had fought before, but that was nothing compared with what was to come in the future. As I considered the future, I was more determined than ever to make our club, our Sanctuary, a true resource for the members of our community, the LGBTQ community.

We wanted to be a light in the darkness that was now descending upon us. We wanted our stories to continue, not only our stories, but all the stories in that big beautiful world that we called the gay community.

I looked at Henry with tears in my eyes. He hugged me, tighter than he had ever hugged me before. "I swear to God, we're gonna get through this. Together," he whispered in my ear.

I closed my eyes as he kissed me, comforted me, wanting to protect me. He knew that I was afraid.

"I love you, Henry."

A Message to Readers
of CLUBBED

Joey, Henry and all the rest of the characters in *CLUBBED: A Story of Gay Love*, want to thank you for reading and sharing in their trials, their tribulations and their triumphs.

I hope you enjoyed the book as much as I enjoyed writing it. All of the characters are a part of me, and I'm so happy to be able to share their stories with you.

You might know that I published this book independently. That means that it's my responsibility to also promote the book, so I'd like to ask a favor of you.

If you enjoyed the book, please give it a rating on Amazon. If you would be so kind as to also write a review, well, that would be awesome!

I also promote the book on Instagram. You can follow me there @robertkarl_inpr

As part of my promotion, I like to show photos of the book taken by readers, wherever they happen to live. I would be thrilled to receive a photo from you, showing the book in some cool location in your city, town, or wherever you live. I would then post the photo on Instagram using the tag #wheresmybookwednesday.

Of course, if you want, I would give you credit for the photos, which can be sent to me by email at robert.karl.author@gmail.com

Again, thank you for reading CLUBBED. Remember, everyone at the club has a story, and every story deserves to be told.

Made in United States
North Haven, CT
13 November 2021

11111742R00138